To request permissions, contact the publisher at
councilofgeeks@gmail.com.

Paperback: 978-1-7326759-9-5
Ebook: 978-1-7372616-0-5

First paperback edition June 2021.

Line Edited by Teresa Grabs
Structure Edited by Robyn Moore
Cover art by Yasushi Matsouka
World Map by Vitor Nunes
City Map by Valeriya Zhukova
Illustrations (Chapters 1, 6, 7, 8, 13,
19, 23) by Natalie Linn
Illustrations (Chapters 2, 5, 14, 15, 25, 26, 29, 30,
33, 34, 36) by Emil Friis
Illustrations (Chapters 21, 32) by Benjamin Filby

Council of Geeks
PO Box 4429
Saint Johnsbury, VT 05819

Dedicated to my Great Queen

TABLE OF CONTENTS

City of Torvec

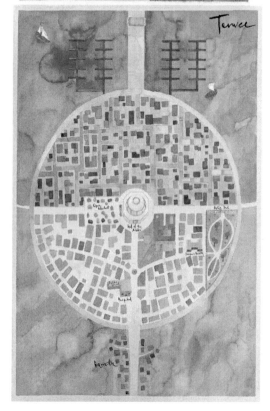

The Lone Continent

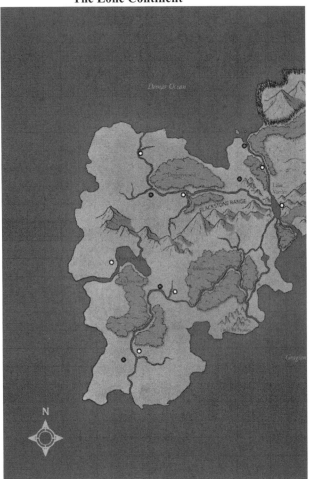

Chapter 1

Farris hugged his midsection and waited for the line to advance. The setting sun cast its pink hue across his fellow travelers' faces as it descended behind the mountains. The other travelers ranged from weather-beaten to well kept, with the latter doing their best not to rub elbows with the former. Farris was worse for wear; his clothes dirt-encrusted and grass-stained from nearly a week of on-foot travel along the Dagrin River. If he'd stuck to the main road, he'd have gotten to this point days ago, but the fear of pursuit had kept him on the more roundabout route.

"That vehicle is worth more than your annual wage, and I'm telling you it would be safer outside the gate within sight of the watchtower than in that stable where any rabble can pry parts off it," snapped a tall, dark-skinned man in a long, bright green coat. He stood with his arms crossed, trying to intimidate the visibly unimpressed Head of the Watch, who was tapping their foot while waiting for him to finish his rant.

"Sir," they said, straightening their brown, leather coat for emphasis. "Perhaps you've not bunked down for the night at an outpost like this before. Look around." They paused and waited for the man to actually look around, which took a few moments before he begrudgingly did so. "See all these walls? These little buildings in here?" they asked evenly. "Notice anything?"

Listening in, Farris couldn't help but look around. They had built the outpost for space efficiency, with a series of crate-like buildings within its twenty-foot-high walls. Watchtowers were spaced evenly along the walls, and one of the members of the watch was lighting torches and lamps.

"It needs a coat of paint and proper lights," smugged the man.

"It's *wood*," said the Head of the Watch sharply. "No metal, nothing running on lightning cages, no combustion motors. We're in the middle of the Wild World, and your motor carriage out in the open all night will attract the Fey."

The man's shoulders slumped; he raised a hand and opened his mouth, but the Head of the Watch steamrolled him before he could get a word in.

"Moving along the road is one thing; they'd ignore that. And if the only danger were that they'd break it down and bury the pieces, I'd frankly let it happen," they continued, seemingly becoming a little taller with each word. Or perhaps the man in the green coat was shrinking. "But Fey taking an interest in something right at our door is a danger to every man, woman, grey, and child in this outpost. So, either drive it to the stables for the night where it's out of sight, or I'll have the watch turn it on its side and drag it there."

Farris smiled as the man in the green coat huffed impotently before storming off out the gate to retrieve the vehicle.

The line began moving forward as the night's boarders were handed bedrolls and directed to the largest building to find a spot to sleep. Farris tensed as he inched closer and closer to the front of the line. There was no reason for the watchman to question his presence or appearance; it hadn't happened to anybody else so far. But at the back of his mind, Farris heard a hissing insistence that he was about to be pulled aside. A bead of sweat dripped down his forehead, which he swiped at hastily. He reached the front, and the watchman didn't even look up from his board.

"Number in your party?"

"Uh… one."

A bedroll was shoved against his chest, and it took a second for Farris to think to take hold of it properly and follow the others to the rest house.

Inside, it was practically empty, aside from the people settling down in groups with their bedrolls. He scurried around a few clusters, headed towards the back, and opened the bedroll. This was hardly luxury accommodations, but it was a step up from sheltering under a tree without covering because he didn't think to grab a blanket when he'd fled. He laid down and rested his head on the thin pillow that he'd been given, smiling up at the ceiling, dimly lit by a few lanterns that dotted the walls. There was little doubt he'd sleep sounder than he had in some time; he just hoped that the night would not bring another dream.

***

The night was cold, yet an oddly warming breeze rustled through the forest's thick covering of leaves and branches. Farris ran his fingers through his sandy hair, brushing it out of his face as he tilted his head back, looking at the sky. The canopy above him parted like curtains on some great stage at the start of a play. The moon was a sliver in the sky, and the stars shone brighter than he had ever seen in his seventeen years of life. After a few moments, he dropped his head. Above him came the creaking sound of the parted trees closing back into their impenetrable canopy.

Faced once more with the darkness of the forest, Farris gripped the mane of his mount, a large and powerful mare. The stars that had lit up the sky did little to penetrate the leaves, now closed in above him. His straining eyes could only see vaguely defined, constantly shifting shadows, yet the mare moved forward at a steady and unbroken pace, somehow confident in her chosen path.

Farris' legs wrapped around her bare middle, and he dreaded the thought of falling off. He squinted in the darkness, trying to force the shadows around him to form more defined shapes. This only made the shadows appear more fluid than before. He swallowed hard as he felt anxiety rising in his chest.

He slowly turned his head from one side to the other, hoping to find some source of light that might reassure him he wasn't completely lost and alone—a glimmer of a campfire, the first hint of morning, anything that might penetrate the darkness even for a second. Unable to bring the murky surroundings into focus, his eyes drifted downward, and he couldn't help but notice a strange quality of the mare that had eluded him up to now. As complete as the darkness around him seemed, she seemed somehow even darker and blacker.

Overhead, the branches shifted again with a slow, groaning creak, sounding like a massive door with hinges that had never been oiled. Amidst this low groan was the faint fluttering of wings. When the canopy above him cracked open again, the pinpricks of starlight caused the damp trunks of the trees to glimmer in a way that should have been comforting. Indeed, he would have expected it to be somehow reassuring, but it wasn't, not even a little bit. It was mocking him. It took a little while before he noticed the mare had quickened her pace, having been too busy focusing on the solidifying scene around him and trying to anticipate what might happen next without panicking at the possibilities. As the sensation of the mare's stead trot sank in, he looked down at her once more. Her coat was impenetrable to the eye, even in the soft glow created by the thin beams of light glinting dancing on the lingering raindrops clinging to the tree trunks, and she was just as ill-defined now as she'd been in the near-total blackness. The mare's coat had no shine, no clear point where she ended, and the night began. Light seemed to simply collapse into her.

As his breath hastened from the fear crawling up into his throat, Farris tried recalling how he came by this mystifying black mare. To his bewilderment, he could not find a firm memory of her before the journey they were on at this very moment. He soon realized he also could not remember where they were going or where they had come from. He could not recall any memory of why he was in the forest at such a time of night. Most disconcerting of all, none of these holes in his memory had struck him as out of place until just then. This thought process was interrupted by a sudden jolt as the mare broke into a full gallop.

The flutter of wings around Farris became louder, and he could hear high-pitched chattering that seemed at once to be in the distance yet also inside his head. He gripped the mare's mane so tightly his hands started to tremble. The path on which they rode narrowed as the trees' branches began to stretch, reaching out to claw at Farris. Gnarled wooden limbs shed their leaves as they reached for him, scratching across his arms and his shoulders.

The pointed tip of one branch cut across his face, and he felt the warm trickle of blood run down his cheek and follow his jawline before dripping off his chin. The drops of blood fell onto the mare's coat, where they vanished, consumed by the darkness of the galloping beast beneath him.

Farris held onto the mare's mane like it was his only lifeline, despite a growing sense of unease about his mount. The beast's hooves thundered as they hit the ground, and the air rushing past his head should have been deafening, but instead, the cacophony of noise was fading into the background, becoming little more than a distant hum. His ears instead rang with sounds that should have been too quiet to detect—the sounds of delicate wings flying against the wind, a gentle thud caused by something leaping from tree to tree. Incessant high-pitched chattering soon dominated his hearing. As the noise gained strength, it took on the qualities of a laugh, but not a laugh like anything he had heard before, rather some strange mockery of laughter. It sounded like an imitation performed by something that had never laughed before.

Farris tucked in close to his mount, pressing his body down tightly against the back and neck of the mare. The beast felt cold as he brought more of his body closer. It was not a sense of cold that would have come from the running animal itself being freezing. Instead, it was as though his own body's heat was being drained from him by the black void of a horse on which he rode. His energy and strength were beginning to slip away when a howling cackle cut through the air behind him. Something landed on his back roughly, nearly knocking him off the mare.

Diminutive hands gripped at Farris' shoulders while a pair of small feet pressed against the small of his back. Sharp thorny toes dug in and held firm while spiked fingers raked slowly down either side of his spine, tearing away the skin and replacing it with searing pain. Through it all, the thing upon his back cackled unnaturally in his ear.

Farris tried to shake the creature off, but the thorns held fast even as the fingers dragged through more of his flesh. He threw his head back to scream, but his lungs failed him, and only a weak whisper passed his lips. He silently prayed to lose consciousness, but every passing second only heightened the painful sensation. A flash of light banished the dark before settling into a less intensely bright pulse, like a heartbeat.

The trees retreated from the flash, and the path widened. Everything lit as if the sun was among the trees, except for one thing.

The mare's coat swallowed up the light that was now illuminating the forest. However, blazing licks of fire had replaced the thick tufts of mane beneath his grasp.

The flames wrapped around the young man's wrists and fingers and held them fast. His skin blistered and cracked, the flesh charred and blackened, like a piece of meat thrown directly into an open flame. Except this meat felt every lick of heat and new blister.

Farris struggled to free his hands from the agony of the fire, but the flames held him as tightly as iron shackles. He looked all around in a panic; soon, his eyes locked onto the head of the mare. The labored breath from the mare's nostrils made the air bend and waver with its heat, and a newly formed twist of blackness ending in a pointed spike protruded from its forehead.

Without any break in its thundering stride, the mare turned its head to one side until its eye met with Farris.' The beast's iris was the same bottomless pit of blackness as her coat, except for a single point in the center. The point was infinitely small and would have been undetectable had it not been made of the purest white light. This point of light burned its way into his very being, even more harshly than the fire of the mane burning his flesh.

By now, the skin on his hands had begun to shrivel and curl back from the heat, peeling away, exposing the muscle and bone, which was also beginning to char. The pain was unbearable, yet he found himself locked in place by that single point of light in the mare's eye. Something was buried beneath the embodiment of rage and pain on which he rode, and it was reaching out. The mare's eye blinked, and the light was gone as Farris awoke.

He opened his eyes to a sideways world. He was lying upon his right side, curled up on his makeshift bed, his forehead drenched in sweat. The shaved logs that formed the resting house walls replaced the sinister trees of his dream. The blazing light of the mare's fiery mane gave way to the dull flicker of candles at the far end of the room. The otherworldly creature was already fading from his mind. The malevolent chattering and fluttering of wings were replaced with gentle snoring and the shuffle of blankets as others slept on similar mats spread throughout the room. Everything had changed, yet the burning pain in his hands remained.

Farris looked at his hands. They were not blistering or peeling as they had been in his dream, but the pain and heat were worse than ever. As he pushed against the floor to get to his feet, there was a crackling sound where he placed his hands. When he pulled them away, he saw the floor blackened and scorched where he'd touched it.

Clenching his left wrist as tightly as possible, Farris worked his way steadily across the room. He silently cursed himself for taking a spot so far from the exit. If he'd only looked behind himself and seen the dozens of people behind him, he might have thought better of it. But it was too late now and winding his way among the densely packed forms strewn about in a way that left no direct path out. Half the lanterns had been allowed to burn out, and the few left cast flickering shadows, so the thick beams that held up the roof took on the haunting qualities of the trees in his nightmares, appearing to bend and weave of their own accord.

By the time Farris was halfway across the room, he was sucking his breath in through his teeth and was nearly doubled over, clutching his wrist and the searing pain to his gut. The heat was beginning to rise in his right hand as well. The pain came in waves, and each time it eased even a little, he looked to the lanterns that stood on either side of the double doors to the outside.

With only a few dozen feet to go, the burning surged up his arm. He gasped and fell to his knees as sweat dripped into his eyes. He was ready to give up, to let it all flow out of him, when the scent of perfume wafted up and caught his nose and shot the reminder that his was not the only life in the room directly into his brain. He gritted his teeth and tried to stand. Holding his left hand to his chest, he reached his right to the ground to steady himself. Through the veil of searing pain, he did not see the bare shoulder of another traveler, poking out from under a blanket. His hand grazed the exposed flesh.

A piercing scream rang out and filled the room as a woman threw back her blanket and cradled the burnt and blistering flesh of her shoulder. Shadowy figures sat bolt up across the room, some rising to their feet while others scooted away or huddled together. The sounds of confusion and fear echoed off the walls, like a harmony to the woman's screams. Another woman nearby lunged toward her, pushing Farris out of the way. She didn't realize he'd caused it, and the fear in the pit of his stomach told him that would only be the case for a few seconds. He bolted to the double doors, holding both hands tightly against his stomach. Puffs of smoke rose as his shirt began to smolder from the heat. He leapt over several forms still on the ground and felt a rush of air as someone reached for him and missed by inches. As he reached the doors, he aimed his shoulder at the crack between them, burst out into the moonlight and open air.

He stumbled to the center of the courtyard. As the burning sensation spread up both his arms and began to cross over into his chest, his vision grew foggy. He looked all around, turning a complete circle as the haze of pain clouding his memory of where the main gate was. There had been a small, shed-style structure near it, but there were at least four of those. In the dim glow of moonlight, everything blurred together in a haze of growing pain. Behind him, screams echoed out of the resting hall; he winced, trying desperately to block the sound out. Watchmen peered into the courtyard from their posts along the wall.

A voice rang out from the halls' open door. "Why is he running?!?"

Farris looked back at the orange glow coming from the doorway and saw several silhouettes emerge; one of them was pointing at him. He shot his eyes around, frantically hunting for the exit and be prepared to bolt in a random direction rather than stay in place. He clutched his hands to his chest, wincing and sweating. A shadowy figure near one of the sheds became lit by an activating shock rod's sparks, accompanied by the sharp clicking of electricity arcing between the rod's prongs.

The fire that was raging just beneath the skin of his arms had spread inward, meeting in the center of his body, and intensified. He knew from experience that he wasn't far away from collapsing.

He whipped his head around, and his eyes finally focused on the twin lamps marking the gate. As figures closed in on him from behind, he gathered every ounce of energy he had left and propelled himself to his escape. He heard shouts from behind him, but he did not dare to look back.

"Stop that boy!"

Shock rods flickered to life from all sides and closed in as Farris forced himself to move forward with everything he had. If he could get outside, he would not be followed. Not at night, not if he made for the tree line.

The heavy double doors reached up the wall's full height, barred with a thick block of wood across them. But next to it was a smaller door, the size of a normal house front entrance, meant for single travelers and closed with a simple wooden bolt. Farris couldn't slow down enough to keep from slamming his shoulder against the sturdy door. The door didn't budge from the impact, and the clicking of shock rods was closing in all around. Farris leaned a hand on the door for support while he pulled back the locking bolt. The wood smoked and crackled under his touch.

Once the bolt was free, Farris pulled the door open and flung himself out into the open air. A jolt of searing heat surged in his chest, and he fell to his knees in the dirt.

"Stop! Don't go out there!"

"Leave me alone!" Farris shouted, pushing himself off the bare ground.

At first, he stuck to the road to put as much distance between himself and the outpost as he could before veering into the long grass that would slow him down. The moon bathed the road, but it all blurred together as he fought to hold back the heat radiating from his hands. It was like trying to hold back a thin door against an incoming tide. His strides slowed as another wave of heat shot up his arms to his chest and began to creep into his throat. There was a loud crack from behind him, and a white electric bolt soared over his shoulder and singed the ground on the uneven road ahead of him.

Now clearly unsafe on the open road, Farris veered off and made for the miles of thick woods which separated the road from the mountains.

Dashing through the tall grass that buffeted the road, he could just make out the thick trunks and high branches of the Everwood. There was another crack of noise from behind him, but this time the bolt only flew into the night sky. Glancing back at the outpost one last time, Farris could just make out several figures wrestling a bolt rifle from the hands of whoever had been firing the shots. None of them made any moves to follow him.

He tumbled over the waist-high stone wall that bordered the tree line and floundered into the darkness of the forest. It seemed to him he only made it a few steps into the woods before collapsing to his knees in among a cluster of ferns. However, one last panicked glance back revealed he'd gone deep enough into the forest the light from the outpost's beacon torches could not be seen.

He tried to get his feet under him but promptly fell to his knees once again. Farris stopped fighting the burning from within and finally let it flow. Flames erupted in the air around him, swirling and coalescing into a whirlpool. Searing heat expelled itself through his fingertips. The last of his energy drained with the fire, and as the blazing flickers dispersed, he went limp and collapsed.

Chapter 2

When morning broke at the valley outpost, the chatter was only about the previous night's fiery incident, with a few travelers pointing out that only one person was hurt. It had started as a fairly accurate recounting by those who were most awake at the time, but it was already changing with each retelling. By the time the gates were opened and the travelers departed, they breathed sighs of relief at surviving an elemental nearly burning the entire outpost to the ground. By the time most of these travelers reached their destinations, they'd be speaking of the "burner" who cackled madly that he would roast them all in their sleep.

The Head of the Watch peered down from the gate tower as the travelers and merchant caravans cleared out. As soon as the last stragglers were clear, they summoned the morning shift sergeant to round up a handful of watchmen to cover up or clear away any burnt leaves or branches as well as check the integrity of the stone wall along the tree line. Everything was to be made as orderly as possible before midday when a fresh wave of foot traffic and caravans would trickle through.

Barrol, the stout and well-tanned shift sergeant, grabbed the first dozen watchmen in sight and put them to work. Fifteen minutes later, he marched out to where a particularly pasty member of the watch was pacing back and forth along the same five feet worth of wall, and had been for the last ten minutes.

"Priya!" Barrol shouted. "At least *look* like you're working!"

"There's nothing to do," Priya moaned. "And I was supposed to come off duty hours ago."

"Then go do nothing up that way." Barrol pointed further along the stone wall.

Priya looked to where his commanding officer was pointing and sighed. "That elemental didn't even hit that bit of forest; I saw where he went in and—"

"Stow it! I don't care anymore. If you're going to do nothing, at least do it far enough away from me where I don't have to deal with it."

Priya shuffled off along the wall, spreading fallen leaves around with his feet as he went and letting his hand graze over the wall's stones. Once he was some distance from the other outpost guards, he hopped over the rather feeble-looking barrier. He ventured to the edge of the tree line and leaned against a thick oak tree, removing a small box from the inside pocket of his dark green coat. He opened it and took some of the black powder inside between his fingers, and rubbed it on his gums, sighing deeply at the sensation. "Hello, Priya," said a voice from the branches above him.

Priya jolted, dropped his box, and pulled a medium-length shock rod from his belt. He instinctively activated the rod and pointed it up at the branches. A short figure, buried in a faded, dark red traveling cloak perched above him. Sunlight glinted off the silver and charcoal band on the figure's right arm. A bright red scarf tucked beneath the cloak's hood wrapped around the figure's mouth and forehead, leaving its deep brown eyes visible.

Priya put the rod back onto his belt. "Damn it, Garion." He leaned down and retrieved his box, grateful its contents hadn't spilled. "Why can't you just walk up and shake hands like everybody else?"

Garion chuckled from his perch amongst the thickest leaves. The only angle he could be spotted was from directly below, looking straight up. "If you really want to be seen speaking to me openly, I could arrange that."

"Alright, alright," Priya muttered, tucking his box away. "I just wish you wouldn't take such glee in scaring me like that."

"I take my pleasures where I can." Garion's gravelly voice rang clearly despite the scarf covering his mouth. "Had a little trouble last night, I see."

"Yeah, we had a burner in the barracks." He leaned against the tree trunk as casually as possible, making a point of not looking up in case anyone was watching. Garion's keen ears would be able to hear him even at this distance. "We got off fairly light, all things considered."

"So, no injuries then?"

"Just one; she'll be ok, though. We actually had more trouble from the badge who took a pot shot at the kid."

"A boy?" Any last hint of courtesy dropped from Garion's voice.

"Huh?" Priya tried to sound nonchalant but frowned at having given a detail for free.

"You said the burner was a kid; was it a boy?"

"I'm not sure; it all sort of happened at once." After a brief pause, he opened his hand and waited. A small bag dropped into his palm; the coins inside jingled as it landed. He smiled and pocketed the bag. "Yeah, I'd say he was probably

16 or 17. Light brown hair, average build... wouldn't have thought much of him, to be honest."

Garion moved some branches and surveyed the clean-up operation again. "So, he made it to the woods before he went off?"

"Yeah." Priya paused and scratched the stubble on his chin. "I'm surprised the fire didn't spread much, to be honest."

"The Fey contained it."

"Do you think they'll retaliate? For the fire?" Priya shuddered. "I mean, I haven't seen crows or anything; that's a good sign, right?"

Garion let the watchman's fear fester for a moment before answering. "Don't know," he said casually. "They can be strange about elementals sometimes. If they have him, that might be enough." He let the uncertainty hang in the air before asking, "Is the marshal still here?"

"What! That no-talent slack shot who almost fired into the trees?" scoffed Priya, tossing his head to the side and scowling. "Nah. He was the first one out the door at dawn. Probably off to lick his wounds and talk about how close he came to catching the one that got away. Damn trigger-happy payday chasing idiots, the lot of them." He realized what he'd just said and coughed awkwardly. "Present company excluded, of course."

"You should get back."

Priya checked around, making sure he wasn't about to leave anything behind. "Any clue where the kid's headed?"

"No idea."

There was a rustle in the branches, and when Priya glanced up one last time, the tree was empty.

Chapter 3

Farris awoke curled up atop scorched and cracked earth. He opened his eyes reluctantly, and the images he saw were little more than vague outlines. A fluttering wing, soft as a flower petal, brushed his shoulder. He whipped his head around just in time to see something small and glowing fly into the blurry outlines of the trees. He placed his hands underneath his chest and pushed up, his muscles wracked with aches as he struggled to his hands and knees. Every limb shook with the effort, his legs trembling most of all, even without properly standing. He winced and tried to get a foot flat to the ground, but everything was giving out.

With a defeated huff, he rolled to the side and propped his back against a charred tree stump. He rubbed his legs to restore proper feeling to them while looking about to get his bearings. He squinted as a ray of light hit his eye. As he shifted his head and blinked the glare out of his eye, he took note of the sharp angle of the sunbeams that broke through the trees. It must be very early morning, he thought.

Then he paused and realized he not only had no gauge for how long he'd been unconscious, but he didn't know which way was east or west. The sun could very well be setting once more. A wind blew through the trees, and he shivered, feeling confident that it wouldn't be this cold if there'd been a full day of sunlight, so it must be morning.

The wind cut through him, and he glanced down at his clothes, which had already been in a poor state when he fled the outpost but were now little more than charred rags. He pulled at the burnt wisps of his shirt only to have it tear away from his torso and crumble to dust. He didn't dare test what was left of his trousers. His boots fared slightly better; the leather was singed but largely intact.

Farris' eyes drifted from his own body to the dry and broken earth around him, which formed an almost perfect circle, about twelve feet in diameter. Outside the circle, trees and grass appeared to have been only lightly touched by the fire he'd unleashed. As he surveyed the damage to the ground around him, he spotted a toadstool at the edge of the circle. His eyes went wide as he looked around and saw similar toadstools dotted around the entire perimeter of the circle. His breath caught in his throat, and he lunged forward. He still could not stand, but he scrambled out on all fours as fast as he possibly could; ignoring how his trousers were crumbling with every movement, he hurled himself out of the toadstool ring. He landed roughly on the grass and lay there panting, trying to calm back down.

After a few deep breaths, he crawled to the nearest tree and propped his back against it, looking back at the toadstool ring with a sigh of relief. Stories of the rings flitted in and out of his mind; stories of people being lulled into year-long slumbers, turned to stone, twisted into beasts, or (very rarely) healed of injuries—stories of Fey magics being concentrated and amplified, sometimes causing miracles but mostly causing mayhem.

Even with these childhood fears swirling in his head, he smiled in relief at being outside the circle.

"Well," he sighed, catching his breath. "That'll get you moving in the morning." He chuckled weakly at his lame joke.

Farris was quick to turn his eyes away from the toadstool ring and take in his surroundings properly. He'd never been inside of the Everwood before, not really. The Dargin River he'd been following in the days before cut through it, but there were always at least several yards of open grass between the river's edge and the forest proper. Despite the area's reputation, he couldn't help but find it beautiful. There were enough gaps in the canopy to allow the warm sunlight to shine through in diagonal beams, lighting up the patches of grass and bits of brush.

There was a twinge of guilt at the realization that he might have burned it all to the ground had it not been for the toadstool ring apparently containing his energies. This had to be the doing of the Fey, but it would have been only to protect the forest. Any safety it had afforded Farris would have been coincidental and unintended. Thinking back to the night before, he couldn't remember seeing the ring or being led to it. He could only remember a haze of darkness and burning pain.

He frowned the thought away and glanced up at the full green leaves over his head. He squinted, trying to catch any movement among the high branches or any other sign of treshen. They were the thing he'd been most wary of, even when keeping to the river. Pixies and recaps were usually little more than nuances, but treshen were notorious for attacking humans who strayed from the well-worn valley trading road. Even merchant caravans had been torn apart, and on rare occasions, the merchants along with them.

With no movement beyond what he'd expected from the light breeze, Farris let his eyes drift down and to his right. There were more stones and rocks that way, reminding him that the Celeste Mountains cut through the Everwood, which meant kobolds weren't out of the question. He didn't think he'd come deep enough into the forest for that to be likely, but he truly had no way of knowing.

A flutter of wings to his left made him whip his head around, but he saw only tree trunks and ferns. The sound of wings meant pixies, which would hopefully be indifferent to him now that he was no longer an immediate threat to the forest. The bigger concern would be dryads shifting about among the trees and ensuring he lost his way, the thought of which reminded him that he was already plenty lost as it was. He wouldn't let his mind entertain the notion of encountering a huldra.

Farris shook his head, stopping himself from imagining every possible threat, and pushed himself up on his elbows before rolling to the side. Something rustled in the trees over his head, but when he glanced upward, he only saw swaying branches and a few gently falling leaves. He took slow deep breaths. He needed to do whatever he could to keep from panicking. Experience had taught him anxiety and fear would only cause the fires within him to build faster. The metallic clanking of a cocking firearm broke the silence. He zeroed in on the sound coming from the far side of the toadstool ring.

Standing among the trees was a tall pale man pointing a bolt rifle directly at Farris. "I was starting to think you were never going to move out of that ring."

Farris eyed the silver and charcoal band on the arm of the man's weather-beaten brown jacket and sighed. Marshal Service. They presented themselves as law enforcers but were much closer to bounty hunters.

"Imagine my good fortune to have a burner practically fall into my lap. Got to love an easy payday."

"There's no warrant out for me." Farris stalled for time. All his energies were spent, and he was defenseless. "Nobody's going to pay you a bounty."

"That hardly matters," the man scoffed. "Sagaris University isn't too far, and I'm sure those lab rats will pay a pretty penny for a specimen as lively as you. The Guild always does."

Farris started to push himself onto his feet, using the rock he had been leaning on for support.

"I wouldn't do that," said the marshal, bringing the sights of his rifle halfway up to his eye.

"Are you really sure you want to fire that thing in here?"

"If I hit *you,* they won't care. All they care about is the trees."

The marshal was halfway around the toadstool ring, taking care in finding each footstep.

"Judging by your aim last night, I wouldn't exactly call you a crack shot," Farris retorted with a smirk. He wasn't sure what his mockery was meant to accomplish, but anything that deviated the marshal's attention from his aim, even slightly, was a good thing.

"That was in the dark at ten times the distance," the marshal snapped back.

As the marshal spoke, a small point of glowing green light hovering a foot or so above the ground caught Farris' attention. It briefly darted back and forth in the air, then disappeared into a moss-covered rock a few feet to his left.

"If you really think I can't hit you, then make a move," the marshal dared, showing no signs of noticing their new guest.

"Alright." Farris gritted his teeth as he heaved his upper body to the left and grabbed hold of a protruding root. Using it as leverage, he swung his half limp legs around and connected with the hollow moss mound. It broke open easily, like an egg hit with a chisel.

A swarm of glowing green insects erupted from the broken mound, filling the air. Farris crawled away as fast as he could. The marshal waved his rifle through the mass of glowing dots trying to shoo them away—some burst in small explosions of light and noise. Most of the swarm headed deeper into the woods, but a small cluster surrounded the marshal and inundated him with flashes and bangs. Disoriented, the marshal slipped on a damp stone. He caught himself on a tree but dropped his cocked rifle. The gun discharged as it hit the ground and a bolt of white lightning fired from the barrel, exploding a sapling birch tree into splinters.

Farris twisted his head and looked back. With his would-be captor still standing, Farris realized crawling wasn't getting him away fast enough. Planting his hands firmly against a bare flat stone, he pushed himself up onto his feet, grabbing at the nearest tree for support as he stood. He wasn't sure how fast he would be on his feet, but it had to be faster than crawling.

After the rifle fired, the marshal froze in place, but he turned his attention back to his target when nothing happened after a few seconds. He pulled a black metal rod from his belt, and with a twist of the handle, sparks flew between the two short prongs at the end of it.

A harsh chattering filled the forest, stopping both in their tracks. Their eyes darted about, but neither could pinpoint the source. Farris wanted to run, but his legs were frozen with fear. The angry chatter waxed and waned in volume as it encircled them. The marshal slowly and deliberately closed the gap between him and the elemental. He disabled the shock rod to avoid attracting any further attention, and in its place, produced a set of steel restraints.

The sound of a snapping branch echoed above them, stopping Farris from picking a random direction to make his escape. A dark form launched itself from the canopy at a sharp, downward angle. He saw the creature briefly after it landed— a treshen. It had a fine coat of short grey fur, stood about three feet tall, with the proportions of a six- or seven-year-old child, and its ears were pointed. Its nose was little more than a pair of nostril slits on its face, and it sported a short tail with a tuft at the end. It flashed a wicked set of jagged teeth at Farris as it hunched down on its legs, with knees which bent in the opposite direction as those of a human and sprang straight up into the cover of the canopy.

The marshal stood, frozen in shock. Four razor-thin gashes appeared diagonally across his face. The marshal staggered backward, stumbling, and landed roughly on the burnt and cracked ground inside the toadstool ring.

Roots and vines erupted from the scorched earth, wrapping around his legs. He pulled the shock rod from his belt, primed it, and pressed it hard against the thickest root. A sharp crackling sound and the scent of burning wood filled the air. The root did not release its grip on the marshal's leg, so he held the shock rod in place, unleashing a fury of sparks until the root blackened and smoke began to rise. It unraveled from his leg and retreated into the ground. With the thickest and strongest restraint no longer holding him, the marshal kicked his right leg free of the remaining botanical captors. He tossed aside the rod, releasing one final spark, its lightning cage depleted, then began using his bare hands to pull at the vines wrapped around his left leg up to the knee.

Realizing the marshal may yet break free, Farris turned to run for it. Upon turning away, he was confronted by a pixie hovering at eye level. It was close enough it could have reached out and touched his nose. It was roughly three inches tall, but this close to Farris, it looked humungous. Its fluttering wings beat the air so fast they were little more than a glowing blue and green haze. Its flawless skin was like polished ebony and emitted a soft glow that blurred its body's details. The small creature cocked its hairless head at Farris and stared at him for a moment.

The pixie smoothly fluttered to the side until it was clear of Farris' head. He followed it with his eyes, eventually turning his head to keep it in his vision. The glow of the pixie's fluttering wings deepened to a reddish hue before it shot forward toward the marshal, stopping inches from his face. He swatted at the creature, but it dove under his hand and flew down to the vine still partially entwined around his ankle.

The instant the pixie's tiny hand touched the vine, it thickened and coiled around the entirety of the marshal's leg with lightning speed. The vine gave a sharp tug, causing the marshal to fall flat onto his back, his head smacking hard against the dirt as he landed. The pixie laid its hands on the scorched earth within the ring, and moss appeared. The moss quickly began to spread throughout the ring's interior. With a series of low creaks and cracks, the trees began to shift and close in around the ring.

The last thing Farris saw before the moving trees completely obscured his view was the moss creeping up the marshal's legs. He turned away and took hold of a fallen branch that was sturdy enough to support his weight before fleeing as quickly as he was able, leaving the sounds of the man's cries behind.

Chapter 4

With the toadstool ring well behind him and most of the feeling returning to his legs, Farris tossed aside the branch he'd been using for support and leaned against a large stone to catch his breath and gather his thoughts. He had to make his way back to the relative safety of the valley road; the trick was figuring out what direction that was. He looked up to try and catch the angle that the sunlight was coming through the leaves. The light wasn't coming in at as sharp an angle as it had earlier, so it was morning at least. He knelt to where a beam of light was hitting a rock, but with a creaking of branches, it shifted and was gone. He hung his head and sighed. He couldn't trust anything that was being filtered through the trees. For all he knew, he could be headed north toward the Celeste Mountains or even east back the way he'd first come.

He shook his head to stop his mind from going down the path that would lead him to dwell on Sagaris University. His self-doubt about whether fleeing had been a good idea battled the choking fear of what would happen if he ever found himself back there. He slammed his palm against the rock he was leaning on and did what he always did when the big picture weighed on him—he focused on the immediate issue of deciding which direction to go.

Climbing a tree in a Fey forest presented many potential hazards—pixies, red caps, and other small troublemakers in the tree hollows, treshen stalking from the canopy, and even the tree itself could be a resting dryad. Any tree in the Everwood could be the last tree someone climbed.

None of this changed the fact Farris needed to get to a high vantage point, so he took stock of the trees around him. Most were either too thin to climb or had branches too far off the ground to reach. Eventually, he spotted one with ashy grey bark and firm branches low enough to work his way up to the canopy. He approached the tree and took a deep breath before gingerly placing a hand on the bark. He held his hand there, trying to sense if the tree was reacting to his touch. At the same time, he glanced up to see if anything was emerging from the small hollows further up the trunk.

"Ok… if anybody's home, it'd be really great if you'd just give me a freebie on this one," he mumbled.

Farris gathered his courage and hoisted himself onto the first branch. He hadn't climbed a tree since his preteens, but it came back to him easily enough. Soon he was making steady progress, being careful not to stray too far out from the trunk. Every few feet, he would pause to listen for any rustling in the leaves. Each time there was only the sound of birds, insects, and a light breeze, so he continued his climb.

It wasn't long before his head broke through the canopy into the sunlight. He shaded his eyes with a free hand and surveyed the area. A stiff breeze whipped his sandy hair around his face. To the north, the sloping peaks of the Celeste Mountains brushed the bottom of the clouds. He adjusted his grip on the branches and twisted around away from the mountains. A wide gap in the trees ran the length of the valley marking where the road lay. He smiled and sighed out a long breath, figuring he could make it to the road in less than half an hour.

One look down and all the tension flooded back into his muscles. It took a few deep breaths to work up the nerve to begin working his way down. Lowering himself from branch to branch, he began picking up speed. Fear kept him steadily dropping from branch to branch. Soon, the entire descent was closer to falling than climbing.

With his haphazard pace, twigs scratched at Farris' bare torso, drawing small traces of blood. With ten feet left to go, he dropped forcefully on one of the branches, snapping it beneath him. He landed with an awkward thud and rolled forward onto the rough ground, then picked himself up and looked around, fearful of what kind of attention he may have attracted. He turned due south, eyes focused, brow set, and brushing leaves off his shoulders and upper chest as he set a determined pace. As he moved through the forest, he would flash his eyes to each side and sometimes even glance up, but he never slowed and never looked back.

Some yards behind him, a crow landed silently on a short branch, its bright yellow irises locked onto Farris. The tree twisted slowly and a pair of deeply set eyes, normally hidden in the bark, cracked open. Both the dryad and the crow watched Farris move away from them. The crow's eyes flashed, and it took flight after the young man, never making a single sound.

***

Farris made better time than expected and was soon at the forest's edge, with only a waist-high stone wall and a grassy field between him and the valley road's well-worn dirt. A low hum and a shifting of gears caught his attention. Coming up the road was a rectangular crate on treads with a small boxy compartment in the front. It was buffeted on either side by egg-shaped personal carriages on large wheels that bounced along the dirt road. They were grey and undecorated, something for utility rather than spectacle.

Travelers on foot, with travel bundles upon their backs and heavy leather boots, moved to the side to make way for the small motorcade. A mother put her hand on a child's shoulder to keep the youngster from wandering back into the road before the motor-carriages had passed. Headed in the other direction was a smattering of oxen-pulled carts, each loaded with goods but covered with heavy blankets to keep sticky fingers at bay. As people passed each other, they nodded and waved, a polite acknowledgment of their shared pathway. Farris sighed with a smile and was about to step out of the woods when he glanced down and stopped short. What little had been left of his trousers had been almost completely torn away by branches.

This was not a time to be emerging from the woods looking like some naked feral youth. He craned his neck to look further down along the road and spotted a wooden caravan that had set up shop not far from the tree line. A bright orange awning hung over a wide window in the side of the caravan. Farris couldn't see what was inside the caravan from this angle, but a merchant had their head out the window with a length of vibrant purple fabric across their arm so the couple at the window could feel it. All three appeared to be making a show of the haggle, with one of the women in the pair jingling a coin purse on her hip and wavering her head back and forth. Behind the caravan, just out sight from the road, was a makeshift drying line upon which hung blankets and rugs. Underneath that line were several small piles of folded clothes.

Staying behind the rock wall, Farris worked his way closer to the caravan. An olive-skinned woman tended a pot suspended over a small fire, her walnut brown hair kept in place by a bandana patterned in swirls of orange and dark green. "Cassia!" came a shout from the other side of the caravan. "I need a sample of the royal fleece!" The woman sighed and stepped away from the pot, reaching down into one of several baskets under the clothesline.

Farris used her distraction to move in closer, narrowing his eyes and trying to pick out what looked like finished clothes and not just fabric samples. His foot landed on a twig, breaking it in two with a sharp *crack*. The woman's head snapped up; she whipped around and ran her eyes along the tree line. Farris dropped to the ground, crouching as low as he could get.

He held his breath, shaking slightly despite his best efforts. He strained his ears, listening for any rustling that might indicate Cassia moving through the grass toward him. When he heard a sigh and a muttering of "damned pixies," the tension finally left his muscles, and he let go of his breath. He lifted his head and peered through the brush just as she pulled out a fluffy blue textile.

As she returned briefly to the pot, Farris started to move again, practically crawling on his belly despite the additional scrapes he was sustaining, not to mention the rapid disintegration of his already shredded trousers. He smelled cooking meats and vegetables coming from the pot. He watched her dip a ladle, and the smell of stew wafted his way on a gentle breeze. His stomach growled loudly, and he laid flat to the ground again to muffle it. She sipped at the ladle and nodded with a smile.

"Cassia!" came a bellow from around the other side.

"Keep your breeches up!" she hollered back. "I'm coming!"

She shook her head as she moved around to the other side, and Farris lunged out of the brush toward the nearest basket of clothes. He knocked it over and spread the clothes out on the ground haphazardly. He grabbed the first pair of pants he saw, dark green as it so happened, and a purple shirt. He turned briefly but longingly towards the pot on the fire but didn't have time to pour a bowl, and the pot would be too hot to grab directly. When Farris' eyes came up from the pot, they settled on a flowing sky-blue skirt and his breath caught in his throat. A tan foot in sandals protruded from the skirt and tapped the ground. Farris' eyes trailed up to a pair of folded arms over a white blouse and eventually settled on the narrowed stormy blue eyes, one eyebrow raised.

For a moment, they stood frozen in place, each waiting for the other to make a move. Farris swallowed, and the noise of it echoed in his ears. He felt like his heart was going to stop dead in his chest as she cocked her head, her eyes wandering up and down. After a moment, she brushed an escaped lock of gingerbread brown hair behind her ear and started to snicker. Farris glanced down at his near nakedness and held the stolen clothes in front of himself, trying to retain whatever dignity he could.

The woman's mouth tensed up, its corners curling upwards even as she fought it. Her face went flush, and she held a hand over her mouth. Farris shrugged weakly and moved backward toward the tree line. When he was about to turn fully toward the woods, the woman waved at him to stop. She bent down, picked up a leather belt, and tossed it at him. He reached out to catch it but lost his grip on the bundled pants and shirt. The woman burst out in riotous laughter.

"Thanks," said Farris meekly, gathering up the clothes.

The woman waved him off. He jumped over the wall into the brush, holding the clothes tightly, and moved away from the laughter to find a spot where he could compose himself well enough to re-emerge and travel the road once more.

Chapter 5

A day's journey away to the southeast, a tall, pale, very severe woman strode Sagaris University's halls. The wide halls were sparsely populated, with class having been in session for some time. When she rounded a sharp corner, she came upon a cluster of half a dozen students in their plain white lab coats and leather shoulder bags. Two of them were comparing notes while three others jostled each other mockingly to the frustration of an onlooker. They didn't notice the woman at first, as the carpeted floor muffled her footsteps that would have otherwise reverberated off the riveted metal walls, polished to a nearly reflective shine. When one of them did take notice, they hastily alerted the others with a sharp whisper, and the group shuffled to the side against the wall as the woman passed, never slowing her stride.

She adjusted her spectacles as she passed by doors leading to lecture halls, the faint echoes of introductory-level lectures drifting out and creating a low hum in the hallway. Lectures on the basic principles of electrical conductivity, on the properties of different mined ores, on the powers of the known Fey species (from minor pests like brownies to the dreaded Morrighan), and much more.

When she reached a set of wooden double doors, she opened one silently and slipped into one of the lecture halls. She glided in among the back row chairs, the highest as each successive row of seats was lower, funneling down a gradual slope to the open space at the bottom of the semicircular room. As she chose a seat and pulled a clipboard and pen from her satchel, she glanced down at the white-haired and blotchy-skinned Professor Lawton at the bottom level of the room his nose aloft, pacing and reciting his well-rehearsed lecture.

"Generations later and the root cause of elementalism is still hotly debated, with few patterns having emerged among those who generate elemental forces." Professor Lawton paced before his students. A student in the front row raised her hand, but the professor took no notice. "Relative youth at the time of the first manifestation has been the only reliable consistency so far recorded."

"Professor?"

Professor Lawton stopped mid-stride and glared.

"Yes? Is there a question?"

The student dropped her hand hastily and shook her head before sinking into her seat.

The woman in the back frowned. The school year was in its third of four sessions, and the fact that only the first three rows were occupied spoke to this. She looked across the empty rows of the back half of the hall, which would have been packed full only five months ago. The first year of study was deliberately brutal, with the earliest classes and fullest schedules, the intent being to weed out those who lacked academic stamina. Only a third of new students made it to their second year, and only a third of those would see graduation and the chance to earn a place in the Science Guild. She could not remember the last time she'd been in a first-year lecture hall and placed two fingers on her temple amidst her short greying hair as Professor Lawton resumed his droning.

"And with elementals only generating a single type of energy, we must disregard the outdated notion they bear any similarity to the mystics and conjurers of the Old World."

The woman at the back scribbled an illegible note onto the clipboard and shook her head. As the minutes marched on at an overladen pace, her fingers kept coming back to her temple to gently rub as if trying to massage the boredom from her mind. She sighed when a low horn reverberated through the room and halls, marking the end of the class session.

While the students fumbled with books and notes and double-checking their schedules, she hastily stood, dropped the clipboard into a worn leather satchel, and pulled on her long, rustcolored coat. She didn't care whether Lawton had even realized her presence. She sidestepped out of the back row of seats and pushed open the double doors out into the corridor, which was already bustling with first-year students moving to their next classes. As she stepped into the sea of students, a young man with maroon cuffs on his white lab coat approached her.

"Professor Raines?"

"Yes?"

"Dean Gartis would like to see you," he said, failing to keep his intimidation out of his voice.

Professor Raines nodded tersely. The young man lowered his head and wound around her to head down the hall. As soon as he passed, she frowned, and after glancing back to be certain he had rounded the corner, she let out a heavy sigh. For the past few weeks, her communications with the administration had been through memos and messengers, which was how she preferred it, but the face-to-face talk was inevitable.

She headed up a nearby ramp, stepping aside for a post-grad in a wheelchair, and then emerged into the courtyard. She blinked as the sun shone down on the three-tiered steel pyramid that was Sagaris. She stood atop the first tier, housing classrooms in its perimeter and laboratories in its center. Small patches of grass with single trees and the occasional bench dotted the courtyard. She paid no mind to the students congregated about in the open air, nor to the ones dashing from the dormitories in the second tier to their classes in the first. She turned to the second tier and walked a direct path to one of the glass-encased faculty lifts along its side.

Once inside the cylindrical lift, Professor Raines closed the steel-framed glass door and removed a key from around her neck, inserting it into a keyhole on the left side of the door. With a grinding of gears, the lift began to rise the second tier's steep side, staying upright even as it went. It came to a shuddering halt at the halfway mark. She slid open a hidden panel in the steel frame that reinforced the lift, revealing a circular impression.

She adjusted her guild ring bearing the university's insignia, a series of interconnected spirals, before pressing it against the impression in the wall and giving it a quarter turn to the left.

The lift restarted, and she took her ring out of the impression, sliding the panel closed.

As the lift neared the top of the second tier, the professor removed her spectacles and replaced them with a pair of shaded goggles from her satchel. Soon, the lift slowed to a complete halt, and she stepped out into a brilliantly bright light. Sun collection panels covered nearly the entire second tier's roof. They helped power the facility, but their reflective frames made them blinding to anyone looking directly at them. The goggles allowed her to safely make out the path that cut through the panels, leading to the third tier that housed the administrative offices.

Sagaris University sat in an open field, buffeted by the Everwood to the north and the Gragient Sea to the south. On a clear day, the mountains could be seen cutting through the heart of the forest. Professor Raines paused between panels, looking out over the Everwood and the Celeste Mountains before continuing through the double doors leading to the administrative offices. Inside, the professor was confronted with another set of nearly identical doors. She kept looking forward as she removed the protective goggles and replaced them with her spectacles. As she did, the double outer doors closed behind her, allowing her to open the inner doors to the reception area. She walked across the maroon strip of carpet to the polished metal receptionist desk. Behind the desk sat another post-grad in his maroon cuffed coat, with a large leather-bound book in front of him.

"Professor Raines for Dean Gartis," she said as she approached the desk, not bothering to hide the irritation in her voice.

He opened the leather appointment book to the corresponding page and nodded. "Yes, he's expecting you, it's—"

"I know where it is." Professor Raines glided past the desk to the left and into the hallway beyond.

Her rust-colored coat flowed behind her as she walked down the hall of polished and reflective metal. After a few turns through the hallway, she arrived at a wooden door with a brass nameplate. Cassius Gartis – Dean of Elemental Studies. She knocked roughly on the door.

With a mechanical whir, the door unlocked and swung open.

The room inside could be comfortably called over-decorated. A deep red carpet covered the floor, while tapestries with swirling yellow, green, and blue adorned the walls. Shelves filled with thick volumes placed alongside polished silver and gold statuettes aided in removing any hint of the university's cold metal construction. Amidst all this, the sandy-skinned and golden-haired Dean Gartis sat behind his large hand-carved wood desk, looking rather like a child sitting at his parent's workspace.

"Draza," he said, smiling and motioning for her to sit in one of the dark green chairs in front of his desk. "Thank you for coming."

As she entered, he pushed a button on the arm of his chair, and the door gently closed behind her. Professor Raines placed her satchel beside one of the chairs before settling into it. The chair was purposefully set low to the ground, allowing the high seated dean to look down on those who sat before him. If they had been on an even plane, she would have been the one looking down on him. "Dean Gartis," she acknowledged coldly.

"So, how was the lecture refresher?" He laced his fingers together and rested them on the desk.

"Should I answer that diplomatically or honestly?"

"I always expect honesty from you."

"Lawton is a pompous windbag. He hasn't changed his lecture more than three syllables since I was forced to sit through it as a student," said Professor Raines as she gripped the side of the chair, just below the dean's line of sight. "There are years of advances he ignores because they don't fit into his outdated prepared speeches."

"Valid points." He nodded. "There's a reason he's still only lecturing the introductory classes, but he has a consistency which is easily built upon. And I feel you benefitted from seeing that. I know it's been a long time since you held a lecture."

"I don't belong in a lecture hall with undergrads," she replied, her fingers tightening around the edge of the chair. "I belong in a laboratory with skilled assistants."

The dean put up his hands and nodded with a smirk. "I absolutely agree with you; however, the board feels you've been cooped up for too long and should be circulated. I know you took the"—he paused, taking a moment to choose his next word with care—"loss of your prized specimen rather hard."

"That was not my fault!"

"It's not a question of fault, Draza." The dean's smirk faded by half as he brought his hands together on the desk and began tapping the index fingers together. "It happened in your lab, which makes it your responsibility. The impact of the incident was far too great to just sweep under the rug." Professor Raines held her tongue as the dean continued. "Adding the disappointing results of your last project, and I've been left with little choice."

Professor Raines leaned against the back of the chair and took a deep breath before speaking. "When can I get back to my lab?"

"I'll try to wrap the inquisition up quickly. However, I'll need you to put in at least two full semesters in the lecture hall. It will show the board you have broader skills than they're giving you credit for, and I also suspect they'll notice a lack of advancement coming out of the elementalism lab without you heading it."

"And in the meantime, I'm put a year behind in my research." She folded her arms and sat up straighter in the chair.

The last remnants of the smirk vanished, and the dean said nothing for several seconds, narrowing his eyes at her. "It's a slap on the wrist Draza, take it and be grateful."

She took another deep breath before making her final inquiry. "What about my test subject?"

"The board feels you've probably acquired most of the relevant knowledge that could be gleaned from that specimen already, so no formal recovery is being mounted at this time." Dean Gartis unclasped his hands and leaned back in his chair. "I wouldn't worry about it. If the subject makes a splash out there, then we'll send a collection team or employ a marshal as needed." The smirk returned to his face, in time with a casual wave of his hand. "And something tells me this particular specimen will have a difficult time keeping a low profile."

Chapter 6

Garion peered down from his perch on a branch six feet off the ground. A thick blanket of bright green moss filled the toadstool ring—except for the human face with its eyes closed and its mouth open. It looked like someone getting one last breath of air before drowning.

The face appeared almost serene, with the pale coloring giving it a delicate look like it might crack if touched. Garion pulled a small vial from the folds of his cloak, uncorked it, and with a steady hand let a drop of red liquid fall and land directly between the closed eyes. As soon as it landed, the eyes shot open and darted in all directions, though the face itself did not turn or move. Soon the eyes settled on the hooded figure above them.

"Hello, Franklin," Garion said.

The first few attempts Marshal Franklin made to speak yielded only slight gurgles. With a great deal of effort, he was able to speak. "G... get me out of here," he said in a strained rasp.

"I'll think about it, but I have a few questions first," replied Garion as he nonchalantly tucked the vial into the folds of his robes.

"P... please, get me out and I..." Franklin paused. "I'll tell you anything."

"I'd rather get some answers first," said Garion, shaking his head. "Then we'll talk about getting you out. Or I could just go; it's not really much difference to me."

"No," whimpered Franklin. "Anything… please."

"Good. Now, who contracted you for the boy?"

"No one."

Garion leaned closer. "Don't lie to me."

"I swear. Spotted him fleeing the…" Franklin paused again. "Outpost. Followed him, easy mark."

"There're no easy marks in the Everwood." Garion shook his head dismissively. He smirked behind his scarf. Hearing that Franklin had only come across the boy by luck meant there shouldn't be any more competing marshals. This sort of thing was why he never took unwarranted work; it was too messy with too many things to go wrong. But debts had been called in, so he had to make do.

A branch near the canopy creaked, and leaves rustled. Garion glanced up just in time to see the silhouette of a treshen leaping between trees. A sharp chattering echoed from several directions. Garion looked around for the best place to jump to.

Franklin saw that Garion was preparing to leap away, and panic flooded his eyes. "Stop… Garion, help me."

Garion adjusted his stance so his bare feet clung to the branch. He fell forward, but his feet held on, so he swung downward until he was upside down and his half-concealed face was hanging inches from Franklin's. "I know you can't move your head enough to look and see this, so you'll have to take my word for it," Garion said grimly. "There's nothing left to help." "What—"

Garion cut him off with a wave of his hand. "This right here," he said as he outlined the marshal's face in the air with a grey finger, "is all that's left. The moss has absorbed the rest of you. The only reason you can even form a thought is because your brain hasn't been broken down yet." "Please…"

"You're already dead; you're plant food. Your brain is firing off residual energy from the moss and a dash of this." Garion removed the vial from his cloak again and dangled it in front of the trapped marshal's eyes before putting it back once more. "But that was only ever going to buy you a few minutes." The leaves above Garion's head rustled, and the chattering started to crescendo. The treshen would descend on him if he didn't move soon. "If you have any last words, better make it fast."

Franklin's eyes began to cloud over. The moss had started creeping up around the edges of his exposed face. His lips moved slowly but deliberately. "Damn you... Half-breed."

"True to form. Goodbye, Franklin." And with that, he swung off the branch and clung to the side of an ash tree on the other side of the toadstool ring. He paused for one last look back at the face of Marshal Franklin embedded in the creeping moss.

Garion clasped onto the trunk of the tree with only his feet as he reached under his cloak and pulled out a tightly rolled scrap of parchment. He unrolled it, scribbled what would look like gibberish to anyone who didn't know how to decode the message, rolled it back up, and tucked it away to be sent off once he was clear of the forest.

His ears pricked up at the sound of a branch creaking and a *whoosh* of air above him. The sound repeated several times in rapid succession.

Garion sprang away from the trunk as a half dozen treshen descended. Some landed softly on the ground while two raked their thorny talons down the trunk Garion had vacated. He leapt for the first branch thick enough to support him, grabbing it with his hands, and let momentum swing his legs forward. He released the branch, landed on the ground, and rolled forward. The treshen pursued him on all fours, but Garion's stride was longer and his legs more powerful as he ran through the forest, easily leaping over whatever obstacles were in his way and never looking back. The savage Fey steadily lost ground and soon gave up the chase. Garion, however, was hot on the heels of his prey, and giving up the chase was something he would never do.

Chapter 7

"Wow."

When Farris crested a hill and spotted the high walls of Torvec, he stopped dead on the road and stared at the fabled "Locket of the Lake." The city was built on the shore of Lake Vaettir, and in fact, the shoreline bisects the city into the cobblestone roads of the shoreside and the canals and elevated walkways of the lakeside. The wall, stone reinforced with shining metal, ran unbroken around the entire city, extending even into the lake itself. From the center point of the lakeside wall, a great dam extended the full three-mile distance across the oblong body of water. Behind the wall, buildings reached up, with an opulent dome in the center of the city. Even the small wooden buildings that buffeted the main road as it reached the city gate seemed to be gleaming in the sunlight.

Farris snapped his gaping mouth closed and sighed a small relief there weren't any other travelers close enough to have seen his literal slack jaw. He started down the hill with a new spring in his step and a renewed sense of adventure, something he hadn't felt since his first day on the run.

As he got closer, Farris puzzled at the fact he didn't see any smoke rising from anywhere.

Torvec was the last large city east of the continental divide not to be powered by the Guild's lightning cages; that was why he'd picked it as a destination. The Science Guild held no direct sway because the city wasn't dependent on their technology to keep the lights on.

The only other way to power a city of this size would have been with combustible fuels made by the Alchemist League to the west. As the road leveled out at the bottom of the hill, he shrugged his concern off by reminding himself he didn't know much about alchemy anyways. The League had been superseded on the eastern side of the continent by the Guild for longer than he'd been alive, and for all he knew, they made smokeless fuels by the barrel.

Farris enjoyed the mental exercise of this train of thought, but his sense of excitement was tempered by reality as he drew closer to the city. He didn't have a solid sense of what to do next once he reached it. The opportunity for him to escape his confinement within Sagaris University had come suddenly; it had not been a part of a grand plan. So, for the last three days, his only real goal had been reaching this city and its port. How he would pay his way, or find shelter within the city walls, or even what his ultimate destination was, were things he still did not know. They'd been filed away as a "deal with that later," but "that later" snuck up on him.

"At least you're out of the wood," Farris reminded himself. "One step at a time."

Trying not to dwell on the forest itself but unable to fully clear it from his mind, he thought of the many stories his mother had told him of the creatures who lurked amongst the trees. He'd already had his fill of the treshen, but there was some small comfort in all the things he hadn't encountered. No sadistic redcaps with their bare pates coated in blood had tripped or snared him. No misshapen trow had thrown rocks at him. He'd not heard the hypnotic voice of a huldra, the very idea of which sent a shiver of lingering childhood dread down his spine. As much as he'd always been fascinated by the Fey and what they could do, his mother had instilled a proper sense of fear. Being older now, he suspected some of his bedtime stories had been embellished, but the lingering fear they instilled remained, and that fear was now bolstered by experience.

Farris frowned and rubbed his hands together for warmth. Though the sun was beating down, a vicious breeze coming off the lake cut through his oversized clothes. He said a mental "thank you" to Cassia for the belt because, without it, the pants would instantly drop to his ankles. He took a moment to look down at his hands as he rubbed them, pausing to touch his upper chest. His fingers were chilled from the wind, almost icy. A slow smile spread across his face, and his shoulders drooped as some of the tension left them. He had yet to accurately predict when his elemental forces would demand release, but there was little doubt he'd be in the city before that happened, and once there, he could find an isolated nook to expel them safely. He looked out to the lake and took a deep, steadying breath. Releasing his powers underwater was an amazing sight, one he almost looked forward to. The flame would cut through the water and writhe about briefly like a fiery serpent before succumbing and burning out.

A smile crept back onto his face, and he perked up slightly. Now he had at least an immediate plan; that's more than he had a few minutes earlier and was something to be happy for. But then he reminded himself just as quickly that all he had was a plan to spin his wheels in the city and didn't have the first clue how he'd get passage on a ship elsewhere or where "elsewhere" would even be. He shook his head, trying to stop the back and forth arguing between his sense of accomplishment and his anxiety, forcing it all back into "deal with it later" because fretting over it was not helping.

Despite his best efforts, his brain needled him with reminders of what'd gone wrong so far, thanks to his lack of a plan. He thought of the woman he'd burned at the outpost just because he'd decided the comfort of a night indoors was more important than the damage he might do. Her scream echoed in his head.

He found himself wondering if he should have let the marshal take him in. At least he wouldn't be able to hurt anybody if he were locked up. The marshal—another person injured because of him. He sighed. Rationally, Farris knew the marshal's fate was his own fault for following him into the Everwood. He'd have found himself in a worse situation than the one he'd fled if the marshal had captured him. He rubbed his arms and told himself the Fey had attacked due to the marshal's actions; he even believed it, but guilt still ate away at him.

A low rumble growing louder snapped Farris out of his head. He sidestepped to the edge of the road, allowing a lumbering crate-shaped motorized cart twice his height to chug past him going the other way. As he neared the city, merchants and travelers making their way to and from the city filled the road. The wind blasted him again and drew tears to his eyes. He clutched the flapping cloth of the oversized shirt, put his head down, and pushed onward.

***

The wind finally started to ease off as he reached the outskirts of Barreth, a small hamlet of inns, restaurants, and supply shops outside Torvec's main gate. The dirt of the valley road transitioned to a cobblestone street with wooden walkways running along either side. It was a pleasant enough place, but Farris was too astounded at the wall's size to notice much about the small wooden buildings he was passing. It's not that he wasn't used to the scale; the Science Guild liked to build big if Sagaris was any indication, but there was something about this wall that left him breathless. Massive plates of thick steel had been affixed to the exterior of the original stone structure. The rivets were almost the size of his head, and yet there was a kind of artistry to the buttresses supporting it from the outside. The thought of how much work had gone into the structure left him dumbfounded.

As Farris made his way toward the gate, he spotted the city's constables' dark blue uniforms at the entrance and tensed. He stepped off the road and pretended to browse the thick cloaks in the nearest shop window while shooting glances at the constables out of the corner of his eye. He saw a trio of broad-shouldered figures, their boots crusted with dirt and carrying heavy packs, and watched as they passed through the gate with little more than a passing nod from a constable. It soon became clear the constables were only there to ensure a smooth flow of traffic and didn't appear to be stopping anyone.

"Just walk through," he muttered to himself. "It'll be fine. Look like you belong here."

He started to move toward the gate again, meandering back onto the road and side-stepping oxen droppings. He pinched his nose closed for a few steps until he found his rhythm again. As he approached the gate, he gave an awkward wave to one of the constables. The man nodded in acknowledgment but otherwise ignored him. Once he was through the main gates, he abandoned the large, open square that greeted newcomers and ducked down a small side street to take stock. Leaning against the side of a wooden building, he looked at the structures around him.

Torvec had been built up in spurts over time, resulting in a mix of drastically different building styles crammed together as staggered periods of growth favored new materials and aesthetics. The wooden building he was leaning against was three stories high, and the third story looked as though it had been added haphazardly after the fact. Directly across the street stood a massive rectangular iron structure, six stories tall, with the building's corners accented with spiked protrusions. Farris found the contrast bizarre yet oddly endearing as he began to wander down the street, taking the first chance to turn west toward the lakeside.

He started to feel like a tourist, a feeling he embraced because it was certainly better than feeling like a fugitive. He passed a cozy little flower shop in a brick building bordered by drab and utilitarian stone housing blocks. Across the street, a couple was trying to wrangle five children and keep them going in the same direction with little success. He drifted by a sidewalk café and needed to restrain himself from snagging an unattended pastry from one of the tables, but the last thing he needed to do was break the law and give the authorities a reason to be interested in him. His stomach grumbled in protest.

Farris ducked down the street next to the café and from there headed toward an alleyway behind the building, hoping to spot a refuse bin where he could find unfinished and relatively fresh meals. Unfortunately, he wasn't the only person who had that thought. A tall man in a tattered coat and torn pants, a woman in a faded dress, and a short individual wrapped in ragged oversized brown robes with a hood that concealed them almost entirely were already occupying the alley. All three appeared to be waiting for someone to come out the café's back door and dispose of something edible, though they kept a few yards clear of the bin itself. Farris frowned; he had no way of knowing if they were together or if they were about to fight each other for whatever scraps appeared, or whether any of them would be willing to share. Given the palpable tension in their stances, he expected not.

He sighed and left the alley, knowing he wouldn't be able to fend off the melancholy that was washing over him. Seeing those three street urchins practically shaking with anticipation of little more than garbage filled him with a sadness he couldn't put into words. It made him even more worried about his situation, and it occurred to him he may be looking at his future. Not knowing what else to do, for the time being, he leaned back against a wall and let himself slide to the ground. If he couldn't get something to eat, he could at least get off his feet for the first time since the toadstool ring.

It was only after Farris took his weight off his legs it struck him just how exhausted they were. The determination that had gotten him here could no longer mask the aches he'd accumulated in his limbs. As he began to rub one of his legs, he heard a metallic clink on the cobblestone in front of him as a man strolled past. Looking down, he saw a tarnished copper coin dropped by the passerby, who clearly thought he was some kind of beggar.

Though the idea he looked like a beggar didn't do much for Farris' ego, he wasn't about to question an unsolicited gift. As he leaned forward on his hands and knees to pick up the coin, there was a flash of light and a sharp *bang* from the alley. He leaned further into the street, trying to see around the corner. The robed figure bolted around the corner, holding what looked like a half-eaten sandwich. A small pale hand shot out from the robes and pushed Farris roughly against the wall with more force than he'd have thought somebody that small could manage.

"Ow!" he yelped as his back slammed against the wall. He slid sideways and landed with his shoulder hitting the cobblestones. He started to straighten up again when he saw the other two from the alley round the corner and give chase, barreling toward him. Farris brought his chin to his chest and covered his head as the man jumped over him and the woman went around him, both shouting in an accent Farris couldn't parse. He uncovered his head and was surprised to see how little reaction this scene had caused. There were two women, one in a bright blue vest, the other in an emerald-green dress that went down to her ankles, glancing up the street at the chase for a moment before turning and walking away, hand in hand. No one else on the street and no one at the café seemed to have noticed. No one came to see if Farris was alright either. They all simply went about their business.

Farris propped himself back up to a sitting position, rubbing his shoulder and adding it to his growing list of cuts and bruises. He glanced down at his chest to see a slight singe on his shirt where the robed figure had pushed him. Touching it, he received a light static shock.

"What the…?"

He frowned and shook his head before reaching down for the copper coin again. As he pinched it between his thumb and forefinger, he noted a tingle in the tips of his fingers. Between the stress of passing through the gate, the hunger, the pain in his legs, and then being knocked over, Farris hadn't really taken proper stock of his energies. He looked from his hands to his surroundings and his mind's eye pictured every wooden cart, door, and building engulfed in flames. He swore under his breath and gritted his teeth through the aching in his legs to force himself onto his feet and begin his search for a safe spot, ideally with water.

Chapter 8

Deep in the heart of Sagaris University's largest tier, Professor Raines stood behind her office desk, rapping her fingers on its well-worn surface. Sunlight had never touched most of the objects in the office, and the artificial light gave everything a sickly green tint, including the professor herself. The shelves that lined the walls were full near to bursting with reference books, teaching texts, and leather-bound notebooks documenting her work. Handwritten scribbling on the notebooks' spines marked the dates and names of various projects she had worked on or supervised over the years. If there were a filing system of any kind, it would not have been apparent to anybody other than her.

Behind the professor's faded leather chair, a stainless-steel work counter jutted out from the wall underneath rows of steel cabinets, most of which bore elaborate combination locks. She turned to an open cabinet and removed a bottle of blue translucent liquid as well as a small glass. She turned back to her desk with gritted teeth and slammed the bottle down next to a small piece of rolled parchment. She took a deep, slow breath before placing the glass down next to the bottle with a lighter touch.

The professor sat down heavily. She poured the blue liquid from the bottle into the glass until it reached halfway, then let it bubble as she unrolled the parchment for the fourth time in as many minutes. It still read the same as it had the last three times she'd checked: Confirmed sighting at valley outpost. Torvec likely destination. If city is reached, subject may be lost. Competing marshal neutralized. Continuing pursuit.

Professor Raines dragged her fingers across the imitation wood surface of her desk, her nails leaving shallow gouges in their wake. She viciously snatched up the parchment and paper with her decoded notes, turned to the wall, and opened a small hatch between the counter and the cabinets. Throwing both parchment and paper into the compartment, she snapped the hatch shut and pressed a small red button beside it. A deep rumbling from the wall and an orange glow at the edges of the hatch came and faded as the items inside were incinerated.

She rose from her desk, leaving the drink untouched, and went to the door. Frowning as she opened it forcefully, she stormed down the short barren hallway to the hub connecting the labs she supervised. Her purposeful footfalls reverberated against the undecorated metal walls. Unlike the lecture halls and administrative offices, the laboratory section had no use for comforts like carpet or portraits. Being here meant working, and anything that didn't aid in the work had no place. From the hub, she headed down a hallway marked "Containment Lab 4." Upon reaching the metal door to the lab, she pressed a button on the wall, and something buzzed from inside. A steel slat slid open, and a pair of young blue eyes set against alabaster skin peered at her. Just as quickly, the slat snapped shut, and the door pulled open from the inside.

The professor walked through, stepping onto the observation deck and leaving her teaching aide to close the heavy steel door behind her. The lab's lighting was much stronger than in the professor's office—rather than the sickly green, everything was bathed in harsh white.

Thick glass encased the observation deck, looking down upon the lab proper. Charred and broken remains of a containment capsule stood in the center of the lab, a twisted skeleton of exploded metal.

This was the first time Professor Raines had been in Containment Lab 4 since the incident, and she looked over the scene with narrowed eyes and tight lips. She gripped the safety rail a few inches from the glass, her knuckles whitening. Scratches and cuts, some still healing, were scattered across the backs of her hands. She looked from those cuts to the exploded capsule, the moment of it erupting in energy and showering her with shards of glass as she'd shielded her face. Her breath was short and shallow; she closed her eyes and inhaled slowly, letting it out in a prolonged sigh before opening her eyes once more.

Lab Assistant Petit, who'd let her in, approached from behind and gave an awkward cough. "As you can see, the observation port was replaced. We've also been able to clean up the loose debris," she said nervously. "However, the board has not yet authorized replacing the containment unit."

The professor hung her head for a moment, glaring at her hands. "I want this lab kept on lockdown until we're permitted new equipment."

"The investigative auditors are still collecting data," Petit replied, nervously tapping her fingers on the backside of her clipboard. "They requested the project notes again… They already have the observation logs, but—"

Professor Raines rounded on her. "Let them collect their own data; they will not be privy to mine."

"But... the board—" Petit stammered, stumbling back a step and clutching the clipboard to her chest.

"Divert all requests for lab findings to me. I will not simply hand over months of research to administrative cronies on the whim of those who have no right to even call themselves scientists!" She paused and drew in a slow breath before continuing in a gentler tone. "Just send them to me, Carolyn. I will take responsibility." She placed a hand on her assistant's shoulder. "Do you understand?" Lab Assistant Petit nodded, and the professor patted her shoulder lightly before departing the lab.

Once she reached the metal door to her office, she took a small key from around her neck and inserted it into a sliver-thin slot just under the plaque with her name and title. Once the door closed behind her, she stood and stared at the glass of blue liquid still atop her desk.

She kept her eyes on the glass as she walked back to her desk and sank into her chair. She reached out and ran her fingers along the edge of the glass. Drinking it would calm her nerves, but it wouldn't change anything. Not really. It would only make her a slightly calmer and duller scientist, and even that would be short-lived. She looked to her shelves of notebooks, shook her head, and let out a hollow chuckle, thinking back to the days when there was nothing she would have ever done to jeopardize her station. But the work she'd been doing—work even her lab assistants didn't recognize for what it was— mattered more than any possible punishment, and if the Guild knew, it could truly cost her everything.

She lifted the glass tentatively, noticing it left a ring behind on the desk. She peered at the blue drink with a sense of longing before setting it back down. Turning around, she pulled the bottle from the open cabinet once again, and with an expert hand, slowly poured the contents of the glass back into the bottle without a single drop spilt. She returned the bottle to the cabinet and locked it. She looked at the now empty glass in her hand for a moment before throwing it full force against the office door, where it shattered into a shower of glistening shards.

Chapter 9

"Damn it, damn it, damn it, damn it…"

Farris was putting a great deal of effort into not panicking, but it was sinking in just how badly he'd gotten turned around since entering the city. The warm tingling in his fingertips was spreading across his hands, which he clenched tightly as he tried to get his bearings. He was on a narrow street, too small for anything besides foot traffic, keeping his head down, avoiding eye contact with the couple coming the other way. He moved quickly to where the next street connected, hoping to spot a sign, street name, or any possible way to determine his location, but found no guidance. A chocolate-skinned woman in a lilac dress glanced at him as he passed, and his eyes shot to his hands to be sure there wasn't smoke coming from them that might have caught her attention. He frowned and looked down both ways of the road, only slightly wider than the one he'd come from, hoping to spot one of the bustling streets that actually had names. If there was any sort of system in place to guide travelers, Farris hadn't been able to work it out. And being well aware that this was likely more reflective of his frazzled state of mind than of the city layout only frustrated him further.

His head shot back and forth several times before noticing a pale, slender person in a green vest furrowing their brow at him. Farris headed to his right, for no better reason than staying still seemed like the worst available option. He fought the impulse to glance back and see if they were still watching him and turned left at the first opportunity. He tucked his hands under his armpits and held his arms close to his chest. Deciding that it was time, he forced himself to ask for directions from the next person he saw. He tried not to let the tension show in his face as he approached a lanky man with honey-toned skin who was leaning against a lamppost on a narrow street, inhaling the fumes from a burning incense stick in his hand.

"Excuse me…" called Farris as he drew near.

"It's my last one; I don't have anymore," the man snapped before turning to leave.

"No, wait! I just need to know the way to the canals."

The man turned back to him and took a deep breath of the fumes.

"New in town, eh?" He smirked before pointing to his right with a flick of the wrist. "Not exactly around the corner, but head that way, and you can't miss 'em."

"Thanks." Farris nodded, keeping his hands tucked under his arms, and turned down the first street running in the direction the man had pointed.

He felt safer on the side streets, but their disjointed, near labyrinthine nature had gotten him lost in the first place, and he couldn't risk it happening again. Accepting the fact that a busier but more direct route would get him to the canals much faster, he glanced down the narrow road he was on, saw one of the wider primary streets, and moved towards it as quickly as he could without breaking into a full run.

When he exited the confines of the narrow side streets and alleys and emerged onto Crown Boulevard, the sun nearly blinded him, and he had to shield his eyes and squint. Many people wore shaded spectacles, and some of the better-dressed folks carried lacey parasols. As his eyes adjusted, he caught the whiff of fresh bread from a nearby bakery. He diverted his way around a vegetable cart, nearly bumping into the customer loading a basket with leafy greens. He kept a steady pace, silently pleading that he wouldn't catch the eyes of the constables as there appeared to be one at every other corner, calmly surveying the street. Every time Farris thought he saw the eyes of a constable glance in his direction, he felt the heat in his forearms spread a little higher and grow a little hotter. He began to sweat but didn't wipe his brow, only tilted his head down and pushed forward.

He wasn't going to make it to the docks unless he ran, and running would give the constables a reason to notice him. The scream of the woman from the outpost echoed in his mind. He winced and shook his head, scattering droplets of sweat onto the stones of the street. His head began to move in rhythm with every step, glancing from shop windows to pedestrians to constables and back to the ground. He forced himself to keep his head down and minimize his increasingly twitchy movements. When he allowed himself to look up again, he saw the street opened into a square.

Where the street had been all movement and bustle, the people in the square were in no rush. Friends chatted around the perimeter, parents sat on benches and watched their children chase each other. And in the center stood a circular fountain with three tiers, and the jet of water at the top reached up into the glittering sun before dispersing out and collecting in the pool around it. The fountain itself was ringed by a metal grating that drained away any excess that spilled out from the children reaching in to try and splash each other. The brimming pool of water at the fountain's base looked just big enough to contain his flames.

He would be caught, but no one would be hurt.

Farris set his jaw and lunged forward but took only one step before the burning shot up his arms into his shoulders in a rush of pain, bringing him to his knees. He looked up from the hard stones. A cluster of people in simple garb were closing in around him, their faces filled with curiosity or concern. A couple wielding matching lace parasols turned to move away while a burly, almond-skinned constable, looking like they might tear their uniform if they flexed their muscles, led a cluster of people towards him.

"You alright there, friend?" came a voice that sounded miles away. "What's your name?"

Farris closed his eyes tightly, using everything he had to keep the fires contained and hoping against all indications that when he opened them, he would still be in the Everwood. As terrifying as that prospect was, it would be better than what was happening now. He felt himself being lifted off the ground.

"This boy's burning up!" hollered the constable.

It was all over, and there was no escape now. Part of him wanted to give up and just let go. He'd already lost, was there any point in fighting back the flame now? The image of all the people in the square flashed across his mind, and Farris curled up a little tighter, tucking his hands under his arms to keep his scorching touch off the person carrying him. A whiff of smoke hit his nostrils as his hands began to singe his shirt.

"Move aside! I need to get him to the ward!"

***

The public ward sat at the edge of the fountain square, but Farris was so focused on holding back the fire, he barely registered being carried into the building and laid down. He only dared to open his eyes for a moment before closing them again. In that brief glimpse, he saw, to his horror, he was on a cot in the middle of a room filled with people awaiting care.

The constable waved towards a woman in a hooded plum-colored robe. The hood was up, obscuring her face. The robe flowed behind her as she responded to the summons.

"Matron, he collapsed in the square. He's burning up, and he wasn't responsive when I asked his name."

"Thank you." She knelt beside Farris and lowered her hood. "You did the right thing. Could you please ask the front desk to send me two orderlies right away?"

The constable hurried back toward the front entrance of the ward. Farris began shaking and shuddering from the effort of keeping everything bottled up. The matron leaned close to his ear and whispered, "What element are you?"

Farris forced his eyes open and looked directly at her. She had short, cropped hair and a carob complexion. Her angular features cast nothing but compassion, but he was too scared to affirm what he was. He only shook his head stiffly as his shuddering worsened.

The matron glanced around quickly before reaching a hand toward Farris.

"Don't—"

Ignoring his plea, she touched her hand to his pale, clammy skin where the neck of the shirt dipped down.

The energy building in his hands and arms was stronger than ever, but the excruciating pain retreated from her touch. A white glow emanated from her palm, flowing into his chest. He looked into her warm brown eyes, and she nodded with reassurance.

"What is your element?"

"Fire," he whispered.

She nodded again and removed her hand from his chest. To his relief, the soothing sensation he'd felt at her touch did not immediately vanish once the physical connection was broken. However, the pain started to return to his hands, where the energies inside of him were most concentrated.

The matron leaned in close to him again. "Close your eyes and focus. Don't let go until I tell you."

Farris nodded his quivering head and shut his eyes in concentration once more. He would need all his strength to keep the flames at bay and steel himself against the returning pain.

The matron waved over the two orderlies. "I need this boy taken to quarantine immediately. Handle him very carefully." She stepped back and allowed the orderlies to take positions at Farris' head and feet. "Use your gloves and follow me."

The cot jutted about as an orderly grabbed each end. Farris kept his eyes closed, trying to keep everything inside. There was a creak of a sliding steel gate, and he was maneuvered into a smaller space that soon vibrated and whirred before lurching into its descent.

The journey downwards seemed an eternity to Farris. The pain the matron had eased was rushing back. He grit his teeth against it as the lift shuddered to a stop, and the orderlies carried him out. The sound of their boots echoed off cold, stone walls, and a chill in the air made Farris shiver despite the heat building in his hands.

The orderlies moved with practiced efficiency down a hall and into a room, gingerly placing the cot onto a metal bench embedded in the wall. The stone walls were bare; there was a flickering light on the ceiling but no window. Had Farris opened his eyes, he would have thought it more akin to a dungeon than anything else.

"Thank you both. Now you two go to the sterilizing showers and be sure you dispose of the gloves. After that, you may return to your posts. I'll make sure he's registered and monitored."

"Yes, Matron Branford," responded one of the orderlies. They both gave very slight bows before exiting the room.

Once their backs were turned, Matron Branford leaned down to Farris and whispered, "Not yet, just hold on."

Her sandals scuffed across the stone as she hurried out of the room. Farris clutched his chest, trying and failing to slow his breathing as he heard a heavy metal door scrape along the floor until its latch caught with a heavy *clank*. For lack of anything else to focus on, he listened as bolts on the outside were locked at the top and bottom of the door. Another wave of burning heat ran up his arms, and he lurched off the cot onto the floor. The cold stone gave him a breath of relief, but it was gone within a second. He curled into a tight, fetal ball, unable to rise from the floor.

He heard more scraping of metal midway up the heavy door as a hatch slid open, and the matron peered in at him. Smoke wafted up from under his arms where he'd tucked his clenched fists; the smell of singed fabric accompanied the faintest crackling sound. He set his jaw and let out a groan—a groan, which, without any intent from him, turned into a rasping scream. Underneath his tightly shut eyelids was a faint red glow.

"Now!" shouted the matron, and she immediately ducked her head back from the open hatch.

Farris let loose the forces inside of him, filling the entire room with fire and escaping through the open hatch as a spear of flame. The matron quickly pushed the hatch closed with the thickest part of her sandal.

The thinner metal of the hatch, and a matching one at the foot of the door, began to glow red, then orange, and then white. Inside, the flames danced and whirled around the room, obliterating the cot before thrashing about wildly, searching for something else to consume. Farris' fingers were rigid, spread out as if having to make room for the fire that poured from and between them. As the last of his energies escaped, he fell limply down onto the floor, and the word faded away; he slept out of sheer exhaustion.

Chapter 10

Farris' thoughts were fractured and hazy as he wandered through a dense forest. The thick cover of trees should have blotted out the sun, but it was as bright as if he were in an open field. He pushed branches out of his way, despite not being sure where he was going. He simply felt a deep-seated need to keep moving.

Soon, he found himself in a small circular patch of grass. The branches around him stretched over, enclosing the clearing in a dome of wood and leaves. Though the sky was almost entirely obscured, the tall grass did not seem to be missing a single ray of sunlight. Looking around, he saw all sides of the clearing walled off by thick knots of thorny vines. Turning to look back the way he came, he stopped short, seeing the yielding branches he had just pushed past were now an impenetrable wall of wicked, thorny bramble.

Farris approached the tightly knit vines nervously, trying to see any way through them. He reached out with his left hand and touched the tip of a thorn, intending to test its sharpness. To his surprise, the vines recoiled, pulling back and forming a small porthole to the forest beyond the clearing. Farris looked down at the fingers on his left hand and saw his index and middle fingers' tips were blackened and burnt. He brought his other hand to his face to compare the two, confirming there was nothing out of place on his right hand. He reached his right hand toward the bramble. His unblemished fingers were pricked and started to bleed when the thorny vines failed to retract. Farris sucked the drop of blood off while reaching out with his left hand once more. He led with the two burnt fingers, and the vines receded until he had an unobstructed path out of the prison-like clearing.

As soon as he was clear, his eyes landed on a fallen form among the trees ahead of him. It curled up upon the ground and was a brilliant white. It was not actually radiating light, yet somehow it was the focal point, all the same. When he drew closer, he heard slow labored breaths and saw the curled form heaving from the effort of breathing.

He still couldn't make out what he was looking at, but as he drew closer, he could appreciate its size. It was too large to be a human or any Fey. Whatever it was, it was in pain and needed help. Farris was about to break into a run to reach it when a sharp call rang out from behind him. He stopped dead and turned toward the noise. He was faced with an abnormally large crow perched on a branch a few yards away. The crow's head cocked to the right, and its beak opened again as if to call out once more, but no sound came. It only continued to glare as it slowly rotated its head until it was cocked to the left. It then leaned forward, and he could see a shock of blazing red feathers running down the length of its back.

The bird's gaze paralyzed Farris, and his vision narrowed to the point that the crow was the only thing he saw with any clarity. He shook his head violently to clear his tunnel vision, and when he looked back at the bird, it was no longer alone. It had been joined by at least a dozen others, smaller and uniformly black, but all had the same unwavering stare fixed directly at him. He couldn't be sure, but he thought each of the birds had different colored eyes.

Farris took a step back and felt a sharp jab in his torso. He looked down to see a dark red spiraled spike protruding from the center of his chest. It took him a moment to realize he was looking at an exit wound, and the spike had run him through from behind. The dark red color was his own blood, now starting to drip off the tip. As the blood ran down and off the spiraled curves, it revealed the color underneath to be a deep and hollow black.

Farris felt no pain. Instead, a numbness spread from the spike throughout the rest of his body. All physical sensation started to leave him, and he slumped forward on the pointed spiral. As his vision faded, he used what little strength was left to lift his head once more.

The crows were flocking to a central point, and in the haze that was overtaking Farris, it seemed to his eye that as the birds swarmed together, they took on a new silhouette. As each one of them came to the focal point, they blended into a mass which, for a brief moment, appeared to be the outline of a human figure with wild, untamed hair. With this final blurred image, he slipped out of sleep and awoke on the cold stone floor of the quarantine cell.

Farris groaned and pushed himself up from the ground to a sitting position as he looked around the room. There were scorch marks on the walls, with the most prominent on two opposing walls from when the force of the fire had forced Farris' arms to spread apart. Aside from the general blackening of the stones and the metal bench, the room itself was largely undamaged. By contrast, the cloth cot he had been brought in on had burnt to ashes. Farris glanced down at himself and realized for the second time in as many days he had destroyed his clothes. This time there weren't even tatters remaining.

"Perfect." He sighed and scooted across the floor, leaning against the wall to make sure he hadn't managed any new injuries.

To his surprise, the cuts and scrapes he'd sustained getting here appeared to have scabbed over and healed up. His eyes fixated on the fingers of his left hand. A small patch of skin on both the middle and index fingers' tips was cracked and seared. The burn marks were not as extensive as they'd been in the dream; however, they were on the same fingers. "Ok, so that's new. And probably not good."

He rubbed his thumb against the burnt patches. The skin was rough and dried out, but it didn't hurt to touch. Looking closer at the index finger, he saw a crack in the scorched flesh which ran deeper than it first appeared. He brought it closer to his eyes, and within the sliver of the crack, he saw the faintest hint of a red glow. "No, no, no, no," he said, shaking his head and removing the finger out of sight, opting instead to focus on more immediate concerns. Such as what fate lay in store for him now that he was conscious.

Taking more time to examine the quarantine cell, Farris noted how dimly lit it was. Glancing up at the ceiling, black soot coated the light. Unfortunately, it was too high for him to reach and clean off, so he would have to make do. A small pile of clothes rested in front of the heavy metal door and appeared to have been slipped in through a sliding hatch at the bottom. He sighed relief at the street clothes. Anything was better than the bright yellow clothes used to designate prisoners.

Farris pulled on the brown trousers and slipped the grey-green shirt over his head. Both fit him considerably better than the clothes he'd been wearing before. The pile had included a pair of leather shoes, and as he laced them up, the wall to his left let out a grinding sound. One of the larger stones slid aside, revealing a basin. Approaching cautiously, he dipped a finger into the clear, cool water and sighed. All decorum removed, he leaned down and slurped directly from the basin. After a few gulps, he submerged his head completely. He came back up, throwing his hair back, letting the cool water splatter against the wall behind him, and drip soothingly down his back.

A loud clanking from the door jolted him from his revelry. A pair of brown eyes peered at him through a hatch midway up the metal barrier. The hatch snapped closed again, soon followed by more clanking and grinding noises as the door was unlocked. He half expected to see city constables with shackles as the door slowly swung open for him to come out of the cell. He moved out into the long, stone hallway, where she glanced up at him and smiled warmly.

"You clean up rather well."

Farris blushed.

"We need to hurry," she said, taking his hand. She began pulling him along the hallway away from the cells. "If you're discovered wandering around, it'll raise more questions than I can convincingly answer."

She led him down a series of winding corridors on a floor that angled slightly downwards. The walls were bare, and after the first few turns, Farris stopped seeing any doors, and connecting halls became fewer and fewer.

"Where are we going?" he asked. Nothing about these halls gave him any indication about what might be at the end of them, and, for all he knew, she was about to dump him back onto the street and lock the door behind him.

"There's a passage to the undercity for emergencies." She continued leading him swiftly and purposefully through the stone passageways. "It's kept locked from this side, so I'm sorry, but I can't go with you."

Farris stopped dead in his tracks, pulling his hand away from hers. "Can't you just sneak me back out the way I came in?"

The matron shook her head gravely. "You're not staff, and you were never officially logged in. If you're spotted exiting the quarantine wing, hospital security will stun you on sight without question." She took his hand in hers once more. "Please, trust me. The undercity's not as bad as you're thinking; I can promise you that much."

Doubts kept flooding him, but Farris let the matron lead him again. "But I don't even know what direction we're going. I'll never find my way out."

The pair stopped at a large circular vault door, and she turned to him. "Listen to me very carefully. If you take your first left, then second right, third right, and first left, that will take you to one of the topside stairwells along the southern side of the wall. Now repeat it back to me."

"First left, second right, third right, first left," repeated Farris mechanically, as if reciting a lesson back to a teacher.

"Just repeat the route to yourself. Don't jostle anybody, and you'll be fine. When you get topside, steer clear of the fountain and the square in case the constable who brought in is still on duty." She released his hand and stuffed a small parcel into one of the pockets of his trousers. "Eat that sparingly. It tastes awful but will keep you going." She took hold of the handle at the center of the circular door and cranked it to the left. The entire metal door rolled itself into a large cubby in the wall.

The tunnel it revealed was dark, but for the spot of light in the distance. Farris could smell the mildew and hear the dripping of water on wet stones. His shoulders tensed up as cold air from the tunnel washed over him.

"That's the junction where you make your first left." She pointed to the light. "Once you're topside, try to stay near the staircase, if you can. I'll be by in the morning. If for any reason you can't stay there, I'll be lunching at the Sprite's Mist Café at noon."

"Wait," said Farris, suddenly realizing he'd lost all sense of the day. "What time is it now?"

"The sun set three hours ago. I'm sorry I can't keep you here until morning, but you'd be discovered at the shift change."

Farris looked down the tunnel and shuddered, rubbing his arms to try and calm his nerves.

She placed a reassuring hand on his shoulder. "Just stay out of sight as much as you can. If you must meet me at the café anybody can tell you where it is, just don't ask a constable. I'll be lunching with someone, so don't approach me, but I'll see you."

Farris met her gentle brown eyes and took a slow cleansing breath, which drained the tension from his shoulders. "Thank you."

She smiled and nodded. "If you feel your energies building up, try to release them as quickly as possible in small doses. Whatever you do, don't let them gain the kind of force you expelled earlier."

Farris nodded. His inherent fear of the fires within himself had created the habit of holding them back for as long as possible, even though he knew the inevitable release would be all the worse. It was an instinct he would have to fight if he were going to remain undetected.

She motioned for Farris to head into the tunnel, which he did, turning back one last time once he was past the door. "Matron Branford, right? I think that's what I heard the orderly say."

She nodded and smiled. "Tomorrow, you can tell me your name. One more time, where are you going?"

"First left, second right, third right, first left."

"See you tomorrow." She smiled once more before pulling a release on the wall, causing the thick steel door to roll back into place.

Farris gathered his courage and turned toward the light. "First left, second right, third right, first left." He repeated the directions to himself as he started down the tunnel.

Architecture was never something he'd taken much interest in, but he knew about the undercity because he'd read about the water sprite who once dwelt in Lake Vaettir. The sprite was said to have rarely left the lake's depths, but when it did, the docks and ships would be torn apart. Citizens would flee into the network of tunnels of the undercity, safe from the watery wrath of the sprite thanks to one of the most extensive drainage systems ever devised.

Farris wondered if it was still being maintained properly as he splashed through a shallow puddle. "First left, second right, third right, first left." He was almost at the junction now, stepping in time with his own rhythmic chanting. He arrived at the light and turned left. "Now it's second right, third right, first left," he mumbled.

He didn't fight his wandering thoughts, letting the memory of Fey stories keep him from worrying too much about what might be around the next corner. Because, if nothing else, he wouldn't encounter any Fey down here. He couldn't remember when the last sighting of the sprite was, but he felt like it had been decades, which probably accounted for why these tunnels looked like they were due for maintenance.

To his annoyance, Farris' mind reminded him now all the undercity was known for was a haven for the destitute, criminal, and the insane. He passed another junction and kept moving forward. "Second right, third right, first left."

The tunnel opened into a cavernous area with a water pool at its center illuminated by electric lanterns spaced regularly around the perimeter. Shooting up from the middle of the pool was a thick pillar stretching up to the ceiling. Glancing upward, Farris saw a large ring of grates at the outer edge of the pillar through which came moonlight and a steady trickle of water.

He realized he was directly beneath the square and fountain where he'd collapsed. He also realized he was not alone. Makeshift housing, some little more than cloth propped up with sticks, littered the underground square's perimeter. The fact it was the dead of night did not seem to matter because the area was alive and buzzing with activity. Pots were bubbling over small fires, clothes were being washed in the pool, and the hum of conversation echoed around him. It didn't seem like some den of misfortune; in fact, it didn't seem all that different from Barreth outside the main gate.

Farris was jostled from behind and snapped out of his thoughts by a walking pile of raggedy brown robes pushing past him. He cocked his head at them, recognizing this as the one who'd fled the alleyway behind the café. His eyes followed the ratty figure, who didn't seem to be attracting any attention. However, he realized his presence had been marked by a leathery-skinned vagrant crouching on the ground to his right. The man was peering up at him while hunched over a small fire roasting a skewered rodent on a pointed stick. The crisping vermin looked only slightly less sickly than the man. Farris gave a weak smile and slight wave, not knowing what else to do. To his relief, the crouched man smiled back and gave a rather haphazard little salute before turning his attention back to the fire.

"Second right, third right, first left," Farris reminded himself, realizing that second right meant going along the wall of the underground square. He stepped around the man with the rodent rotisserie and followed along the stone wall. He passed by openings to other tunnels, counting them off as he went.

"Third right, first left."

He turned into the third tunnel and continued long enough that he started to doubt the final left turn was ever going to present itself. He started to doubt if he'd gotten it right but pressed on simply because it was the only direction he had to go. Finally, a tunnel appeared to his left, and looking down it, Farris spotted stairs lit with moonlight.

"Finally." He sighed. Moving closer, however, he noticed rain pelting down onto the stone steps. "Of course, because it can't be too easy."

Farris leaned against the wall of the tunnel to think. It would be a total downpour up on the street level, and the last thing he needed was to catch a cold. His stomach growled and ached. The first thing to deal with was the empty pit that was his stomach. The smell of the cooking rodent had done more to remind him of his hunger than he'd have thought, considering how unappetizing it had been.

He reached into his pocket for the parcel Matron Branford had given him. Unwrapping it, he found what looked like a cross between a loaf of bread and a small brick—it had the appearance of the former and the texture of the latter. Taking a bite proved difficult, and even when he got a bit off, he almost spat it out. It was rough and mealy and quite possibly the single most unpleasant thing he'd ever had in his mouth. Nevertheless, he chewed as quickly as possible and choked it down, tucking away the rest to save for a true emergency—like dying in the desert because no other circumstances would be worth it.

With nothing else to do but wait, Farris headed back to the square where at least he wouldn't feel quite so alone. Perhaps he could find a place comfortable enough to wait for daybreak. He shivered a little as he walked and wondered if he'd be able to work up the nerve to ask any of the under-dwellers about borrowing a blanket.

Chapter 11

In the morning, as the sun was peaking over the eastern mountains, its rays did not touch Garion as he worked his way through the tunnels of the undercity with grim determination. Sneaking into the city had been simple enough, but he'd lost almost a day scouring the docks and alleyways. Busy cities made for harder tracking, especially when trying to avoid being noticed by the constabulary.

He exited the rounded tunnels into the underground square, pausing to take in a slow breath. The tight tunnels agitated him, and he needed to regain his cool. The first rays of light were shining through the grates that surrounded the fountain. Long-term residents of the undercity were letting their hand-cranked lights die out. Many were still sleeping on stoops and in corners while others milled about or bathed themselves in the pool.

After his cleansing breath, Garion was able to focus. He closed his eyes and let his other senses drink in the space. He had little trouble picking up on the distinct crackling energy of an elemental in the area: a crisp charge to the air undetectable by anyone else, feeling like a hot needle poking the back of his neck and heating up as he zeroed in on it. He moved along the wall and stopped short when he felt a sparking jolt hit his senses. He was picking up on more than one elemental signature. He moved quickly on the stronger of the two trails.

A broad-shouldered woman with ebony skin kept a keen eye on Garion from the shadows as he worked his way around the perimeter to the opposite side of the square. He moved in straight lines, side stepping as needed, but otherwise ignoring them even as he drew the attention of more sets of eyes with his presence. His keen nose caught a whiff of ash and smoke, something that to a human would just signify a small flame like a cooking fire. But there was a spark, something sharp and pulsing just underneath that smokey smell, something that Garion could pick up and recognize for the elemental energy it signified. Garion grinned as he broke into a run and dashed toward a curled-up form resting against the wall. He leaped and clung to the stone just above the mass and viciously tore away the ratty blanket covering it, revealing a dirt-encrusted man with a scraggly beard.

The man yelped. Garion snarled as he sniffed the blanket in his hand. Throwing the blanket aside, he grabbed the man by the throat and hoisted him up violently onto his feet.

"I… I didn't do anything, I swear," the man blubbered.

"Where did you get that?" Garion growled, pointing to the discarded blanket.

"It's mine; I didn't steal it."

"Who else used it?" demanded the marshal, shaking the man roughly.

"Just some kid… he looked cold, so I lent it to him. He—"

Garion pulled him in closer until the man's eyes were only inches away from the narrowed slits peering back at him from under the scarf and hood.

"Hey!" shouted the broad-shouldered woman, rushing over to the scene with a cluster of others close behind to back her up.

"Where is he?" asked Garion slowly and deliberately, completely ignoring the small mob approaching.

"I… I don't know. He gave it back and left a little while ago; I didn't see where." He looked to his side. "Cecily! Get him off me!

"You drop him right now!" Cecily ordered, now nearly close enough to reach out and touch Garion.

Garion squeezed the man's neck tighter, causing the under-dweller's eyes to go even wider. The complete lack of concern on Garion's part was enough to stop Cecily's advance for now. He looked back into the man's eyes. "Where was he when he was using the blanket?"

The under-dweller pointed a trembling hand to a nook in the wall a few yards away.

Garion released his grip, and the man collapsed to the ground, coughing and sputtering. Cecily rushed over as Garion sprang from the wall and latched onto a pillar several yards away, then to the nook the raggedy man had indicated.

In the nook, Garion's thin nostrils flared, and the hair at the back of his neck stood on end. There was a tension around him as if the air itself had been compressed and warmed. His eyes searched the area and landed on a scorched spot on the ground. Behind him, other residents of the undercity were coming to the aid of the abused man, one of them dabbing up a small trickle of blood from his neck with a bit of cloth. Some glared at Garion, but none moved to confront him. The hunter touched the blackened bit of stone and vanished down a tunnel.

***

Farris smiled and reveled with the sun on his face, barely noticing the light breeze on the side street where the stairway had led him. All things considered, the undercity and its residents were not nearly the frightening things he had imagined.

At the same time, he was ready to put the entire city behind him, to say nothing of this damp and not entirely pleasant section of it.

Having the sky visible overhead relieved much of the tension in his limbs. The undercity, the quarantine cell, the canopy of the Everwood, the steel enclosures of Sagaris—enough was enough. If he were ever able to build his own home, he'd make the entire ceiling a skylight and never feel locked up again. He smiled and settled onto a stoop not far from the stairwell.

It wasn't long before he was tapping his foot and wondering when the matron might arrive. He'd check a watch if he had one, but without it, he opted to watch the clouds for a bit and hope time was passing faster than it felt.

"A watched sky never changes." He frowned at having repeated the same words his mother regularly chastised him with, even though she wasn't much more patient than he was most of the time.

"I'm patient when it matters," was the response she'd always give when Farris would point this out.

Thoughts of his mother brought a wave of conflicting emotions. Love and affection, butting heads with frustration and rebellion, and through it all, he felt that longing that comes with knowing he would probably never see her again.

"We live, we learn, we leave." Farris quoted from his favorite storybook of traveling adventurers his mother had given him and sighed.

He rubbed the fingertips on his left hand together, noting the tingling sensation. He'd released several small bursts of fire throughout the night, being sure to do it in a nook where he wouldn't be seen. The matron had been right; smaller bursts were much easier to control, though he did need to release it more frequently. Farris leaned his head against the wall and grumbled at the fact he'd had to be told and hadn't figured it out on his own. But at least this way, he could direct them where they would do no harm, and that mattered more than his pride.

Farris glanced around, hoping to spot some sign of the matron, but when she failed to appear yet again, he left to find somewhere to release a little fire. He was the only one out on this narrow street, but there were plenty of doors someone could come out of or windows through which he could be seen. Ducking down a dead-end alley, he quickly found a spot out of sight behind a large metal container that smelled of refuse. After checking over his shoulder to be certain nobody was looking, Farris pointed his fingers at the stone wall of the alley. A bright, thin line of fire extended out from his fingers. It lashed against the stone, leaving dark marks on it. It reminded him of a whip he'd once seen a rancher use to round up a herd, a very faded memory from early childhood.

"I wonder." He experimented with moving his fingers around and found the line of fire reacted very much like a whip. He chuckled, and after a few more cautious swings of the short fire whip, the flame flickered and sputtered out as the last energy was spent.

"Whoa. Really wish I'd figured that out before."

He looked at the burnt markings on the tips of his fingers with a newfound and undefinable sense. Pride or wonder didn't seem right; it still terrified him, after all. But, for once, it was something other than fear and shame. The word 'awe' crossed his mind several times, and he accepted it was the best he could come up with, for now.

"Ok, don't get cocky," he told himself as he turned to exit the alley. He still didn't know how much control was possible, but the idea there was any to be had at all gave him the excitement of discovery and hope no matter how he tried to keep a lid on it. Just before exiting the alleyway, he heard voices from the direction of the stairwell.

"Don't treat me like I'm the one who did anything wrong!" snapped a voice.

Farris peered around the corner, his eyes locked onto the blue uniforms of three constables, clustered with their backs to him and all facing a frazzled looking pale man in well-pressed pea-green robes with silver trim. His stomach tightened, and his mind raced, but there was no other way out of the alley, so he froze in place.

"Sir, we only asked that we take this conversation off the main road," said the muscular ivory-skinned officer with corporal stripes on the shoulder of her double-breasted uniform. She spoke evenly as she wrote down a statement as the other two constables stood behind her, arms folded, their uniforms a brighter shade of blue to hers.

"I told you, I didn't see their face!" The merchant threw his arms up in exasperation.

"Remy, you need to take a breath," said one of the lower-ranking constables.

Remy took a breath and looked past the corporal to the officer who'd addressed him. "Mordin, can't I just do this with you?"

The olive-skinned officer shook their head, and Remy turned back to the corporal and frowned.

"Look, you're going to have to bear with me," he said, pausing to rub his eyes as if trying to scrub out the frustration. "I prefer people I know, corporal…?"

"Benevolence," replied the corporal.

Remy scoffed and shook his head. "Seriously?"

She raised an eyebrow at him, and Remy cleared his throat awkwardly. "Does it really take all three of you to take notes?"

"Catching a criminal is rather difficult, Mr. Callum, if we don't know what we're looking for," Corporal Benevolence pointed out. She put pen to paper again. "So, from the beginning, please. What exactly did you see?"

Remy took a deep breath, though it did little to calm him. "I was just heading back to my shop from Risen Sun Bakery. I was practically run over by this…" He waved his arm in a circle, trying to find the words. "Walking pile of rags. Little bastard didn't say 'excuse me' or anything; just skittered off. I only had to take a few more steps to realize my coin purse was missing."

Farris ducked his head back and let out a restrained sigh of relief as he leaned against the wall. He reminded himself that he needed to not assume every authority figure was looking for him; the stress was the last thing he needed.

Corporal Benevolence nodded as she checked her existing notes and jotted down a few new ones. "Continue."

"I tried to follow, but they got ahead of me, and I lost them back where I waved you down," Remy concluded, gesturing out to the main road.

Mordin chimed in, pointing at the stairs that led down to the tunnels. "Do you think they went to the undercity?"

"Isn't that your job to figure out?" snapped Remy.

"Hey now," said Constable Mordin, "let's keep it civil; I'm trying to help."

"I'm sorry Mordy… Look, I've seen that little rat around for the past day or two. Thought they were just a beggar, not a thief."

"Alright," said Corporal Benevolence. "I've got your address, and I'll be filing the report within the hour. Since you said you've seen them around here before, Constable Dormin will stay here and conduct a few interviews. Constable Quentis will do a preliminary sweep of the immediate undercity tunnels. We'll do all we can, and we will question any possible witnesses, but

I should warn you the undercity residents aren't known for being forthcoming."

The merchant sighed again and hung his head as the corporal tore off a small piece of paper from her notepad.

"This is your case number if you have any questions." With that, she turned to her companions, pointing Mordin down the stairwell as the other began to knock on the nearest door. Corporal Benevolence put an arm around the merchant and escorted him back to the main street.

Farris' shoulders slumped as he let out a sigh. "Just great." Even if the constables had no reason to question him, he didn't feel safe staying by the stairwell anymore if they were going to be investigating.

"Sprite's Mist Cafe," he repeated to himself before strolling out of the alley as nonchalantly as he could, sticking his hands into his pockets and picking a spot toward the end of the street to focus on so he wasn't tempted to glance over at the constable going door to door. Fortunately for him, the constable was being yelled at by an aging man yelling about what hour it was, so his departure went completely unnoticed.

Chapter 12

Professor Raines seethed outside her office as a team of lab assistants poured over her notebooks. Dean Gartis had finally stepped in and asserted his authority; now, there was nothing she could do but stand by powerless as her notes were scrutinized, disorganized, and marked up. The professor resisted the urge to check on the one notebook she'd stashed and hidden under her rust-colored coat.

"And you were present at the event itself?" asked Deacon, the fresh-faced amber-skinned inquisitor standing beside her. This snapped her attention away from the mess being made of her office and back to the interview she was being forced to undergo.

"Yes," she responded bitterly.

"I would appreciate it if you could walk me through what happened," he prompted, not bothering to look up from his notepad.

Professor Raines motioned to her office. "I was going over a backlog of reports on elemental subject L9 and—"

"Why was there a backlog? Were you distracted by other things?"

She gazed down at the inquisitor, frowning. He couldn't be more than a few years out of his graduate studies and flush with newfound authority, which he had yet to truly earn. "I had been focused on the energy signature detection project. There was great pressure to deliver a functioning prototype, and other things fell by the wayside."

He noted her response. "No other distractions?"

Professor Raines shook her head, and Deacon nodded for her to continue.

"In going over the daily logs, I noted there was no record of energy release from the subject in three days. I summoned my TA—"

"That would be Lab Assistant Petit, correct?"

"Yes. She—"

"How long has she been your assistant?"

Professor Raines tightened her lips and drew in a slow breath. "Two years."

"You get along with her?" Deacon inquired with a raised eyebrow.

"We work well together."

"And she hasn't been a distraction for you?"

The Professor's lip curled into a snarl, and her eyes narrowed. "No, nor has any other assistant or colleague of any gender in the entirety of my time at this university. Such things are *not* where my interests lie."

He made another note. "Very well then, Lab Assistant Petit was summoned…"

"She confirmed the logs were not an oversight, and the subject had not released any elemental energies in nearly 72 hours."

"And this concerned you?"

Professor Raines folded her arms; this was becoming insulting. "There is no record of any elemental holding back their energies for more than thirty hours, and that was with extreme physical distress. This subject had more than doubled that. Yes, it was a point of concern."

"What happened then?" asked Deacon, still looking to his notepad.

"I went to Containment Lab 4, where the subject was being held and observed."

"Walk me through, please."

Professor Raines began walking down the hallway to the laboratory hub, and the inquisitor followed behind, still focused on his notepad. As the pair arrived at the containment lab, the professor frowned at the open door and the bustling administrative assistants on the other side of it. Two were making sketches of the obliterated containment capsule, while another five were stationed about lab observing the equipment in use and the records on hand. Inside the pockets of her coat, Professor Raines clenched her firsts hard enough for one of the healing cuts between her knuckles to re-open.

"And when you arrived, that is when the explosion occurred?" Deacon asked as he glanced down from the observation deck.

"Yes. The release of energy was far beyond anything that had been registered before, and containment was… not sufficient." She ran her fingers over the cuts and burns on her hands left by the shattered glass and explosive energy. Her breath caught in her throat as she looked down at the mangled containment unit, prompting her to turn away.

"Why do you believe the emergency enclosure measures failed?"

"You know why they failed," snapped Professor Raines, whipping her head around at Deacon.

"Yes, we do, but I wish to hear your thoughts on the matter all the same." His lips twitched into a slight grin.

"The emergency measures should have kicked in when the explosion blew out the power. However, those measures operated on the assumption at least the backup generators would continue to function." Professor Rained spoke slowly and pointedly as though she were trying to get through to the thickest student in the class.

"The blast and the energies sent through the system were sufficient to knock out power in the entire structure. That meant safety protocols took priority over containment procedures, and all doors automatically opened to allow evacuation."

"I trust you understand how fortunate you are no other subjects escaped."

"You say that as though it were luck," retorted Professor Raines. "All other subjects were still held inside intact containment capsules—an open door did them no good. Are we finished here?"

"For the time being, but I would like to know one more thing." Deacon glanced up from his notes to look up at the professor's face for the first time since they'd entered the containment lab. "While we appreciate the scene of the incident was not disturbed, why did you resist allowing this inquisition access to your notes and laboratory?"

She looked down at the younger man, meeting his eyes and not blinking. "Because I'm protective of my research, as anyone of experience would be. I have no intention of compromising the integrity of my work unless it is deemed truly necessary. I did not feel it was necessary." She kept her gaze locked on him.

After an uncomfortable moment, Deacon cleared his throat and turned back to his notes. "Yes, well, the Dean didn't agree."

"And *that* is the only reason you're anywhere near here right now."

Deacon began flipping through his notes for no reason other than to have an excuse not to look her in the eye. "That'll be all for now," he said with a slight cough before venturing down to the containment lab proper. Once there, he began barking orders at those under his direction.

Professor Raines spun on her heel and marched out of the lab.

When she'd put distance between herself and the containment labs, Professor Raines reached into her coat and confirmed the notebook was still there. The inquisitors could pour over everything else, but they couldn't have this. Like all Guild-issued notebooks, it was virtually indestructible, with pages and binding treated to fend off the effects of fire, water, or even tearing of pages. Had she been caught removing it from the scene of an active inquisition, it would have cost her professorship, if not more.

Professor Raines continued through the halls until she reached a heavy steel door. She opened a panel in the wall, pressed her guild ring to the exposed notch, and turned it a quarter turn to the right. The steel door slid open quietly, revealing a stairway. She descended quickly as the wall slid back into place behind her. A desk, staffed by a very pale and bored-looking clerk gazing into a book on his lap, sat at the bottom of the stairs.

On the desk were a faded nameplate displaying "Technician Doccen" and a leather-bound logbook sitting open with a pen beside it. Doccen didn't look up as she approached; he merely reached out a finger and tapped on the registry log. "Name, rank, requisitioned vehicle, and destination, please," he said lazily.

Professor Raines said nothing; instead, she pulled a small pouch from her coat pocket and dropped it on the logbook, where it landed with a muted thud. A tiny amount of glittering powder puffed out the top when it hit, even though the draw string was pulled tight.

Doccen glanced up at the pouch briefly before letting his eyes drift down again. He reached out, took the pouch, and placed it under the desk. "Nothing bigger than a two-seater, please. Larger vehicles are harder to cover for."

Professor Raines breezed past him to the underground station where the rail cars were kept. Her steps echoed across the large, man-made cavern, its stone walls smooth and curving up to the ceiling. In the center of the space was the start of the electrified rails, which branched off to several different tunnels leading to research outposts and other universities. The stale air smelled of engine oil, and the cavern was silent but for the sound of air coming down the tunnels. The cars themselves hung from the ceiling, suspended by large metal clamps.

She approached a series of levers on the wall, laid out in a ten lever by five lever grid with the handles color-coded. She pulled the appropriate sequence, and behind the wall, an engine hummed, and gears turned. She watched as a small, single-seat car was lowered from the ceiling and placed onto the track by the clamp, which promptly retracted back to the ceiling. The car was little more than a rectangular metal box sporting a thinly cushioned chair in front of a control panel. She quickly climbed in, locked the door in place, and set to work on the dials, knobs, and levers in front of her. She deftly set the controls but held off on initiating the sequence. She leaned back in the seat, pulling a small scroll and scrap of paper from her coat pocket, and compared the coded message on the scroll to a scrap of paper onto which she'd decoded it. "Subject has reached Torvec. Collection difficulty increased. Assistance requested."

Professor Raines stuffed the scroll and scrap of paper back into her pocket and pulled the lever at the side of the chair, starting it along the path she'd programmed. The motor whirred as it drew the needed power from the lightning cage, peaking in volume and pitch before shooting the car into the polished stone tunnels. Professor Raines was pushed back hard in her seat, but her expression did not change as intermittent lights blurred past her on her way to the closest research station to Torvec.

Chapter 13

Farris had a thankfully easy time finding the Sprite's Mist Café, getting clear directions from a friendly woman selling flowers from a basket. It turned out to be a dining spot of some note along the main artery, which led from the shoreside gate to the fountain square. The sign made it look like the large looping letters "Sprite's Mist" were rising out of foaming waves. Farris thought it looked a bit overdone as he looked at it from across the street.

His eyes kept drifting up to the sign not to have it look like he was surveying the diners, which was, of course, exactly what he was doing. Most of the dozen tables on the café's patio were occupied by two or three diners exchanging pleasantries, with only three having a lone occupant. These were the tables Farris was trying to focus on nonchalantly, remembering Matron Branford said she was meeting someone.

There was a pallid-looking man in a grey suit, reading a newspaper with a face that looked like it hadn't smiled in a month. In the shade of the awning was an elderly umber man who appeared to be having trouble cutting up his food but also didn't look like he was going to ask for help, with his jaw set and his eyes narrowed in determination. At a corner table sat a freckled young woman in light brown slacks that matched the vest she wore over a white shirt, her red hair was in a bun and she kept peering up and down the street and seemed to be waiting for somebody.

Farris sat on the lip of the building he'd been leaning against and tapped his feet on the stone walkway. He didn't have a watch, but he'd heard the hollow ringing chimes of noon a few minutes earlier. Glancing up the street once more, he spotted a plum-colored cloak hurrying along the sidewalk, and his heart nearly leapt into his throat. If the matron spotted him, she didn't do anything to show it as she breezed past the young woman in the corner table and took up a seat across from the man with the paper, which he folded up and placed on the table.

Though the street was narrow enough that Farris had a good view of the pair, he could not make out the conversation over the noise of the street. Their body language and gestures looked relaxed and casual. He had to keep reminding himself to look away or down at the ground now and then, so he didn't look like he was gawking. He started making a more detailed assessment of the man. He'd never been good at guessing ages, and he appeared neither particularly old nor especially young. The suit was well-tailored, he wore matching gloves, and his dark grey overcoat was hung over the back of his chair. There was also a cane with a dragon's head design on the handle resting against the table next to him.

Farris was snapped out of his concentration when the man made a flourish of putting his newspaper up between himself and the matron, which she responded to by snatching it away with a frown on her face. Between the street's general noise and the boots landing on the stone roads, he couldn't even catch snippets of their conversation. "Lip reading," Farris muttered to himself. "Need to figure out how to read lips."

Whatever they were talking about, it looked like they'd started disagreeing. The matron was passionate and energized by whatever point she was arguing; the other man appeared more resigned and annoyed. When she lit up with an air of excited triumph, Farris assumed she'd won whatever the argument was.

When the two rose from their seats, and the man gathered his things, Farris was hit by the anxiety that comes with uncertainty. When they left, was he supposed to follow them? Were they going to come over to him? Had she even seen him? His rising nerves made him clench his teeth, and he felt a slight tingle in his fingertips.

Once the pair left the table, they crossed the street toward him, and Matron Branford made a point of catching his eye before nodding her head to the alleyway the man had already headed down. Farris scrambled to his feet but made special effort to walk rather than run to the alley. Nobody else had taken much notice of him, and he didn't want to undo that by dashing about. However, he couldn't help but pick up his pace once he'd turned down the alleyway.

Once he spotted them, Farris followed a few feet back, taking slow, drawn-out breaths to help him remain calm. Though he felt safe around Matron Branford, the man was a new factor, and he found himself very nervous about making a positive impression. The pair led him around a few tight corners to be better isolated from the active city streets. They seemed to know were going, even in this labyrinthine maze of back alleys.

When he rounded the final corner, he almost ran into the man, who'd stopped and turned to face him. Farris took a step back as the man looked down at him skeptically. He stood his ground as best he could, not wanting it to be obvious that he was intimated. He felt a little better when he glanced over to the much kinder face of Matron Branford for some sense of reassurance. She smiled and nodded in a way that communicated everything was going to be ok.

"What's your name?" the man asked with disinterest.

"Farris," he replied, happy for an easy starting question. "Farris—"

The man held up a hand. "Just your first name, the less I know, the better. I'm not going to tell you my name because you're going to forget me as soon as you possibly can." His tone managed to be both insistent and cold at the same time. "Clear?" he asked with a raised eyebrow.

Farris nodded, though he couldn't keep himself from frowning. As much as he appreciated any help he could get, he'd already concluded this was a man he'd actively avoid under any other circumstances.

"I know you two have met," the man said, gesturing to Matron Branford. "She doesn't care if you know her name because she's got more heart than self-preservation instinct. That's *not* a condition we share."

Farris nodded again. Despite his growing distaste for the man standing in front of him, he found himself tensing with excitement. For the first time since his initial escape, he felt the kind of genuine hope that comes with being helped and having a plan. He'd always assumed being out in the world meant he would be completely on his own and having evidence to the contrary did more for his spirits than he could have imagined. And this feeling only grew when Matron Branford smiled and lowered her hood, reassuring him he wasn't alone with the warmth in her eyes.

"I'm not going to put you up anywhere," the man said emphatically. "You'll have to manage that yourself. However, I should be able to secure you passage on the water if you can lay low for the next day or two. Do you think you can manage that?"

"I think so," said Farris, who couldn't help but wring his hands a little and give away his lack of certainty on this point.

"We'll see…" said the man with a doubtful frown. "Which direction?"

"What do you mean?"

"There're five rivers feeding into that lake," said the man with an irritated sigh. "It'd be helpful to know which way you'd prefer to go."

Farris had honestly not thought this far ahead. He'd always known getting to Torvec would give him options, but which of those options he might choose had all been continually filed under "deal with it later." Not to mention somewhere in the back of his mind, he'd expected to have been discovered and captured before this point. "North," he blurted out after a brief mind racing moment. It was completely arbitrary, but he had to say something.

"Alright then, up the Ilyria it is." The man nodded. "If I pull some strings, I could get you all the way to the Demar Ocean if you want to press your luck. Though if you're smart, you'll be off the boat long before that."

Farris furrowed his brow, trying to work out exactly what was being implied. The man saw he wasn't getting it.

"Keeping your... condition hidden for as many days as it would take to reach the ocean would be no small feat."

Farris relaxed his face and nodded. He started to second guess himself and wondered if he should have picked another direction, but upon quick reflection, it seemed like one direction was as good as the next. He was going to be on his own no matter which way he went.

He'd always wanted to travel north when he was younger, to sail out and see the edges of the Frozen Sea, or wander the Sale Cliffs, or see the Bramble. Why not take the opportunity?

"Now, once I've secured you passage—"

The man stopped short at the sound of bits of stone falling down the side of the brick building to his right. He stepped back and looked up, scanning the top of the building. Farris and the matron did the same just in time to see a few bits of loose debris tumble from the rooftop like marbles dropped by a careless child. They stepped to one side as the pieces skipped down the edge of the wall before breaking into smaller pieces on the ground. All three went silent as they scanned the edge of the building for any sign of what might have caused the fall. Farris squinted, half expecting a shadow to suddenly move and a signal a squad of constables into the alley. Instead, he saw a black bird fly across the gap from one building to the other.

After a few moments of silence and stillness, the man leaned in closer to Farris. "I'll get the travel information to Selane," he said in a whisper. "So, wherever you hole up, be sure she has a way to reach you. Whatever I get is going to have a narrow window. If you miss it, I'm not getting you another ride."

"Thank you," whispered Farris. "I wish there was something I could do to repay you."

Matron Branford smiled while the man straightened up and frowned.

"There is," he said. "Don't come back."

Simple enough, Farris thought to himself. He didn't have much reason to want to return here, and he definitely had no desire to see this unpleasant man again.

"You go find your hidey-hole, and I'll see about your accommodations," the man said as he brushed past Farris toward the way main road. "I hope you're not expecting first class because you'll be lucky to get a wooden crate."

Farris looked to Matron Branford for guidance, unsure if he was supposed to split from them right away. She motioned for him to follow her terse companion, and he followed at as much distance as he could get away with. The alley widened as they neared the street that housed the café, and she took up a position walking right alongside Farris, who gulped nervously when her shoulder brushed his. Part of him wanted to extend his fingers out and brush them against the dark skin of her hand. He fought this urge back and cleared his throat awkwardly. "So... Selane was it?" asked Farris, unable to think of anything else to say but needing to fill the silence.

Matron Selane Branford nodded with a smile but said nothing.

"And you're... like me?" he asked, thinking back to the soothing white glow from her hands from the day before.

"No, I'm like me," she said with a smile and a bouncy shrug. "But I suppose there are some similarities."

"It's just... I've never heard of... what element are you?" Farris blushed, not knowing if this would be considered a personal question.

Selane shrugged. "I'm not sure what you'd call it, but it seems to help ease people's pain."

"I didn't get to tell you my full name."

"Don't want to hear it!" the man hollered over his shoulder as he reached the point where the alley emptied onto the street.

As soon as the man stepped out from the shadows, a small figure wrapped in tattered rags bumped into him. The man took a step back into the alley and brushed dirt off his vest and trousers as the figure scampered off. As he did this, he touched a now empty chain dangling from his vest. He turned back to Farris, his face tense with anger. "You want to repay me, boy?" Farris nodded reflexively.

"Catch that urchin!" The man turned and launched himself out of the alley, gripping his cane tightly as he ran up the street.

Farris looked to Selane, a bit thrown off by how quickly this was happening. She motioned for him to follow. "Go on."

Farris ran out of the alley, following the man in his pursuit of the thief.

***

From the rooftop across the street from the Sprite's Mist Café, Garion had watched Farris wait on the street below him. The marshal had been waiting too, waiting for his quarry to step out of the public eye where he could be secured and removed from the city in secrecy. But when Farris had ducked into the alley in the company of two others, all Garion could do was track them silently from the rooftops.

The marshal leapt from building to building in near silence as the trio ventured into the more secluded alleyways. When they finally stopped, the marshal peered down at them from seven stories up. Even his keen ears could not make out what was being said from this height, but he could take an educated guess.

If Farris were being helped, it made it even more imperative that Garion end the hunt quickly, even if it couldn't be done in complete secrecy. He crouched at the edge of the rooftop and prepared to make a rapid descent into the alley to grab the young man by force. He stopped short when he heard a distinctive high-pitched whine behind him. The marshal slowly stood and turned around with his hands raised. As he turned, his foot knocked a loose bit of the roof's edge down into the alley, the flakes of stone skipping along the alley walls down to the street.

Garion found himself facing a dispatch of three constables, one of whom was pointing the offending rifle in his direction. The one in the center stepped forward, an olive-skinned woman wearing a uniform several shades darker than the others, which sported the gold collar lining on her jacket, indicating a sergeant. As she stepped forward, a crow shot out from among the plants on a nearby rooftop garden. All three constables ducked low as the crow flew a tight circle over them before soaring inches over Garion's head. The marshal shifted and ducked, catching a glimpse of the bird's piercing yellow eyes.

The constables stood back up, the one with the rifle taking aim once more. The sergeant motioned for the other constable to check the garden for any other signs of crows as she scanned the sky for the bird, spotting a black speck as it flew out beyond the city wall. She relaxed her shouldered and lowered her eyes back onto Garion.

"Marshal Cole," said the sergeant, stepping forward and not needing to raise her voice to assert her authority. "I would ask you to accompany us to the Hall of the Arbiter."

Garion folded his arms defiantly and narrowed his eyes at the constable aiming the rifle. A slight tremor in the constable's grip told Garion his reputation was already known. "I'm really rather busy at the moment."

The third constable returned from the garden, and the sergeant made a small gesture which prompted them to draw their rifle from the holster on their back, though they didn't aim it yet. "Right now, this is a civil request."

"Then I suppose this is me civilly declining."

The sergeant frowned. "If you want to make it official, I could arrest you on suspicion of unwarranted hunting within the city limits."

"You could try." Garion unfolded his arms.

The sergeant made another gesture, and the second constable aimed their rifle at Garion, with a steadier hand than their compatriot. "Nevertheless, I ask again that you accompany us now."

Garion shrugged and raised his hands. "Let's try to keep it brief at least, alright?" He turned to his right and strolled casually to the edge of the roof, the armed constables tracking his movement as he did so. "I know the way."

"Marshal Cole, you are meant to be escorted by us," objected the sergeant.

"You'll slow me down, and I don't have the time to waste. If you want to note in your report, I didn't wait for you, go right ahead. But I'm going straight to where I've been requested, so I hardly think it's worth the paperwork." The sergeant gestured again, and both constables re-holstered their rifles. Garion gave a half-hearted salute and leapt down to the adjoining rooftop and proceeded directly to the Hall of the Arbiter at the center of the city.

Chapter 14

The rag-encased thief skittered between people, carts, and the occasional small animal on the busy market street. The thief's small size made darting around obstacles an easy task, but the sounds of hard footsteps giving chase were not far behind. As Farris and the man followed through the street, each had to find a way around the many obstructions the city presented. Being younger and nimbler on his feet, Farris closed the gap between himself and the short pile of rags more rapidly.

The man followed closely but seemed to realize he was at risk of being left behind. "Make him take the second right!"

"How?"

"I don't care!" With that, he broke off and veered to the right down a narrow side street, leaving Farris on his own to figure out how to make the pile of rags take the next upcoming right turn.

His mind raced as fast as his feet. Running out of time, he did the only thing he could think of. "Stop! Thief!"

Hearing the cry, a large man stepped directly in the middle of the road with outstretched arms. The rags skidded to a stop and ducked as the large man made a grab for them, then darted off to the right, down the side street.

Farris followed, tossing back a quick "Thanks" to the large man, who wasn't invested enough to join in the chase from here.

The side street was much narrower than the main road and was also devoid of people. Brick and stone walls rose high and gave the street a very claustrophobic feeling, compounded by a scarcity of windows.

The street took a sharp right with no other options of where to go, and even as the thief made the turn, Farris was gaining. Once around the corner, he saw the other man coming from the other direction. The only way for the thief to not run directly into him was to take an even tighter alley that broke off to the left.

Once the thief had taken that turn, the man called out victoriously. "Gotcha!"

Farris met up with the man at the turn just thief had taken, seeing that the fleeing pile of rags had been forced into a dead end with nothing but sheer walls and a few scattered empty crates. He, and his slightly out of breath companion, were now blocking the only means of escape.

The thief had their back to a steel wall at the other end of the short alley. The lump of rags at the top covering their head darted back and forth, looking for a way out.

The man moved into the alley and started to close in. "You have something that belongs to me," he growled. "Give it back, and *maybe* I won't turn you over to the constables."

Farris followed a few feet behind.

The thief crouched and shook, head darting about as they approached, but the older man continued to move forward unabated. "Take my watch out of whatever dirt-encrusted pocket you've put it in and give it back to me," he demanded. "Now," he added in an unsettlingly calm tone.

As they got closer, the thief shifted back and forth, looking for an opening that didn't exist. Farris frowned, sensing the situation was becoming much more hostile than it needed to be. He pushed past the man and put his hands up to the thief to show he was unarmed. "Look," he said. "We don't want to hurt you. We just want what you took."

The man glared at Farris for pushing past him but held his stance.

"We don't want to turn you in," Farris said. "And if you just give the watch back, I promise you we won't do that. Everybody will go on their way like it never happened."

Once Farris was within a few feet of the thief, he held his hand out with his palm up. For a moment, the thief looked directly at him, and he could see a pair of pale blue eyes peering out from under the tattered brown hood. There was a slight crackling, and a small hand shot out of the pile of rags and pressed against Farris' chest, electricity arcing between the fingers like illuminated webbing.

Before he had a chance to react, the hand touched his chest, and Farris was thrown backwards violently. He ricocheted off the stone wall and collapsed onto the ground in a tightly curled ball, clutching his hands against his now singed chest.

The hand pointed to the other man, who dove to the ground as a bolt of lightning surged through the air above his head and scorched the wall at the far end of the alleyway. The thief broke into a run, leaping over Farris and darting around the man.

Farris clutched his chest, breathing in hard gasps and taking great pains to uncurl his body enough to watch the thief flee. However, his eye quickly turned to the man who had already picked himself up from the ground. The man angrily pulled the grey glove off his right hand, revealing an index and middle finger that could only be described as withered and decrepit.

The fingers looked ancient, almost mummified, and the flesh sickly and sallow. Farris watched as the man thrust his uncovered hand forward and from those two fingers shot a tendril of empty blackness. It wasn't a shadow, it was far too solid, but Farris couldn't think of any other point of reference for what he was seeing.

The tendril rocketed outward and wrapped around the legs of the fleeing thief just before they escaped the alleyway. A high-pitched cry cut through the air as the thief's legs gave out instantly, and the raggedy form fell into a heap. The tendril started creeping further up the fallen form as though preparing to completely wrap around the crumpled pile of clothes. With a groan and a face screwed up in concentration, the man retracted the blackness back and reabsorbed it into his shriveled finger.

Farris painfully picked himself up, his chest stinging with each breath and a visible burn on his shirt where the thief had touched him. He used the wall for support at first as he made his way over to the fallen heap of rags at the other end of the alley. The man, who Farris couldn't help but now think of as the "Shadow Man," clutched his exposed hand at the wrist until the tendril was completely recalled. He replaced the grey glove, bent down to retrieve his fallen cane, and quickly moved toward the thief.

The Shadow Man easily reached the thief before Farris and yanked back the hooded robe, exposing the head of a frantic woman, maybe five or six years older than Farris. Her platinum blonde hair was wild with static, and her porcelain complexion looked as though she hadn't seen full exposure to the sun for years. She reached a hand toward the Shadow Man, but he caught it at the wrist. Electricity arced between her fingers, though less intensely than before.

He held onto her wrist and, with his other hand, grabbed the collar of her robes, pulling her forward so her face was only inches from his own. "Give it back," he said slowly and deliberately.

The woman gingerly reached into the folds of her rags and produced the man's watch with her free hand. He let go of her wrist and snatched it from her, releasing his hold on her robes as soon as he had it. This sent the young woman crashing down onto the ground, her legs useless as though all strength and vitality had been drained from them.

Farris finally caught up to the pair, but the Shadow Man didn't seem to have any intention of sticking around. He quickly inspected the watch, paying no mind to the thief at his feet. Finding the watch free of damage, apart from the broken chain, he put it in his vest pocket and strode toward the open end of the alley, stepping over the fallen woman with as much regard as he might give to a pile of garbage. He looked back briefly to Farris. "Come on," he ordered.

Farris shook his head and reached down to the woman, placing a hand on her shoulder. Immediately she twisted her shoulder away, and as she did, the front of her robe shifted and dipped lower. Farris gasped and stepped back, slamming his back against the wall. A crackling wall of blue lightning sat just below the woman's collar bone. It was brightest at the center and grew dimmer as it spread toward either shoulder before giving way to normal flesh. It was not a truly solid wall but rather a tightly knit series of electrical lines, as though bolts of lightning were crisscrossing her chest. Though the bolts ran close together, there were occasionally small gaps in between as they pulsed with energy. Through the gaps, Farris saw exposed inner tissue and what looked like organs. It was as though the lighting was holding her together where the top of her ribcage should have been.

"Wait," Farris called out to the Shadow Man, who sighed heavily before turning to look back.

"What is it?" the older man asked in annoyance.

"She needs help," replied Farris, motioning towards the woman on the ground.

"She's dangerous."

"So are you! I don't know what you did to her, but she can't stand up."

The Shadow Man crossed his arms. "She'll regain the use of her legs in less than a day. And she should be grateful she got off so easy. Now leave her." He started to turn away once again.

"No!" Farris shouted with enough force in his voice to stop the Shadow Man in his tracks. "If somebody comes back here before she can move, then she'll be found, captured, and who knows what else."

The Shadow Man frowned. He squared his jaw and looked to Farris like he was seriously considering leaving both in the alley. He pointed a gloved finger at the woman. "Look at her! She's clearly on the run. I guarantee you she's being hunted. This is not my concern." He stared Farris down with a scowl.

"Yes, it is. Maybe what she is or what she's running from isn't your concern, but it's your fault she can't move. If she gets dragged away by the constables and handed over the Science Guild because she can't run, then that's on you!"

The Shadow Man sighed heavily and hung his head for a moment. He looked from the young man to the grounded thief and then back again, sneering with disdain. "This is why I don't help people," he grumbled as he stepped toward the pair. "They're never happy."

As the Shadow Man came closer, Farris knelt beside the woman. With her legs not working, she didn't make any move to try and get away from him but tensed as the two men closed in on her. Farris was careful not to make any quick movements that might startle her. "It's ok, we'll help you," he said soothingly. "I'm Farris. What's your name?"

The woman only shook her head in response.

The Shadow Man chuckled. "Well, she's smarter than you are, at least." He tucked his cane under his arm and knelt next to the woman. "Keep your sparks to yourself; otherwise, I'll just leave you both here," he said flatly.

The woman nodded, after which the Shadow Man took hold of her arm and slung it around his neck. Farris took the cue and did so with her other arm, so as the two men stood, she was supported between them. He winced as the muscles in his chest strained and ached in the spot he'd been shocked. The Shadow Man's greater height made the whole thing a bit awkward, but they were sturdy enough as a team to keep her up. The woman's legs hung limp and useless in the air between them, thanks to her being even shorter than Farris.

"This is going to be cumbersome at best, and we're going to have to stick to the side streets," the Shadow Man said as the trio maneuvered themselves out of the dead end. Thankfully, the street it connected to was still empty. "You'll have to pardon me," he cautioned before reaching down and adjusting the woman's robes, so they covered up the arcing lightning of her chest. Once he was satisfied she was properly covered, he pointed down the street, and the three started to move.

It took a few yards before Farris matched the Shadow Man's rhythm and kept pace. For his part, the Shadow Man made no accommodations and left it to Farris to figure out how to hold up his end of navigating with the woman in tow.

"You're already more trouble than you're worth, you know," the Shadow Man said to no one in particular. "So, let's try to keep this as short and painless as we can." The Shadow Man led the awkward threesome through the side streets toward an unknown destination.

Farris didn't like the unease that came with not knowing where he was being led, but his only other choice was to be alone again, and even companionship as dysfunctional as this was a better alternative to that.

Chapter 15

Inside the gold-domed Hall of the Arbiter, Garion brushed past an attendant without breaking stride and pushed open the double doors to the receiving hall. He was almost always the shortest person in any room, but in a space as excessively large as this, he appeared positively minuscule. The receiving hall, with its columns lining the walls, and its pristine marble floor, was far larger and grander than it needed to be; a relic of a time when those holding the office of Arbiter had hopes to transform the role into something closer to the inherited royalty of the Old World. That never came to pass, but the marble-floored hall remained all the same.

Garion strode down the long blue rug which formed a walkway to the desk at the far end, even as the attendant he'd bypassed scrambled in behind him, blubbering apologetically.

The Arbiter sat behind her desk, her bronze skin contrasted against her ornamental white robes with gold trim, all topped off with a frown. On either side of the desk, each holding a ceremonial spear, stood the Silent Guard, the elite forces of the arbiter sworn to never speak while on duty or repeat anything they hear within the hall. One of them took a defensive stance in front of the desk, brandishing his weapon, while the other left his spear standing upright in a small notch on the floor while he smoothly drew a bolt rifle from the holster on his back and aimed it at the approaching marshal.

"Arbiter Lorac, he wouldn't let me—"

"It's all right, Kae," said Arbiter Lorac. She placed two fingers against her the white hair at her temple, trying to cut off a rising headache. She waved a hand dismissively and said, "At ease, boys."

The Silent Guard returned to their positions on either side of the desk, and the attendant darted back out the way they'd come, closing the doors behind them. Through all this, Garion never slowed his approach. He came to an abrupt stop at the end of the carpet three feet away from the marble desk, buried under scattered documents and a map of the city.

"What are you doing here, Garion?" Arbiter Lorac asked, already sounding exhausted by this conversation.

"It was my understanding that you wished to see me, Good Lady," Garion said with syrupy politeness.

"Don't be an ass. And take that nonsense off your head," snapped the arbiter, shooting a finger at his hood. "I'll tolerate your sarcasm, but you will not address me with half your face covered."

Garion's posture lost a bit of its strength. He took in a slow breath as he reached up and lowed both his scarf and hood. His face's skin was an ashy grey, and his pulled-back hair was only a slightly darker shade of the same color. His ears were pointed, and his face was nearly flat, with only the slightest bump to denote the bridge of his nose. "Apologies," Garion said, revealing jagged teeth which clamped together like a steel trap when he stopped speaking.

"Dare I ask what happened to Sgt. Harmon and the other constables I sent to escort you?"

"They couldn't keep up." said the marshal, narrowing his eyes and smirking. "I expect they'll arrive within the next ten minutes or so with their tails between their legs."

Her lips tightened, and she drummed her fingers in sequence on the desk. "What are you doing in my city?"

"I'm not on official business if that's what you're asking."

"I *know* it's not official," Arbiter Lorac said, raising her voice. "I received no request to honor an open warrant. So, one more time, why are you hunting here?"

"What makes you think I'm hunting, Good Lady?" Garion asked innocently.

"Drop it, Garion, you're trying my patience." snapped the arbiter, smacking her hand on the desktop. She paused to let the sound reverberate off the marble walls, scowling at Garion the whole time. "I don't pretend that the under-dwellers are as privileged as the rest of us, but they are still citizens of this city, and you have no authority to harass them! Do you understand me?"

"Yes, Good Lady, I understand."

"Garion, you've done well by me in the past, even gone above and beyond expectations. I don't forget those things," She adopted a more diplomatic tone. "I'm willing to overlook this… incident. I'll even give you two days to conclude your business in the best way you see fit, uninterrupted and in the open if you choose." Lorac paused to let the offer sink in before adding, "After that, you can consider your goodwill with me to be completely spent, and I *never* want to see you in this city again without a declaration and a warrant. Not even for a holiday."

Garion nodded gravely but said nothing.

"I'm well aware that both your superiors at the Marshal Service, as well as your clients at the Science Guild, consider me to be the big fish in a small pond, but they would do well to remember it's still *my* damned pond."

After a pause, Garion gave a terse little bow.

"You're dismissed." She waved her hand, picked up a pen, and turned her attention back to the reports and other matters awaiting her.

Garion gave a small bow before pulling up his hood once more. He turned and headed down the carpet toward the double doors. When he reached them, he paused with his hand on one of the heavy brass handles and glanced back to the arbiter. "By the way, Good Lady, were you aware you have fey-eyed crows in your city?"

The arbiter stopped dead and slowly placed her pen back on the desk. She looked up at Garion incredulously.

"Lest you think me an instigator, that escort you'd sent to collect me can verify this. One was on the roof where they found me, so I'm sure they saw it as well, provided they were paying attention." Garion pulled his scarf back up to cover the lower portion of his face and yanked the door open. On the other side of the door stood the same three constables who had confronted the marshal on the roof, looking out of breath. Garion smiled behind his scarf as he glanced up at the sergeant. "I think she'll probably want to see you right away."

As if on cue, there came a bellow from the receiving hall. "Harmon! Get in here, now!"

Sergeant Harmon and her two constables scurried into the receiving hall and closed the door behind them.

Garion hurried out of the Hall of the Arbiter so as not to waste any more time. He had no reason to doubt Lorac would keep her word about allowing him to hunt unencumbered for the next two days. Nevertheless, he took more than a little pleasure, knowing he'd just given the arbiter something much bigger to worry about.

Chapter 16

The Shadow Man led the trio through the labyrinth of back alleys and side streets for what seemed like ages. The odd sight of the two men propping up a woman with no use of her legs meant keeping away from busier streets with more prying eyes. Being the shorter of the two men, Farris was carrying more of the weight of the woman who hung between them and was starting to wonder how much further he would be able to go. He'd suggested at one point the older man could carry the woman himself, but that idea yielded nothing but a withering look and a scoff. For her part, the woman did little to either help or hinder their movement. Farris might have thought she was resigned to the situation if the clear tension in her arms and back had not made it clear, this was no less frustrating for her. Finally, they emerged into a wide road, with a line of mid-sized trees splitting it into two halves. Glancing down one way, Farris saw the fountain he'd collapsed while trying to reach the day before.

"That way," the Shadow Man said, nodding his head in the opposite direction from the one Farris was looking.

Farris turned his head and was immediately greeted with the sight of a building looming large in front of them. The structure itself wasn't actually all that tall, only about four stories tall with a pitched roof, but the massive double doors, which were, in fact, the entire front wall, made it seem far bigger and more imposing than it might have otherwise been. The doors, made of red-tinted wood, were ornately carved with burnt marks on the edges of the designs to help them stand out to the eye. There were various features in the carving, trees, mountains, small figures along the bottom, but a huge image of a dragon dominated the majority of the door. One of the creature's wings covered the upper two-thirds of the door, its long, curled neck rearing back as its clawed feet dwarfed the mountains. It appeared that at any moment, it might detach itself from the woodwork and fly off into the wild. Farris recognized the dragon's iconography immediately as one of the most feared creatures of legend — Tamaleon, the Death Breather. He didn't know why this image would be on any building, but he at least took comfort in the fact it was clearly not any kind of detention facility.

Farris had little time to linger on the carving as the Shadow Man moved them along insistently. As they drew closer to the building, Farris saw a much smaller door down in the lower right corner, built into the much larger doors. The Shadow Man directed them past it and took them into the narrower street that ran along the building. The structure's side wall was carved stone, with a 7foot-high ring of riveted metal running along its base. Past the building, Farris could see the open green grass and small hills of a park.

The Shadow Man took the woman's arm from around his neck and helped lean her against the metal at the building's base. Farris kept a hand on her to ensure she was still supported and wouldn't fall over. With her hood up and obscuring her face, he had no way of knowing if this was appreciated or not, and she hadn't spoken a single word.

"Stay right here," the Shadow Man ordered. "This is an emergency escape point." He indicated a panel in the metal wall which blended in almost seamlessly. "It can only be opened from the inside, so I need you both to wait here until I get it open."

Farris nodded and tried not to show his discomfort at the prospect of being left alone with the woman. Even though this narrower portion of the street was as empty, it made him nervous knowing a major street and a park were on either side of him, both with people who might decide to come down the street at any moment.

"You need to pay attention and be ready to move quickly," warned the Shadow Man, his words snapping Farris' mind back to attention. "Normally, that door being opened sends a relay to the constabulary that there's an emergency. I can open it under the guise of a system test, but it can only be open for ten seconds. After that, I won't be able to open it again in the same day without activating the relay and notifying the authorities." The Shadow Man turned and headed to the front entrance, not bothering to confirm his instructions were understood.

Farris wondered if he might have been hoping they wouldn't get through the door in time, and he'd have an excuse to leave them behind. He frowned and took a moment to adjust his grip under the woman's arm. He was trying to keep her leaning against the building in a way that would look as natural as possible. He leaned in and whispered to her under her hood. "Can you feel your legs yet?"

The woman shook her head and gave no other response. Even with the other man gone and nothing else to do, she did not want to talk to him. Farris sighed and waited for some sign the emergency escape was about to open. As one minute turned into two and then three, he looked back and forth down each side of the street to be sure nobody was taking notice of them. As he was turning his head from the park to the square, he stopped when his eyes landed on a crow perched on a second-floor railing across the street. He thought he caught a glint of yellow in its eyes.

As Farris squinted to try and get a better look, he was snapped back to the present as the panel in the wall slid to one side, revealing a corridor. Without hesitation, Farris heaved himself and the woman through the gap. In his hurry, he didn't maintain the best grip on her, and the pair stumbled awkwardly to the ground once they were inside. Farris did his best to cushion the woman's fall with his arms. The panel slid shut behind them. Looking up from the floor, Farris saw the Shadow Man shaking his head.

"Very graceful," he said, looking down at them.

"Sorry," Farris said, his cheeks red with embarrassment.

"Just help me with her." The Shadow Man stooped down to help bring the woman up more or less onto her feet. Farris picked himself up and helped carry her through a series of corridors. The Shadow Man was in as much of a hurry now as he had been on the main street, which led Farris to suspect there were others in the building who might spot them.

The trio soon found themselves heading down a hallway with only one door in the middle of a blank wall. On one side of the door was a vibrant potted plant that stretched up taller than Farris. Once they reached the door, the Shadow Man heaved the whole of the woman onto Farris without much warning.

Farris found himself pressed up against the wall by her unsupported weight, but he did manage to keep her up and was a little proud of himself for having managed that.

The Shadow Man flipped up a panel on the wall next to the door and fiddled with some gear work inside. There was a mechanical whir, and the door swung open. He reached over and gathered the woman entirely in his arms and went into the room looking like a man heaving a particularly unwieldy bag of laundry. Farris skittered in behind just before the door swung shut behind him.

Farris found himself looking at a lavishly decorated office. A carved wooden desk with intricate details depicting dragons with their tails curled around the desk legs sat in the center of the room. There was a carving of a cracked egg in between the dragons. The room was decorated in warm colors giving it an inviting feel. There were two cushioned chairs in front of the desk and long sofas parallel to the side walls with a low rectangular table between them. The two side walls were almost entirely made up of segmented bookcases, with only the occasional painting, mirror, or small statue to break up the continuous lines of leather-bound books.

The Shadow Man laid the woman down on one of the sofas, taking the time to ensure her still weakened legs did not end up in an awkward position. Once she was down, he moved to the desk in front of a panoramic window looking out over the park. Farris didn't get much chance to take in the view before the Shadow Man pulled the heavy curtains over the window. The room dimmed a moment before a gentle glow emanated from a seemingly random smattering of the books on the walls. The effect gave a full and even lighting to the whole room. It threw Farris off for a moment before he realized the glowing books were simply cleverly disguised lamps. Out of curiosity, he reached out to one of the volumes and found it a well-carved and painted piece of the wall itself. He tested another book on the shelf below, and it pulled out, proving itself the genuine article. Glancing at the rows of tomes, Farris estimated about half of what he was seeing weren't even real books. This entire room was about image more than function.

"Boy!" the Shadow Man hollered, taking off his grey coat, revealing a matching vest over an immaculate white shirt. "Swap that plant for the one in the hall." He waved a hand at a corner near the window, which housed a very sad-looking plant. It was tall enough that it must have once flourished but now looked like it had suffered severe neglect, its sparse leaves dried and brown with barely a hint of life in them.

Farris went over and crouched down to lift the plant by its pot. Given the poor state of the thing, it proved to be quite light and easy to carry. It left a trail of fallen leaves behind as he moved it to the door. Once there, he didn't see a handle on the door itself and was about to ask what he should do when, behind him, the Shadow Man reached into one of the desk drawers and pulled a hidden lever. The door swung open inward, nearly hitting Farris. He took the dead plant out into the empty hallway. The new plant, being full and healthy, was significantly heavier, and it took notably more work for him to get it through the open doorway. Once he was back inside, the Shadow Man flicked the lever again, and the door swung shut.

Farris carried the plant as best he could to the corner where the old one had been, setting it down in roughly the same spot. Looking up, he saw the woman had managed to prop herself up in the corner of the sofa where the arm met the backing. She'd drawn back her hood and was watching the Shadow Man intently.

Glancing over, Farris saw the older man seated in the chair behind the desk, gripping the wrist of his right hand, once more unshielded by a glove and looking withered and sickly. Once the plant was in place, he turned to face it. "Get out of the way," he ordered.

Farris moved quickly to a spot behind the unoccupied sofa, across from the woman. The Shadow Man released his wrist and pointed his wizened fingers at the plant. Once more, the black tendrils emerged, though with less force than in the alley. They moved lazily, like the currents of a shallow stream. Once they reached the plant, the two tendrils entwined themselves among the branches, and the leaves began to change from a vibrant green to a dirty brown. It was as though the very life was being pulled from the plant. After less than a minute, the tendrils lost their grip on the plant and fell limply to the ground before retracting into the Shadow Man's fingertips. Once they had fully returned, he cracked his wrist and moved his fingers about.

Farris stood slack-jawed. There was no question he'd had just witnessed elemental energy, but it was unlike anything he'd ever seen or heard of before.

The Shadow Man turned in the chair and appeared annoyed by the stares he was receiving. "Once I let a little out, it's not easy to hold back whatever's left," he said, pulling the glove back onto his hand.

He stood and moved around the desk toward the other two. Farris instinctively backed away, placing his back to a wall and keeping the sofa between them. The woman gave no indication of fear; indeed, she appeared intrigued by what she'd just seen.

The Shadow Man approached her and knelt by her leg. "Do you mind?"

She shook her head, and Farris watched as the man lifted the rags covering her legs, revealing her glaringly pale skin. It had obviously been quite some time since she'd had decent exposure to the sun. He put a hand around her left shin and squeezed it gently.

"Do you feel that?"

"I think so."

Farris jolted when he heard her speak. She'd made such an effort to not say anything to him; he'd come close to assuming perhaps she lacked the power of speech at all. By contrast, the Shadow Man appeared unfazed.

D r e a m s o f F i r e | **173**

"Good," he said, placing her leg down on the sofa. "You'll regain feeling soon. You'll have full use by morning." He went back to his desk and sat on the edge of it, folding his arms. "And as soon as you do, I need you to leave."

The woman nodded before leaning forward to cover up her bare legs with her ratty robes once more.

"What about me?" Farris asked somewhat hesitantly.

"You, I'd like to have gone even sooner, if I can manage it," the Shadow Man replied tersely. He unfolded his arms and went around to the other side of his desk and presently produced a short glass and a heavy corked bottle. He yanked the cork, which made an audible pop, and poured about half of the orange liquid left into the glass, which wouldn't amount to much more than a single swallow. As he recorked the bottle and placed it back in the drawer, he continued. "Things are about to get crazy around here as they prep for dinner service and the evening show." He threw his head back and gulped the contents of the glass. "So, until that's settled down, I don't want either of you leaving this office."

The references to dinner and a show set off a lightning bolt of realization for Farris. Though he hadn't known an exceptional amount about the businesses of Torvec before coming here, he'd heard of the famed Dragon's Breath entertainment hall. He felt a little foolish for not putting the pieces together earlier when he'd first seen the massive carving on the front doors. Farris wondered if this Shadow Man was the owner of the building or simply a manager. In either case, it was clear from the opulence of the office he held considerable sway. Farris thought it curious the man, who'd so guarded his identity, let "dinner and a show" slip and thereby hint at what this place was. Then again, thought Farris, he might have assumed the building would have been recognized by the front door alone, and there was no point in hiding where they were.

That train of thought was interrupted when a loud buzzing sound rang out for a few seconds. A square panel on the top of the desk slid to the side, and a small device with a spool of paper rose. It made some clicking sounds, and a section of the paper moved through the device, coming out at the bottom with writing on it. The Shadow Man tore the paper off the inscriptor and ran his eyes over the short message that had been written on it.

"I have to deal with something." The Shadow Man pulled the lever which opened the door, and marched toward it, looking even more severe than usual. As the door started to swing closed, he turned back. "Try not to kill each other while I'm out."

The door closed, and Farris felt extremely lost. After a pause, he looked at the woman on the couch and gave a meek wave and an awkward smile, unsure of what else to do. She didn't smile back, but she did give a very terse single wave of her hand. After that, the room lapsed into an uncomfortable silence.

Chapter 17

Riding atop her saddled mount, Professor Raines saw the glint of sunlight reflecting off the wall surrounding Torvec. The subrails brought her as close as Research Station #42, and in an ideal world, she'd be in a motorized vehicle right now, but the vehicles were inventoried and tracked, while the stables were far laxer. Horses were kept at the station for use when researchers needed to travel quickly through areas with active Fey populations, as the Fey never took kindly to machines invading their forests. While riding a horse was no guarantee of safety, it at least meant the forest denizens were less likely to pay any mind.

Professor Raines had not ridden in years since she traded in field work for lab work, but she had not forgotten how. The familiar feeling of the animal underneath her gave her a renewed sense of urgency, bringing back memories of outrunning kobolds as they sprang up from the ground.

Having spotted the city, she allowed her steed to meander to the edge of the Ilyria River where she dismounted, and he drank. Keeping one hand on the reins, she put the other into her satchel to grip the smuggled notebook once more.

Feeling its leather-bound spine, she gazed down the river, to the lake it helped feed, and to Torvec's distant metallic glint. From an inner pocket of her coat, she pulled out a small monocular that let her get a closer look at the city.

The great dam and its water traffic came into focus and reminded her Farris could well be on board a ship already. Professor Raines frowned and turned away from that line of thinking. She looked east at the stretch of open field standing between the road she had been riding and the edge of the Everwood. She saw a figure move at the edge of the trees and squinted through the monocle. A tall, blonde woman caught her eye, pulled up a green hood, and vanished among the leaves and shadows of the forest. Even with the figure gone, the professor could see dark forms moving, shaking the branches as they passed to the south in the direction of the city. The sight left her unsettled and more than a little curious, but there was no time for this, and whatever might be happening, she took it only as a reason to keep to the road and not drift toward the trees.

She glanced to the horse, which by this time had drunk his fill. Professor Raines pulled an apple from a saddle bag and fed it to the eager animal. As it ate the treat, she remounted and, once the horse had finished its apple, steered the reins toward the city. With a kick to the haunches, the horse began its journey to Torvec once more. Her rust-colored coat whipped about in the wind behind her as she rode, and the denizens of the forest kept pace in their parallel journey.

***

In the grand opera hall of The Dragon's Breath, Garion stood with his arms folded. He looked out over the tables and chairs, among which the staff were milling about, arranging place settings, and sweeping the floor. The staff activity was concentrated closer to the stage, a fair distance away from Garion. Some of the staff would glance at him, but none looked for more than a few seconds, nor did they address the tables closest to him. Normally, nobody besides staff and talent would have been admitted this far ahead of the evening service, but when Garion had requested entrance, Auria, the fair-skinned house manager, made the call it was better to have him inside and out of the public eye. Having him wait outside where any passerby could spot him was how nasty rumors started, and part of Auria's job was maintaining the hall's reputation as well as its day-to-day functions.

Even though Garion's robes fell in such a way as to almost hide his feet completely, the tapping of his foot on the hardwood was heard clearly throughout the hall's finely tuned acoustics. As the tapping sound echoed in steady rhythm across the entertainment hall, more and more of the staff kept shooting glances at its source. Four members of the security staff stood positioned within a few yards distance of Garion, with the largest standing directly beside Auria. Garion's eyes roved about the room as his foot continued to tap. Auria sighed, checking a clock on the wall and wishing her employer would get here already. But the tension was escalating fast, so she approached the impatient marshal, tucking an errant strand of curly red hair behind her ear and clearing her throat to get his attention.

"I've notified him of your arrival," she said in a professional tone. She smoothed out her flowing skirt as a nervous habit. "Perhaps you'd like to wait in one of the side rooms?"

Garion snapped his head towards the manager, and his eyes pierced right through her. "If he wants me to wait, then I will wait where I am," he said sternly. "I'll not be shuttled off by lackeys."

Residin, the largest member of the security team whose muscles showed quite clearly through his black shirt, stepped between Auria and the marshal. "Hey!" he bellowed. "That's no way to talk to a lady." He stared down at Garion and, easily being two feet taller than the intrusive hunter, it looked almost comical.

Garion scoffed and shot another look at the house manager. "That's no lady," he intoned mockingly.

Auria stepped back and scowled as the rest of the room went silent. The eyes of staff members flicked from Auria to Garion, the former straightening up and glaring down at the latter, who made no movements at all. The silence was broken after Residin looked from Auria back to Garion before growling and swinging his white-knuckled fist down with tremendous force. Garion leapt deftly to the side with almost no visible effort. The fist flew through the air and slammed into the hardwood floor with a *crack* that echoed across the room. Residin howled in pain and gripped his cracked and broken hand. Other members of the security team moved in on Garion from all sides. One of them dove from the side, and Garion leapt upward and tucked in his legs just enough for the lunging man to pass under him and barrel into one of his fellow guardsmen. Both tumbled to the ground roughly, landing in a heap.

Even before Garion's feet had touched down on the floor, a meaty hand was reaching for his neck. Garion reached out and grabbed the approaching limb at the wrist and used it as leverage to change his direction in midair. He rolled across the arm's length, swinging his feet up onto the guardsman's brutish shoulders, and then pushed off them. The guardsman was sent crashing to the floor, and the elusive marshal flipped backwards to the wall, where he clung to the vertical surface like an insect.

One of the guardsmen still standing grabbed a chair and hurled it at Garion's perch, but the chair connected only with the wall where it broke into pieces as Garion dropped back down onto the ground. He skittered away from the wall before the debris could land on him.

In the commotion, none had noticed the grey-suited hall owner arrive, spot Garion, fiddle with an inscriptor located in a cubby near the stage, and finally step out fully into the open area. The fallen guardsmen were picking themselves up and looked ready to attack again when his voice bellowed across the hall. "Enough!"

All eyes shot to the other end of the hall.

The Shadow Man marched across the floor, staff scattering to clear a path. The guardsmen had frozen in place, and even Garion now stood at attention rather than in an attack-ready stance. The man stopped briefly as he passed by Auria. "Are you alright?" he asked, placing his bare left hand on her cheek for a moment. Her eyes gave him his answer, and he quickly pushed forward toward the marshal. "You wanted to see me?" he asked as he came to a stop a few feet away from Garion.

"I think that you and I have some things to discuss."

"I have nothing for you, Garion. I know who you're after, and she's not here."

"She?" asked Garion with a slight cock of his head.

The hall owner glanced about with a frown. "Perhaps we should speak in private," he said more quietly. He gestured toward the doors to the backstage areas through which he'd arrived.

Garion nodded and said nothing.

The Shadow Man looked past him, shooting an angry look at his security team, who were nursing sore bodies and hurt pride. "I'll deal with you lot later," he said before leading the way straight back.

Garion followed, managing to keep pace with the much taller man despite having a significantly shorter stride.

The silence left behind was deafening until Auria clapped her hands to snap the staff out of their stupor. "Clean it up in here. We're still on the clock."

Chapter 18

In the office, silence persisted between the woman and Farris. He was standing behind the couch across from her, where she sat with her legs up on cushions. Farris intermittently tapped his fingers on the back of his sofa. He had been trying to avoid eye contact, not knowing how that might be interpreted. By contrast, the woman had no issue starring directly at him when she wasn't surveying the rest of the room.

The longer the silence went on, the harder it became for him to think of any way to break it. His natural awkwardness around girls wasn't doing him any favors, and the fact that this woman had the ability to zap him with lightning didn't help. In his mind, if he opened his mouth and said the wrong thing, she'd just blast him into the bookcase. Part of him insisted that was ridiculous, and she was probably just as afraid of him as he was of her. Unfortunately, that wasn't the part of his mind winning the internal battle with the part that told him doing nothing was his only safe option.

So, the silence remained, and if anything, it was becoming oppressive. Farris' grip on the back of the couch tightened minute by minute. He'd started staring at the ceiling when a loud sigh brought his attention to the woman seated on the other side of the room.

"Poena."

Farris' eyes went wide, and his body tensed. He had a sudden urge to duck for cover behind the couch. "Uh…"

"It's my name."

"Oh… well… pleased to meet you?"

Poena smirked ever so slightly at his open display of discomfort. With the initial tension broken, she reached down, lifted her legs from the sofa one at a time, and placed her feet upon the floor. She took a moment to gather her strength before hoisting herself up onto very shaky legs. She turned around and leaned forward to use the couch for support, which put her back to Farris. He started to move in to help, but she heard him coming and waved a hand at him to stay where he was, which he did.

It took her several minutes to work her way around to the back of the couch. Her legs seemed to be equal parts stiff and weak. However, she eventually made it to the bookshelf on the wall. She began to examine the books keeping one hand on the shelf itself for support. She started to reach out and touch the various titles to see which ones were real and which ones were decorative. As

Farris had suspected, it was proving to be a roughly even split.

Taking the cue it was alright for him to move about more freely as long as he didn't intrude, Farris relaxed his posture and walked across the room toward her. He didn't go right up to her but leaned against the bookcase a few feet further along the wall from her. "It's a nice name," Farris said, almost cringing at such a canned response. "Um… why didn't—"

"I didn't say my name before because I didn't want the other one to hear it. Somebody who won't give me their name has no business knowing mine." She glanced over her shoulder at the awkward young man. "That being said, you give yours out a little too freely."

"Sorry," Farris said, trying not to blush. "I'm not exactly used to being on the run. You seem to be more of a natural at it." He furrowed his brow at what a strange compliment that was, but it was out there, so he opted to roll with it. "Been doing it long?"

Poena shook her head as she turned her attention back to the bookcase. "Not really. I just had a great deal of time to plan things out."

Farris noticed her fingers were lingering on the spines of the books, at least the real ones. It was as though the tomes brought about memories of another life before this one. He was starting to feel a little more at ease around her as he felt her own guard dropping, at least a little bit. The sense of ease was cut abruptly short by the same loud buzzing sound they'd heard before.

Farris turned to the desk as the panel slid open, and the inscriptor rose up as it had before. The buzzing stopped, and the device clicked and scratched for a few seconds before spitting out a small piece of paper. When it finished, the pair glanced at one another. Poena nodded her head toward the desk insistently. Farris shrugged walked over to it, tearing the bit of parchment off the end. With the message removed, the inscriptor retracted back into the desk, and the panel slid over the top of it once more. He read the parchment as he walked back towards Poena.

Hide. Wall left of windows. Pull 3rd book from right, up 4, push 5th book from left and up 3 at the same time. H4V2. Door will open. Go now.

Farris stopped dead in his tracks, his face went white, and he looked at Poena in a panic.

"What is it?"

Farris couldn't find the words and instead thrust the message into her hands before turning to the wall. The bookshelf was sectioned off into squares of four shelves each, there were eight such squares across the width of the wall, and they went up three squares high to the ceiling. The instructions had given him a sense of what position the books to pull were in on any given squared-off segment. However, he had no idea what square he was meant to be pulling them from. He assumed the "H4V2" was meant to clarify this, but his racing mind couldn't make sense of it. He started to push and pull at books in a panic.

"Farris, stop!" Poena shouted, having read the message. "You'll get everything out of order. Now just let me think."

Farris stepped back from the bookshelf, panting heavily. He could feel the heat starting to build in his fingertips. He closed his eyes and took a few slow deep breaths. This wouldn't dissipate the energy that had already built up, but with luck, it might slow the accumulation of more. When he opened his eyes again, after slowing his breathing, he saw Poena examining a shelf. She tried pulling and pushing the two books, but one of them didn't move at all. She glanced at another segment of the shelves and worked her way over to it.

Suddenly there was a loud *thud* from the hallway as though something had been slammed into the wall next to the door. Muffled voices could be heard, the thick door preventing them from being intelligible.

Farris turned to Poena with a pleading look on his face, but she didn't have time to be comforting. She positioned herself at the segment she'd been moving to and placed her hands on two books. She pushed one with her right hand while pulling another with her left. Both books shifted, and there was an audible clicking of gears as a section near the middle slid back then to the side, revealing another room.

Farris dashed over to Poena, took her arm, and slung it around his neck. Part of him feared she might shock him for his trouble, but there wasn't time to dwell anymore. The pair moved as fast as they were able to through the open passageway. Outside the office, the voice of the Shadow Man came through loud enough that Farris was able to make out, "This is not the arrangement!" The muffled response was less clear, but Farris could make out something about "favors called in." That was all he caught before he and Poena stumbled into the secret room.

They were in what appeared to be a private bath. The floor was tiled and in the center was a large circular tub embedded in the floor. There was a soft white glow coming from the walls giving the room a moody but even lighting.

Looking around, Farris promptly spotted a readily apparent lever near the doorway. He wasted no time in pulling it, causing the bookshelf segments to slide back into place and seal up the room once more. With that done, he helped Poena over to a marble bench that ran the length of the wall and helped her sit down.

Farris heard the slam of the office door outside the bathroom. He went back and pressed his ear to the closed panel, but the voices were even more muffled than when they were in the hallway. With a sigh, he took a step back and put his hands on his hips. Now that he'd stepped back, he noticed what looked like a circular window in the wall. He approached it nervously and peered through it out into the office. He ducked his head away and thought back to the room. He couldn't remember having seen a window, but there had been a mirror. And if his memory wasn't failing it, that mirror is where this window appeared to be.

Farris gathered himself and stepped back to the window, which was concave, and took in a surprisingly wide, though somewhat distorted, view of the office. He saw the Shadow Man talking to a short figure in red travel robes and a cloak. His eyes landed on the silver and charcoal armband that marked the short figure as a marshal. He turned to Poena, intending to wave her over to see if she knew this person but stopped short when he saw she was tightly gripping the bench he'd left her on, her knuckles turning white.

She was looking at the floor and shaking slightly. He began to move towards her, but when she heard his footstep, she shot a pained look at him. Gritting her teeth, she shook her head at him. The electrical webbing between her fingers had started to snap and pop fiercely.

At first, Farris thought it was because she'd seen the marshal, but glancing back at the window, he realized she couldn't see out of it from where she was. Looking around the room, it sunk in there were no windows and no apparent doorway besides the one they had come through. In their desperation, they had allowed the Shadow Man to place them in a room from which they could not escape without detection.

Farris clenched a fist, remembering the mention of an "arrangement" he'd heard mentioned. He didn't know what kind of arrangement the Shadow Man would have with a marshal, but all possibilities seemed bleak.

He returned to the window where the marshal was staring back at him. Most of the marshal's face was covered by a scarf and hood, but the grey tint on what little skin was visible made Farris' skin crawl. After a few agonizing moments, the marshal turned away from the mirror once more. There were a few more muffled words spoken between the Shadow Man and the marshal, which Farris couldn't discern.

The Shadow Man reached for the lever on the desk; a quick pull on it opened the door out of the office. The marshal turned to leave, stopping to throw back one final unintelligible remark before exiting. Farris' clenched fist began to tremble, and his face tensed into a scowl as he watched the Shadow Man approach the bookcase and activated the sliding panel door. Farris took up a position directly in front of the door as the sound of gears signaled its imminent opening.

Once the panel opened halfway, Farris launched himself out of the room, fist first. He connected with the Shadow Man's jaw, a small puff of smoke wafting up from where his fist had landed.

The Shadow Man stumbled back until he caught the desk. He looked more surprised than injured as a hand shot up to the red patch of skin on his jaw where Farris' smoldering fist had made its mark. The young man swore and gripped at his hand, his fingers and knuckles throbbing from the impact.

Behind him, Poena rushed out of the bath. She hit the back of the sofa so hard she practically doubled over it, panting and sweating. The Shadow Man made a small show of straightening his vest and rolling his shoulders back.

"I'd ask what that was about, but I doubt you could even answer that," he snarled. He moved toward Poena, reaching out a hand. "Are you—?"

"Keep away from her!" Farris planted himself between them.

"Giving orders now, boy? Feeling like a man all of a sudden?" He took a step toward Farris, who put up his fists in response.

A small bolt of lightning shot between the two men with a resounding *crack*, scorching the wall. Both stopped and looked over at the Poena. Her hand was extended, having just let loose the shot. She was still panting, but she kept her hand extended out, ready to unleash another blast. The two men looked at each other, and each took a few steps. Once there was more distance between them, she lowered her hand accordingly.

The room fell silent until Farris found his voice. "What kind of arrangement do you have with him?" he asked as calmly as he could manage.

"I don't see how my business dealings are any of your concern." The Shadow Man folded his arms.

"He's an elemental hunter, and you clearly assist him. I think that is definitely my concern."

"Youth." The Shadow Man sighed. "Always leaping to conclusions based on the minimum number of facts."

"Don't patronize me."

The Shadow Man scoffed as he walked around the furniture to give the other two a wide berth as he inspected his jaw in the mirror. He touched the burnt patch of skin gingerly and frowned. "Garion doesn't hunt elementals exclusively. He hunts whoever he's contracted for, just like any other arm of the Marshal Service." He walked back to his desk. "You're right; I have helped him. I'm privy to a great deal of information as to what goes on in this city, and I get it quickly. If I have information that will help him find a fugitive faster, I provide it to him. But this is for criminals. I don't turn in elementals whose only crime is simply existing."

"Why should we believe that?"

"Because I'm still the only one who can get you out of this city in anything other than the locked cell of a collector tank," he said flatly, settling into the chair behind the desk.

"What do you get out of it?" asked Poena.

"He will notify me if a warrant is ever issued against me," the Shadow Man said with resignation. He slumped a little in his chair, as though being forced to say out loud just how precarious his place in the world was made it a physical burden.

"All this so you can have, what? A day's head start?" snapped Farris, who had gone back to cradling his sore fingers and knuckles.

"I really don't care what you think of me." He straightened in his chair. "But think for just a few moments about what might happen if the Guild got hold of somebody like me. This is not a matter of ego. The forces inside me are something no one should have." He swiveled his chair away from the other two. "I probably shouldn't even exist."

Farris found some of his righteous anger leaving him, as the man he'd been so set against now appeared small, almost meek. He also hadn't taken the time to truly think about what he had seen the Shadow Man do to Poena and then the plant. It had been filed away in his brain under "worry about this later." But now that he stopped to actually examine what he'd seen the man do, it begged a very obvious question. "What element are you anyways?"

"I don't know. And I don't want to know."

The room lapsed into an uncomfortable silence. Farris noticed the rhythmic ticking of a clock on the wall, which felt like it was getting louder with every passing moment. He tried to think of something, anything to say, just to break the quiet. He was visibly relieved when Poena did it for him.

"So, what happens now?" she asked plainly.

"Well," the Shadow Man said, standing from his chair. "I'd really love to get both of you out of here, but it's too likely that Garion is going to stake out the building for at least the rest of the day. So, you'll be staying here longer than I'd ever wanted."

"And if we'd rather not?" Poena asked.

"Don't."

"So, you just expect us to trust you?" Farris scoffed as he folded his arms defiantly. "When you can turn us in at any moment?"

The Shadow Man walked to the bookcases opposite the hidden bath, turning back to face the pair with his back against the shelves. He took another slow breath. "It doesn't matter if you trust me," he said. "You should realize by now I can't turn you in. The fact that you don't know my name is moot because you know where I work and what I am. I need to make sure you get out of this city in one piece because if you're caught, you'll point them straight to me."

"I wouldn't do that," Farris insisted.

"You're young and naïve enough to believe that. And I'm old and experienced enough to know better."

Farris glanced back at Poena. He wasn't sure what he'd hoped to get from her, but all she offered was a resigned shrug. He took a breath and turned his attention back to the man at the bookcases, then took a few slow steps toward him and extended his hand.

The man looked at it quizzically and, after a moment, reached out to shake it.

"Farris."

"Tamaleon."

This caught Farris off guard, as suddenly the carving on the front of the building and even the name Dragon's Breath took on new meaning.

"Like the drag—"

"Yes." Tamaleon let go of his hand and looked past Farris to the woman leaning on the back of his sofa.

"Poena. And you'll forgive me for passing on shaking that particular hand. Even with a glove."

Tamaleon smirked and turned around to face the bookcase. He performed a similar trick to what had been done to open the bath, and in turn, another panel slid aside just like the one before. Farris noticed the gears of this one creaked and groaned as if they were unaccustomed to use. Once the panel slid to the side, it revealed a lavish bedroom.

"I can bring you something to eat in a little bit, but after that, the best thing for either of you is getting some sleep," Tamaleon said as he walked into the room.

Farris followed in behind him, and after a moment, Poena followed and placed a hand on the door frame to compensate for her still stiff and unreliable legs. Where the left wall met the ceiling, there was a continuous window about two feet tall running the length of the wall. It was too high up to be looked out of, but it was catching just a bit of the orange light of sunset. Even through his shoes, Farris could feel how soft and plush the carpet was under his feet. There were exquisitely carved furniture pieces, including a vanity, a bureau, and matching side tables. Most impressive of all, though, was the bed itself. It was easily the largest bed Farris had ever seen and sported a massive headboard that stretched up the wall to the window. Carved into the headboard was a scene similar to that on the front of the Dragon's Breath. The finely carved dragon could either appear to be guarding over the sleeper or about to attack them, depending on the angle it was viewed from. For all the amenities that Farris saw, it did not escape his attention that there was no sign of the wear and tear that would come from regular use. Everything appeared pristine, like a finely preserved museum piece.

"Probably more than you're used to, but I'm sure you'll find a way to get comfortable," Tamaleon said, turning back toward the doorway. He paused and indicated a lever embedded in the wall near the exit, next to another window looking out into the office, as there had been in the bath. "This will get you out," he said, resting his hand on the lever. "Do you remember the books to open the other door?"

Farris had to break himself out of the slight spell the finely furnished bedroom had put him under. He stammered, trying to remember precisely the books that had been used. He hadn't thought to be paying attention at the time.

"Never mind." He turned to Poena. "You remember?"

"Of course," she said with a nod.

"Good." Tamaleon turned back to look at Farris once more. "I'd ask you to let go of your fire into the bath and not burn my sheets. And if you wake up feeling… overheated, then you know where you can go."

"And me?" Poena asked with a raised eyebrow.

Tamaleon sighed and rubbed the back of his neck as he thought. "If I can find you a spent lightning cage, will that be enough until morning?"

Poena shuddered at the mention of the cages, rubbing her arms as if trying to ward off a chill, but she nodded all the same. Tamaleon brushed past her back into the office. Poena was quick to follow him out, and Farris took the cue and exited the bedroom behind them. As he exited, he saw Tamaleon grab his coat and pull the lever at the desk to open the office door, moving quickly to the exit.

"What about you?" Farris blurted out, suddenly wondering why he cared enough to ask.

Tamaleon stopped at the door and turned back. "I have to make sure your passage north has been secured. Besides, I don't sleep." With that, he exited the room, and the door swung closed behind him.

Farris turned back around and saw Poena pulling a volume from one of the shelves. Farris couldn't make out the book title from where he was, but it was thick and hardbound. If he were to guess, it was probably a reference book of some description. She wobbled slightly as she carried it to the sofa, where she sank into the cushions and shut out the world as she opened it.

Farris decided to leave her to her comfort zone and looked at the shelves to see if there was anything that might catch his eye. Most of the books, real and fake, appeared weathered and vintage. Half the time, the title on the spine was so faded Farris couldn't make it out at all. The ones he could read had titles like "The Locket of the Lake: A History of the Vaettir Dam," "Artifacts of the Old World," and "Architectural Evolution of Torvec." Even to pass the time, none of these held any appeal for him. Then he spotted a thick checkered board propped up in a corner of one of the higher shelves. He stretched out to grab it and brought it down with a smile.

Farris settled on the couch across from where Poena was reading. He set the board down on the table between them and lifted the checkerboard top to reveal finely carved wooden pieces, each in a perfectly fitted velvet-lined nook. They were representations of armaments and weaponry (battleships, canons, riflemen, and so on) on one side and Fey creatures of the wild (dryads, kobolds, trow, nixies, and more) on the other.

He smiled as he began taking the pieces out and setting them up on either side of the table. With each piece he picked up, he'd pause to take a look at the intricate detailing. His mother had taught him to play Clash at a young age, but he'd never seen pieces as finely carved as these. As he set down an armored dreadnaught on the other side of the table, he looked up and saw Poena was letting the book rest in her lap unread as she watched him. Farris motioned to the board and raised his eyebrows.

"Alright. But I get to be the Fey."

Chapter 19

The yellow-eyed crow glanced about from its perch atop one of Barreth's numerous inns. It looked to the Torvec's main gate, now closed to be reopened at dawn. It peered down at the figures beneath it, its sparkling eyes lingering on the tall woman in a long rust-colored coat as she dismounted from a visibly tired horse and entered the inn. The crow looked out from the small village to the darkness of the woods and the shadowy mountains beyond. Its eyes flashed, and it took flight toward the edge of the Everwood.

The bird's eyes pierced the deepening darkness as it glided from civilization to the wilds of its true home. Crows existed somewhere within the in-between—they were as much a part of the Fey as they were members of the animal kingdom. While the Fey enjoyed a symbiotic relationship with most plants and animals, with crows, it was something deeper.

In the times of the Old World, warriors believed seeing a crow before a battle was a sign their own death was imminent. Some still held the belief that any human who harmed one of these birds would meet a swift and brutal end inside of a year, though they were a minority as most now chalked the entire notion of omens up to superstition. Even the ardent skeptics of the Science Guild found themselves uneasy around these black birds, and in a city like Torvec, the appearance of a crow was something authorities took very seriously, if only for the unrest it stirred.

It had never been clear what percentage of the crow population acted as direct agents of the Fey. Much as any tree in the Everwood could be a dryad, any crow could be serving the mystical forest denizens. Most humans would never get close enough to see the colored glint in the eye that would identify a Morrighan crow.

As the soaring black bird neared the tree line, it fixed its eyes upon a figure standing on a stump at the forest's edge. The alabaster figure was draped in a long black feather cloak. At first glance, she appeared quite youthful, bordering on child-like, but there was something ancient about her presence that ran deeper than her physical body showed. Not that any could even guess at the age of the Morrighan.

Her long, wild hair was several vibrant shades of red. At the root, it was almost orange, but over the length of each strand would subtly darken into deeper shades of red until it was obsidian black at the tips. It resembled nothing so much as the bright flames of a fire fading into the blackness of night. Any foolish enough to look into her eyes would have noted something odd about their color. They would be best described as grey sky eyes, but there was a glint to them that was almost imperceptible, just in the corner of the iris. This glint, when it could be seen, was constantly shifting in color: starting with green and then shifting across the spectrum to blue and purple, into orange and red, then a pure black and back again.

At first glance, the Morrighan appeared more human than Fey. Her average human height and build was something her black cloak of feathers could not hide. Her origin was the subject of great debate amongst Feyanic scholars. Some believed she had once been a human who had been brought into the fold of the forest folk ages ago, during the days of the Old World. Others contended she was the last of an extinct breed of ancient Fey, stubbornly refusing to pass from this world. Still, others argued she may not be a single being at all but a visual projection of the Fey collective. Regardless of where she came from or what she was, there was no question she held sway over the mystical denizens of the forests that no other being could match.

The Morrighan stood stiff as stone at the edge of the forest. Indeed, no one could have been blamed for mistaking her for some sort of carved and painted ornament were it not for the breeze off the lake teasing her hair. Behind her, the branches and leaves rustled as shadowy shapes leapt from tree to tree and chattered incessantly; the treshen were restless. Mixed amongst the grey treshen of the Everwood were some with burnt orange fur and even one or two a shade of dirty ivory. They had traveled east from the Drakonwood and Dimwood, respectively, summoned to this place in anticipation of what was to come. A number of the trees themselves shifted, marking agitated dryads. The colorful wings of pixies flitted about in the dark, hovering in the air but never staying still for more than a few seconds. Some of them landed on the cloak's black feathers for a moment before flying away, much like a child might poke at a sleeping dog on a dare. Still, the Morrighan stood vigilant and unmoving.

The yellow-eyed crow began a descent as it neared the tree line, a slow dive toward her. The trees went silent as the dryads stopped swaying, the pixies settled onto branches, and the treshen ceased their chatter. The bird landed lightly on the stump besides the woman. She opened her cloak ever so slightly, exposing ghostly pale flesh. The crow ducked in under the cloak, which was dropped back into place behind it. At that moment, the glint in the Morrighan's eyes flashed yellow, and she saw all that the bird had seen during its time in the city. After a few seconds, the subtle glint in her eye once more began to shift and change colors, the yellow now added to the pallet of hues.

The activity in the trees behind her picked up once more, building in intensity. Treshen leapt from branch to branch and shook the leaves impatiently. The glow of pixies flitted in shades of green and blue but most predominantly red. The trees themselves leaned forward as though they might uproot at any moment and begin marching on the city. The Morrighan tilted her head to the sky and let out a single shrill cry. It was not a cry any one being should have been capable of. It sounded like a chorus of creatures— birds, wolves, bears, and even snakes all calling out in unison. The cry quieted the forest behind her, and all fell silent once more. It was not time. Not yet.

Chapter 20

Poena won the first game quite handily, and after breaking for Farris to release his fire into the lavish, hidden bath, she'd been poised to sweep the second match as well. A mid-game strategy change turned things around, and Farris claimed victory by a narrow margin. The pair began to reset the pieces as they picked at the plates of food Tamaleon had brought them during the final stretch of the first game. Farris hadn't expected much more than bread and water, but the full and finely prepared meal that was provided reminded him of the kind of business he was in. Poena had picked her plate completely clean while he had some scraps left, mostly leaving behind the vegetables.

As the two reached for their last game pieces, their hands grazed, and Farris received a slight shock. He pulled his hand back instinctively, and Poena shrank into the couch, lowering her head.

"It's ok." He offered a weak smile, but she didn't look up to see it.

Things went quiet as they began another game. The first game had been conducted in near silence. Things had loosened up a bit in the second, but they only talked about the immediate situation on the game board, grumbling or gloating as appropriate. He'd hoped things would ease enough for them to have a real conversation for this game, but now he feared that wouldn't happen. The sense of things relaxing was gone. He took a breath and gulped.

"Do you play often?"

"I used to play to pass the time between classes," Poena said, keeping her head down and moving a nixie diagonally across the board.

Things went quiet again, and Farris' shoulders drooped as he resigned himself to the fact that would probably be all he was going to get by way of conversation. So, when Poena asked her own question in the middle of his moving an alchemy, he nearly dropped the piece in surprise.

"What about you?" she asked, glancing up through her shock blonde hair.

"Well…," Farris' head wavered back and forth for a moment. "My mom taught me how to play when I was pretty young. She didn't really have time to play it with me much, though." "I can tell." Poena snickered.

"Oh really? And what does that mean?"

"It means"— she removed a trow from the board and flipped over the checkered space to show it taking an underground position—"that you don't think more than a few moves ahead."

"Maybe not." He slid his marshal off to the left side, and plucked her huldra off the board. "But you get pretty rash and flustered if I manage to do something you weren't expecting." He smiled, and looked at the carved figure in his hand, turning it around to see the hollow log shape of its back before hastily putting it down.

"That one scares you," said Poena, a note of intrigue in her voice.

"I just…" started Farris, looking away. "When I was little, if I was outside I kept thinking I heard their song, that they'd lure me into the woods. Turn me into…"

"I think every kid gets the fear of being a treshen put in them," said Poena as she shifted a storm sprite to a rear guard position.

"I suppose," sighed Farris. He studied the board for a moment. "See, you're already playing defensively because now you're worried I'm going to do something unpredictable." He smirked as he brought a shock canon front and center.

Poena frowned, but there was a playfulness behind it. That playfulness vanished at the sound of the office door unlocking and swinging open, and it failed to return when Tamaleon entered the room wheeling a box the size of a traveling trunk, mostly concealed by the coat he'd draped over it.

The door closed behind him as he pushed it next to the couch where Poena was seated. "Will this do?" he asked, gesturing to the box as he took his coat off it.

It was a lightning cage. Developed by the Science Guild, who carefully controlled the availability of the device and held tight the secret of how they were filled with electrical energy. Once charged, it could be used to power everything from lights to motor carriages. It had horizontal notches on one side and an indentation on the top.

"Yes, that will do."

Tamaleon gave a terse nod. He looked at the two people in his office as he draped his coat over his arm, his gaze lingering on Poena. "If you've had enough of those rags," he said, straightening his vest, "I can get you something fresher."

"No," Poena replied without hesitation. "When I'm like this, people ignore me."

Tamaleon seemed to understand and accepted the answer. "You won't see me again before morning." He pulled the door lever at the desk. "Try to sleep. Depending on what arrangements I can make for passage out of the city, we may have to move quickly once the sun is up." He turned to the open door, stopped, turned back to Poena. "Are you trying to leave, too?"

Poena cocked her head at him. "I... I'm not... I don't... I mean."

"If you want passage, it'll be with him," he said, pointing to Farris. "I can probably arrange for two of you, but I'm not booking individual trips. So, it's north with him, or it's nothing."

Poena looked back and forth from Tamaleon to Farris. Farris offered an awkward smile; Tamaleon's offered only impatience. After a breath, she looked at Tamaleon and shook her head.

"Suits me," he said. "But you leave my sight when he does." And with that, he exited the office, and the door closed behind him.

Alone together again, Poena turned her attention to the board once more. She silently picked up a dryad sapling and placed it in a new position.

"You know," Farris said, then immediately stopped. He hadn't actually meant to say anything out loud, but it seemed even worse now to not push forward. "It would have been ok if you'd... wanted to come with me." He stared at the board.

He glanced up, and Poena met his eyes. She shook her head slowly, and there was no sense of judgment in her expression. "I'm not...," she started and stopped. Now it was her turn to pause and gather her thoughts. "I'm not really ready for… people." She glanced over at the lightning cage. "Can we pause the game for a minute?" "Yeah, of course," Farris said, leaning back in his seat.

Poena stood up from the couch and walked over to the lightning cage. Small bolts of lightning arcing between her fingers as she rolled up the raggedy sleeves of her tattered robes. At first, she reached out both hands towards the indentation on the top of the box, but upon comparing the size of both hands to it, she let her right hand drop to her side. She stretched out her left hand and held it a few inches above the indent.

Her robes shifted, exposing the electrical energy dancing across her chest once more. Farris blushed as if he were watching something that was supposed to be done privately and instinctively turned away just as electricity began to pulse from Poena's hand into the box. Even turned away, Farris could see the flashing and hear the crackling as the energy poured into the cage. When the sound died down, he glanced back to see Poena settling back onto her spot on the couch. The notches on the side of the box now lit up blue.

With Poena looking to the board again, Farris remembered it was still his turn. He made a hasty decision and moved his guard tower to capture her gargoyle. Looking up, he saw her shake her head at the move and noticed she hadn't moved the robes to cover up the web of energy just below her collarbone.

"You can just ask, you know," she said as she reached out to put her kobold in a position to be able to take either Farris' tower or his cannon with her next move.

"Erm." He moved to spare his cannon, accepting he'd lose the tower. "Why do you…?" He started to speak but realized he didn't know how to word his question.

"Have this?" she finished for him, gesturing to the white and blue electrical lines that crossed her upper chest. He nodded, and she took his tower. "I held it in for too long," she said, her shoulders slumping as she spoke. She glanced up at her opponent. "Have you ever held it back for so long that it built up the length of your arms and started to pool in your chest?"

Farris nodded. The times he'd restrained himself the longest before releasing his fire had resulted in exactly what she described—the feeling that the energy was joining at a central point in his chest because he wasn't letting it flow.

"Me too. And I kept holding it. I held it until I honestly thought it would kill me. And when I let it go…" She rubbed her hands together, which crackled with static. "I suppose it couldn't flow out my hands fast enough... so it made a new exit point."

Farris couldn't help but place a hand onto his own chest, shuttering at the thought of it. "Why would you...?" he started to ask but abandoned the question when he saw how tightly she was clenching her hands together. Instead, he brought his motorcade around to pin down Poena's treshen.

They played for another hour, and without words passing between them, the tension in the room diminished on its own as they eased into the rhythm of play. By the time they agreed to call it a draw, the sun had set on the other side of the lake. Farris began to place the pieces back into their storage slots in the board.

Poena went to the window and looked out at Aelig Park, lined with softly glowing streetlamps that gave off just enough to make stars difficult to pick out in the sky above. "He was right, you know," she said, turning back to Farris.

"What about?" he asked as he glanced over at her and closed up the board.

"We really should try to get a good night's sleep."

"Suppose so." He saw the wisdom in it but couldn't shake the feeling; it felt like admitting defeat in some way he couldn't quite define in his head. Rather than ponder this feeling, he placed the board back where he'd found it on the shelf and walked over to the couch and began rearranging cushions.

"What are you doing?" Poena asked from the bookcase, which she'd already activated.

Farris glanced from her to the couch and back again, his mouth hanging open for several seconds. "I'm just… making up a bed?" he said, turning it into a question at the last minute.

"I mean… If you really want the couch, that's fine. It's just…" She stopped and looked into the large, lonely bedroom, then back at Farris. "I'd rather not be alone."

Farris stood hunched over the couch dumbfounded for several seconds before straightening up, not even bothering to put the cushions back the way they were. "I… I thought you weren't ready for people."

"I'm not ready to have expectations of them," she said. "But tonight, I'd prefer the company."

"Alright," he said, with a slight squeak in his voice.

Poena smirked and walked into the bedroom. Farris followed in behind, his mind racing. He really had no idea how to read this situation or fully grasp what was or wasn't expected of him. He couldn't form a coherent thought. His brain kept jumping tracks from fear of the marshal to questions about Tamaleon, to more questions about Poena, to confusion about the immediate situation, and back again. His face looked like he was in a bit of a trance.

"Door," Poena said over her shoulder.

Farris turned back and pulled the lever to slide the panel back into place. To assuage some of his own paranoia, he pulled it again to make sure it would open the room from the inside. The panel started to slide open, and he put the lever back to the closed position one more time, having satisfied himself they hadn't been tricked into trapping themselves in the room. When he looked back, Poena was raising a blonde eyebrow at him.

"Just... checking," he said, with a weak shrug.

She nodded with a chuckle before turning around and walking to the edge of the massive bed. She began to remove her hooded robe, which made Farris tense up even more than he already had. However, he relaxed once he realized it was only a top layer over an under layer of similarly ragged robes, which she wasn't taking off. She sat down on the edge of the bed, feeling the mattress.

Farris walked around to the other side of the bed. Once there, he removed his shoes, pulled back the sheet and blanket, and sat with his back against the headboard before placing the coverings over his legs. Poena did the same, pausing to press a button on a nightstand which caused the lights in the room to slowly dim as she scooted down until she was laying on her back, looking up at the dragon carving that loomed over them.

"Like I said, no expectations," Poena said as the lights finished dimming, and the pair were left with only the soft glow of streetlights coming in through the window at the top of the wall. "I've been alone for... longer than I'd like. I just want another person here. Just... just here."

Farris thought about his own time being confined, his movements restricted, and his interactions minimized. He nodded to her before realizing it was too dark for her to see. "I understand," he said softly.

The mattress shuttered as Poena rolled onto her right side, facing away from him. Farris let himself slide down under the blankets properly before rolling himself onto his left. Behind him, Poena shifted and pressed her back against his. He tensed at first but soon relaxed, finding comfort in the continuous reminder of her presence. His eyes adjusted to the dim light, and in the empty darkness of the room, the lavish trappings suddenly felt hollow and unappealing. He didn't have to dwell on this thought as exhaustion finally caught up with him. He fell asleep quickly, if not peacefully.

***

Professor Raines sat on the edge of her rented bed at the inn. The room was small and sparsely furnished; it didn't need to be anything more as no one ever stayed more than a night in Barreth. It was a stopover, not a destination, and there was little point in offering lavish accommodations. She frowned at the layer of dust along the windowsill of the only window in the room. There was a nightstand with a drawer that likely hadn't been opened in years. The mattress was stiff and unyielding, offering only slightly more comfort than she might have had being on the floor.

Not that it mattered. She wasn't accustomed to comfort anyway.

The room was dark, despite the electric light on the nightstand. It was still turned on, but no power ran through its workings. Barreth was not technically part of the city, but businesses there were permitted to draw electrical power from Torvec on a restricted and tightly controlled basis, with most buildings going dark shortly before midnight. This was yet another reason nobody stayed there unless they'd missed the gate's open hours. Even those who operated the few businesses in the hamlet usually kept homes in Torvec and worked in shifts, so none had to be subjected to enforced darkness for more than a few days at a time.

Not that it mattered, she didn't need the light.

She'd replaced her normal spectacles with a green-tinted pair from a small collection of colored lenses in her satchel, each one allowing for a different kind of altered vision. From granting color to the colorblind, to magnifiers, to the Guild's precious Feyglass used to make the lingering energies of Fey magic visible to the human eye. The green lenses allowed her to see through the darkness. The world seen through these lenses was an ill-looking green that put most off from bothering with them unless they absolutely needed to. Nobody would choose these over natural or electrical light.

Not that it mattered, the hue was only marginally sicklier looking than the greenish lighting in her own office.

Professor Raines glanced out the window of her undersized room at the wall of Torvec; the wall's top edge glowed softly from the lights within. Her eyes lingered on the wall. Ages ago, the wall guarded against the aggression of would-be conquers. Now, it guarded against the Fey.

The wall mattered because it was keeping her from recovering what she'd lost—what had fled from her.

She looked down at her lap, at the open notebook she'd brought with her. The record and notions she would never allow to be looked at by any other guild member. Not for any reason, even if it meant what knowledge and data it held would be lost forever. Officially the small tome did not exist. It was not an official log; it had no file number, nor was it assigned to a specific project. The book mattered, and only she had ever used it, reviewed it, or held it.

She turned through the pages, looking at her scribblings through the green tint of the lenses. There was nothing new that she would glean from these notes. This didn't stop her from running her fingers over the notes on elemental manifestation progression, energy containment, experiment outlines, and data collected covertly while working on other "approved" projects. All this data was in service of a goal the Guild did not know, a goal she could not let them know.

The only goal that mattered.

Chapter 21

In the middle of the night, Farris stirred with no sense of how long he'd slept. Despite falling into sleep quickly, he'd been fading in and out of slumber for what felt like hours, though it could have just as easily been a few interminable minutes. Unable to settle, he sat up, being careful not to disturb Poena. The glow of streetlamps was still coming in through the window along the top of the wall. It wasn't much, but it was enough that Farris could make out the shapes of the side tables and the shadowy outline of the lever that controlled the door. As he dropped his legs over the edge of the bed and slid onto the floor, he gripped the soft rug with his toes. He'd expected a chill once he was out of the covers, but instead, there was a soft, radiant warmth all around. The sensation was pleasant, but he frowned, nonetheless. He shuffled over to the lever and fumbled with it until the door slid open, granting him passage into the office.

Exiting the bedroom, Farris blinked his eyes adjusted to the surprisingly bright glow coming in from the windows. He moved past the desk to look out at the park and stopped in his tracks, his eyes going wide. Towering flames engulfed the park and were reaching up into the night sky. Still groggy from poor sleep, he'd thought the warmth he felt was his own fire, but he'd been feeling the heat of a raging inferno outside. For all he could tell, the entire city of Torvec might be burning.

Farris stood in silent disbelief. This wasn't real; it couldn't be. He pressed his hands over his eyes and shook his head. He knew this was a nightmare; there was no possible way it could be anything else. He smacked himself across the face and opened his eyes again. The vision of the burning city remained, no less surreally terrifying than before. He thought he could hear sounds of shouting and possibly the wail of a siren, but it was impossible to be sure because all noises seemed to be fading into the background— all except for the crackling of the flames.

The sounds of the fire and of the park being burnt away into nothing were starting to overtake every other noise that Farris should be hearing. But the sound of the flame wasn't getting any louder; rather, everything else seemed to be dropping off until the popping sounds of burning wood and the muffled roar of heat was all he could make out.

"Just wake up!" Farris shouted.

But he didn't wake; instead, his feet carried him to the window without any conscious input from him, and with similar independence, his hand reached out to touch the glass. The instant his flesh made contact, the flames turned in his direction. All the fires spread across the once lush park began leaning toward him. The tips of the flames, which had been licking at the sky, bent and pointed toward the hand at the window. Farris stood mesmerized. A tiny part of his brain told him to run, but something held him in place. Something deep inside was drawing the flames to him, and whatever that thing was, it wanted this. His breath came in short gasps as the tips of the blazing fires inched closer.

The many fiery tips at the ends of the flames began to join, forming a single spike-like point. The spike reached out and touched the glass where Farris' hand was, and in that moment, Farris himself was the fire. He could feel the full extent of the blaze. He felt the trees of the park smoldering. He felt the air being choked by smoke. He felt the snap of each ignition. It was almost serene. That was until he felt the harsh cracking of flesh caught in the fires. He felt it bubble and peel as it burned to a crisp. It was the flesh of those unable to outrun the destruction. He felt the burning choke of smoke in a hundred sets of lungs, desperate for air and finding only smoldering pain. He felt eyes well up with tears to ward off the smoke before those tears began to boil away in the heat. He felt the fire consume it all, leaving only ash in its wake.

Farris pulled his hand back from the window, panting heavily and sweating, shaking his head to rid himself of what he'd just felt. When he looked to the window once more, panic gripped him as the point of flame that had touched the other side of the glass did not retreat in kind. Instead, it started to bore through the window like a drill. He could see the glass melt and drip away as the sharp point of fire pierced its way into the room. Farris turned to the bookcase that hid the bath and began to frantically push and pull at combinations of books.

The fiery spike twisted its way through the room, moving ever close to him. He took a slow breath, forced the world to slow down, and pictured what Poena had done to open it the day before. His eyes snapped open, and he adjusted the appropriate books. The bookcase door slid to the side, and he dashed inside just before the fire touched him. He quickly pulled the lever on the inside, and the panel closed once more.

Farris backed away from the closed passage. He heard the spits and crackles of wood catching fire from the other side of the doorway. It didn't sound like it would last for very long, and he wondered what he was thinking coming in here instead of fleeing the office outright. Not knowing what else to do, he turned to the bath and saw that he was not alone. There was a woman in the bath, her back to him. Her wet hair, a bright red darkening to black at its tips, created a clean line down the center of her back before fanning out in the water.

Farris furrowed his brow and moved toward the bath. His bare feet echoed across the tiled room as though he was wearing steel boots. The woman began to turn to face him, and as she did, black blotches appeared on her shoulder blades and spread rapidly across her back and arms. By the time she was facing Farris, the blackness had engulfed her torso and formed a cloak covering all but her head and neck. The cloak seemed unaffected by the bath water. Her hair, heavy with water, began to curl and spring outward as if drying in a matter of seconds. Farris couldn't stop himself from continuing to move closer to her, even as his heart seized at the sight of her rising out of the bath and standing atop the surface of the water.

She glided to Farris, and a thin, delicate, and deathly pale hand emerged from the cloak. It reached out and touched the side of his cheek. Farris shivered at the cold touch, but his limbs didn't respond to his desperate pleas to flee. She looked directly at him, her cloudy grey eyes seeming sad, almost apologetic. Those eyes shifted to look over Farris' shoulder. He scrunched up his face in concentration until his body finally responded, and he turned around, only to freeze up again by what he saw.

The pointed spire of flame had pierced through the doorway without a sound, and its tip was only a few feet from him. This time no matter the effort and concentration, Farris couldn't force himself to move. He could only watch as the fiery spike inched closer to him. As it cut through the air, the burning red hue darkened, and the spike began to twist and contort. Soon, it took the form of a gnarled and wicked-looking horn.

Farris stood frozen on the spot, unable to even shift his eyes away from their rigid fixation on the approaching tip of the horn. With his eyes focused so intensely, he barely registered the shadowy form that took shape behind the encroaching black horn. The black mass solidified into the shape of a great horse—a fierce and powerful mare.

Farris' mind exploded with orders being sent to every part of his body: orders to scream, to run, to drop to the ground, to do literally anything but stand there rigid and unmoving. But he didn't budge even an inch as the tip of the horn pierced his chest. In that instant, he felt the fire explode inside of his chest. In that same moment, the black mane and tail of the mare were replaced by violently dancing flames. The walls of the room broke away in heavy chunks, and the flames that had been consuming the city surrounded him from all sides. His breath burned in his lungs. He felt the horn penetrate deeper into his flesh and the walls of flames fell in on him. Fire and pain consumed him, replacing any other sensations or thoughts he might have had. He was the fire, no longer a man at all. He felt his body burn away, replaced entirely by the flames. He finally screamed, but only the roar of the fire came out.

Farris awoke in a cold sweat, curled up in a tight ball on the edge of the bed. He lay still and heard nothing but the pounding of his own heart in his chest, like a war drum. He turned his head and looked up. Above him, the light coming through the windows was faint and welcoming, the first light of early morning. Craning his neck back, he saw Poena still facing away from him on the other side of the bed, her shoulders gently rising and falling as she slept. He turned back and slowed his breathing, reassuring himself that he would soon be safely on a boat heading away from this city. He tried to convince himself that the nightmares were just stress and would leave him when he was out of the reach of his pursuers. He even began to whisper, "It's ok. I'm ok." He said over and over, hoping that repeating it would make it true.

Chapter 22

Poena was still in bed when Farris decided to get up for the morning, though he wasn't certain she was actually asleep. For want of anything else to do, he went into the office where he fumbled with the books for a bit before opening the way to the bath. His sense of privacy overrode his paranoia, and he pulled the lever to close the door behind him before shuffling off his clothes. His muscles eased as he stepped into the warm water and sank in up to his neck. He relaxed and watched the strands of fire snake out from his fingers, flick about back and forth in the water, and eventually fizzle out as the added heat created a cloud of steam around him. Despite its part in his dream, he found the bath to be the most unambiguously pleasant thing he'd come across since entering the city. The bath felt private and secure, in stark contrast to the loneliness which permeated the grandiose bedroom.

When Farris reemerged into the office in a fog of steam, with his damp clothes clinging to him and a towel draped over his shoulders, he saw Poena in a chair with a book. Movement by the desk made him stop short and whip his head around. Tamaleon paid him no mind, and therefore missed Farris' frown. He still couldn't bring himself to trust this man, and it was only pure necessity keeping him from abandoning the other elemental's "help" and striking out on his own. Looking back to Poena, he noticed two plates on the table in the center of the room, one with cooked eggs, bread, and a sausage, the other picked clean. He'd spent more time in the bath than he'd intended, and now he hoped the food was still warm.

"Morning. I have your travel accommodations, and I'm happy to say you'll be departing this afternoon." As Tamaleon spoke, he went to his desk unlocked one of the larger drawers. He opened it up and removed the heavy bottle with a small pool of orange liquid at the bottom. It gave a hollow clunk as it was placed onto the table, the fluid in it barely enough to coat the bottom of the bottle.

"Thank you." Farris didn't know what else to say at this point. He had half expected Tamaleon to come back with constables to remove him for good. He couldn't help but be surprised at the man's apparent sense of honor, reluctant though it may be.

Tamaleon uncorked the bottle and waved a dismissive hand at Farris. "Don't thank me until you're well away from here." He sighed. "When you're too far for me to hear you, then you can thank me to your heart's content." He slumped into the chair behind the desk, which had his long coat draped over the back, and took a short glass out of a drawer and poured what little liquid was left in the bottle into it.

Now that Tamaleon was seated, Farris noticed he appeared far more worn down than the night before. "Long night, I take it." He felt like a burden, and part of him was trying to think of a way to repay this man, just out of common courtesy. However, another part of him knew full well the only thing this man wanted was to never see him again. And that much was mutual.

"Yours doesn't look like it was much better," Tamaleon said, motioning to the bags under Farris' eyes that betrayed his fitful night.

Farris nodded. Tamaleon traced the rim of his glass with his finger. There was a pause that hung heavily in the air before he asked a question that had been weighing on him ever since he'd entered the city and started encountering other elementals. "Do either of you ever have nightmares?"

Poena looked up from her book. She nodded solemnly but said nothing.

Tamaleon's finger stopped tracing the glass, and he looked up at the young man. "I used to. I had to pull in a few more favors than I would have liked, but I got you passage and a spare bunk on a cargo ship going north." He stopped and sipped the liquid, immediately grimacing.

"Sorry I robbed you of your bed."

"I told you," Tamaleon said with a note of irritation. "I don't sleep." With that, he downed the rest of the liquid. His face skewed in disgust for a moment before he put the glass and empty bottle back into the side drawer, pausing to remove a folded piece of paper from his pocket and drop it into the slender top drawer before locking them both. He seemed rejuvenated; there was a bit more color in his face and less of a slump in his shoulders than there'd been only moments before.

"What was that?" Poena asked, indicating the bottle as it was being put away.

"That… was very expensive." He turned to look Poena in the eye. "You never did tell me if you want to join this one on his pleasure cruise away from here."

"You're right. I didn't."

"Well," Tamaleon said, raising his eyebrows. "This is your last chance because otherwise, you're out of here on your own. What's it going to be?" Before she answered, there was a loud buzz, and the inscriptor rose from the desk. This buzz was distinctly higher pitched than the ones Farris had heard the day before. "That would be from the main gate," Tamaleon said as the inscriptor spat out a new message. He reached out and removed it from the device. His eyes skimmed over it quickly before he glanced up at the two others in his office. "It seems a member of the Science Guild just entered the city," he said as he crumpled up the paper and tossed it across the room. "At this point, I don't know which one of you is causing all the bother but let me thank you for reminding me why I don't get involved." He stood and began to pace.

"How many informants do you have?" Farris asked, sounding more impressed than he'd intended.

"Enough. What concerns me is that whoever this new person is, they probably didn't want to be noticed. If it were official business, they would have registered at the gate rather than sneak through. My contact only just noticed that the saddle on her horse had the Guild's insignia."

Farris followed the man to the other side of the long office while Poena picked up the crumpled paper and opened it up to read it.

"So, what does this mean?" asked Farris.

Tamaleon frowned. "This means that I need to find somewhere else to put the two of you. I have to assume that Garion is working with whoever just arrived. Most importantly, we just need to lay low."

There was a light thud from the other end of the office. Both the men turned their heads and saw the window open and the curtains blowing from the breeze. There was no sign of Poena. Tamaleon ran to the window with Farris close behind. Looking out the window, the pair could see her as she vanished around a corner.

"We need to get her back. If she's caught, she'll lead them all back here." He pulled the lever that opened the office door. "I just know she's going to do something stupid."

Farris followed close behind as Tamaleon ran out of the office, leaving behind the message from the inscriptor. It gave a physical description of the Science Guild member who had entered the city—female, spectacles, rust-colored coat, short dark hair, tall.

***

Garion watched the Dragon's Breath from his perch atop the Merchant Arms across the street. He saw the rag-wrapped figure drop down from the office window, his grip tensed, and his eyes narrowed. His shoulders slumped when the figure landed, and the hood fell back to reveal a young blonde woman who promptly ran off. Garion frowned and bared his teeth. Tamaleon was still the best lead he had, having seen him with Farris in the alley the day before. Even if he wasn't personally hiding the burner, he almost certainly knew how to find him. If Garion was patient, Tamaleon may well lead him to the boy.

A few moments after the woman had fled The Dragon's Breath, Tamaleon peeked his head out of the open window and almost immediately ducked back inside, not closing the window behind him. Garion scrambled down the side of the Merchant Arms. From there, he leapt into the branches of a tall ornamental tree and from there to the Dragon's Breath roof. Reaching the roof of the entertainment hall, he tucked his head and rolled as he landed. He came up out of the roll and ran to the back end of the building; once there, he paused to give his keen sense of hearing a chance to confirm the room was vacant. Hearing nothing, he scaled down the wall and swung himself into the open window of the office.

He crouched in the empty room, shaking his head as he was briefly overwhelmed by the lingering energies of multiple elementals. One was the familiar deep sinking sensation emitted by Tamaleon but mixed among that were traces or discharge which had not been there the day before. He closed his eyes and focused, blotting out the world and zeroing in on the new sensations. His face twitched as he picked up the stinging static of electricity, and just below that the faintest hint of crisp smokiness which marked elemental fire. It was barely enough to trip his senses and wouldn't make for much of a trail on its own. Garion grunted, shook his head clear once more, and began to search the room, keeping low to the ground. He scanned the room and spotted the inscriptor's message on the floor, and quickly read it. His face fell behind the scarf, and he crunched the paper in his fist.

Garion turned and hopped onto the open window's sill, but as he was preparing to drop to the ground below, his eyes caught a violet-eyed crow in a nearby tree glaring at him. Unable to break from its stare, he felt himself pulled into the bird's eyes in every possible sense except physically. A call echoed through the dark corners of his mind—the call of the Morrighan. Every wild animal mixed with the harshest wind, the most forceful waterfall, and the rumblings of the earth. The call wasn't in his ears but in his very being, pulling at something deep inside. Deeply suppressed hatred welled up inside, a hatred he fought every day to bury as deeply as he could, a hatred of everything humans had built, everything they had destroyed, and a hatred of how human he still was.

He was being called to battle.

Garion finally tore his eyes away from the crow and shook his head, trying to clear out the jumble of anger and rage he'd just been subjected to. When he looked up again, the crow was gone, but the feelings lingered. His blood boiled, and he wanted nothing more than to quiet it, to calm down, to find his center again, but he didn't have the time. Instead, he fed on it as he propelled himself out the window.

He rolled as he landed on the grass and scrambled on all fours before leaping onto the side of a nearby building. He took a series of small jumps up the vertical wall to the roof and, from there, sprinted across the rooftop and began leaping from building to building. Any pretense of stealth was gone; the battle cry that resonated within his soul had no use for subtlety. It took every bit of willpower to keep his focus on his mission and not succumb to the wild urge to destroy the monuments of human progress that surrounded him.

His only goal was to get to the main gate ahead of the elementals, but the awakened rage within him needed more than that. It wanted retribution for the incalculable sins of humanity.

It demanded vengeance.

Chapter 23

"You go directly to the main gate, to the fountain, and then left down the central artery," Tamaleon said hurriedly, pointing the direction to the fountain square. "She went a side route, I'll try to catch up to her, but if I don't, you need to be there to head her off, got it?"

Farris nodded, knowing there simply wasn't time to make a case for any other plan. The two split, Tamaleon sprinting to the maze of side streets while Farris made a direct dash to the fountain. He didn't have time to think about what attention his running might attract, opting to focus on the road ahead and nothing else. He arrived at the fountain square, barely pausing to pivot and head down the main artery that led to the main gate square. He darted around the wide main road dodging pedestrians, sidewalk stands, and the occasional small motor carriage. His legs were beginning to protest, and his lungs were starting to ache with each labored breath. But he kept his mind focused on his destination and pushed as hard as he dared.

The pedestrians thinned as he neared the main gate square. With his eyes dead set on the road, he caught the flash of a shadow, too large for any kind of bird, move diagonally across the street a bit ahead of him. He looked up just in time to see Garion's faded red cloak land on a rooftop before disappearing from sight. A flash of panic gripped his stomach, and for the next few blocks, Farris kept glancing back up at the buildings for any sign of the hunter. His mind raced; part of him was screaming to turn back, while another pushed him to keep going. He took one last frantic glance at the rooves before gritting his teeth and forcibly off his fears under "deal with this later," and tried to fuel the panic into his legs.

When he was about to enter the main gate square, Farris' eyes locked onto a long rust-colored coat, and his brain slammed the brakes. He skidded to a stop and ducked down a tight alleyway, leaning his back against the stone wall and clutching his chest as his heart felt like it was about to beat right through his ribcage. The fear of his frantic sprint building up his fire needled him from the back of his mind. Farris closed his eyes did everything he could to quiet his thoughts and regain focus. After a minute, he slowed his breathing enough that he dared to peek his head around the corner. Again, he saw the tall, bespectacled woman in that distinctive long rust-colored coat carrying a satchel: Professor Draza Raines, his mother.

She was moving from the check-in station at the main gate and marching diagonally across the square toward a side street. She moved with purpose, and Farris knew immediately that purpose was him. When the power went out at Sagaris, the lights had gone out, replaced by dim guide lights along the floor, and the door to his room in his mother's living suite, normally locked, had swung open. Farris thought back to how his mind had practically torn itself in two as his desire to leave his confinement battled with his fear of what that would do to his mother. In the end, he had to leave. He'd been confined and hidden since his first elemental manifestation, and the thought of that being his life had been enough to propel him out of the door, following the guide lights to an exit point and fleeing the university. But he'd never said goodbye, he hadn't left any kind of note, he had simply left her behind. And now she was here, looking for him.

Farris ducked back into the alley and took a deep breath while leaning his head back and looking up at the sky, hoping that some inspiration would come to him and tell him what he should do. Instead, he saw the marshal's shadow spring effortlessly across the gap of the alleyway. Farris gulped and glanced back out at the square. Not seeing any sign yet of Poena or

Tamaleon, he cautiously stepped into the open and began to work his way toward where he'd seen his mother heading. He kept to the perimeter with his back to the walls of the buildings.

Farris worked his way around the edge of the square until he came to the side street the professor had gone down. He peered around the corner and saw his mother and the marshal. She towered over him with a scowl on her face, her hand motions terse and rigid as he stood with his arms crossed. Farris couldn't make out what it was they were saying from this distance, and he couldn't see any cover that would allow him to get closer without being noticed.

He ducked his head back out of the side street and pressed himself against the building, frowning. Thinking back to how easily he got lost in the winding streets, Farris had little doubt there would be some other alley or connecting street. He glanced to his left and saw a tight gap between two buildings. He furrowed his brow in thought, fearful of getting himself lost again. He poked his head around the corner one more time to see the pair still there. He swallowed his fear, ducked back, and squeezed himself into the gap. As he worked his way down, he saw what he'd hoped for: the gap led to an alley that connected into the side street. Once in the alleyway, Farris peered out into the street again. He'd actually gone past them, and they were now between him and the main square, but the important thing was that he was close enough to be able to hear. He pulled his head back and was relieved to find he could still make out the conversation with a little straining.

"If you couldn't send me somebody with hunting experience, then you should have left it at that! *You* being here is a liability."

"I'm not a child, Garion. I refuse to sit idly in that iron tomb when he might be lost for good. I will *not* allow that to happen."

"Fine. But I can't promise that I can protect you."

"Protect me? Just get me to him, and I can bring him in myself. He won't harm me. He wouldn't dare."

Farris shuddered, knowing how right she was. He didn't think she'd try to harm him either, but if push came to shove, he knew in his heart he would be the one to fold.

"The boy is not the only thing you should be worried about. That lightning bug of yours is here. The one that exploded out of containment and shut down your university."

"I've told you already I don't care about her!"

"Maybe not, but she's here. And I think she cares about you."

A sound caught Farris' ear, a kind of dull roar, not loud but growing. He gathered his nerves and peered out into the street, looking past the pair he was eavesdropping on and out to the square. He could see people scurrying about, looking confused or panicked, and the shouting from the square was getting louder.

Poena stepped into view at the point where the street met the square. Her raggedy hood was down, and the crackling energy across her chest was plainly visible even from this distance. Poena stopped dead as she spotted the professor and the marshal. She let out a violent shriek and thrust her hand forward. A hissing bolt of lightning arced out at the two figures. Garion shoved Professor Raines down behind a set of stone stairs leading out of one of the buildings. The lightning shot through the air and connected with an abandoned wooden cart further down the road. The cart exploded on impact, showering the street with splintered wood.

Farris had ducked back into the alley when the lightning had cut through the air past him. His heart was racing as he scurried back to the gap that led to the square and squeezed his way back out until he was in the open again. By this time, the square itself was almost completely empty, with residents and visitors alike having fled Poena's rage. There was still a smattering of onlookers around the periphery, but all looked ready to run away at any moment.

Poena stood at the entrance to the side street, waiting for a clear shot at her targets. Farris moved toward her, hoping to talk her down but with no clue how to do it. Before he made it more than a few feet, he found himself pulled back roughly by a heavy hand on his shoulder.

He turned his head back to see a large muscular constable towering over him, one of three who'd just arrived on the scene, who shoved him backwards, causing the Farris to stumble a few steps up the sidewalk. "Get off the street, kid!"

Farris stood helpless as they pulled out shock rods, which arced and crackled with their paralyzing energy. Poena glared at them but held her ground.

The large constable who'd roughly handled Farris made the first move, lunging forward with the tip of his shock rod leading the way. Poena twisted around and caught hold of the end of it. Even from this distance, Farris could hear the crackling buzz of the rod as it discharged its payload up her arm. She didn't even flinch. She glowered at the constable, who stood there dumbly, unsure of what to do with his apparently useless weapon. Poena jerked her arm slightly and fed the electrical energy back into the rod.

The large man fell to the ground clutching his burned and bloody fingers, some of which had been snapped backward by the explosion. One of the other constables made his move and connected the end of his rod with Poena's spine. He must not have fully registered what happened to his fellow and was functioning off experience that told him this hit should render her unconscious almost instantly, but it didn't. Instead, the energies of the rod simply drained into her.

She glanced back for a moment and discharged a small bolt into the second constable's chest, knocking him flat on his back.

By this time, the third constable had tossed his own rod aside and, in its place, extended a metal baton. Poena saw the drawn weapon and fired a bolt of electricity at him. He dove forward under it and rolled towards her, springing up from his roll and swinging the baton viciously. She took a step back, turned her face away, and the edge of the baton grazed across her cheek. She discharged another bolt into the man's stomach, and he dropped straight to the ground, doubled over in pain.

Farris braced himself against a wall, his mind raced with ideas, but it was simultaneously paralyzed by an inability to land on the best course of action. Poena had to be stopped; not only was she a danger to those around her, but the longer she stayed in the square, the more time the constabulary had to bring its full force down upon her. Fear held him back. Fear that in her anger, she would only see him as an obstacle to be pushed aside or obliterated, fear that they would both be captured, fear that he was about to watch his own mother cut down. There was no way to know if anything he did would help or only make it worse, but he had to do something. He clenched his jaw and moved toward Poena, only to have his arm caught and yanked back.

Tamaleon glared. "Don't add your idiocy to this," he snarled, pulling Farris to the other side of the square.

In the side street, Professor Raines was still ducking down behind the stone stoop while Garion began scrambling his way up the building's wall toward the roof. Poena let loose another bolt, this one aimed at the marshal. He made a vertical leap up to the roof, leaving the bolt to burst against the wall below him and crack the brickwork. Professor Raines covered her head as stone shards rained on her head. She peered over the stoop and squinted at Poena, whose last blast was noticeably less intense than the first.

Poena gritted her teeth and looked back at the discarded shock rod on the ground some yards behind her. She reached a hand to it, and her face screwed up with concentration. The rod began to spark at the tip, and the electrical energy still contained in it shot out of the device and into Poena's hand as though yanked harshly on a fishing line. The electricity crackling across her chest and between her fingers intensified.

Farris was dumbfounded at what he'd seen Poena do, even as he continued to try and pull away from Tamaleon. Distant shouting and the hard stomping of boots caught his attention. He still wasn't sure how to deal with Poena, but a plan to keep more constables from pouring into the square formed in his head and gave him a burst of strength. He twisted his arm out of Tamaleon's grasp and dashed to where the main street fed into the square.

A fruit cart near the corner where the street met the square stood abandoned when its owner had fled the chaos. He grabbed the handles on its side and rolled it into the street before heaving it onto its side, spilling its contents of fruits and the soft straw bedding. He bent down, placed a hand to the nearest patch of dry straw, took a deep breath, and let loose a small flame. It caught fire with ease, and the flame spread quickly to the cart in a fiery barricade, higher and hotter than natural fire would have produced, blocking the end of the street. Farris gritted his teeth, and sweat dotted his brow as he clenched his wrist and forcibly stopped his elemental energy from escaping.

Turning away from the fire, Farris was face to face with Tamaleon once again. He grabbed Farris roughly by the front of his shirt and slammed him against the nearest wall. One sight of Tamaleon's two withered fingers froze Farris in place. Tamaleon's eyes smoldered as he raised a shriveled, blackened index finger to his lips and shushed Farris into obedience.

"Professor Raines!" Poena bellowed down the side street. "Come out and answer to me!"

"I never meant you harm!" she shouted back from her cover behind the stoop.

Above them, Garion made a leap from one rooftop to another, now at the edge of the square.

Poena let loose another bolt of energy that blasted the corner of the roof to pieces. "Keep your dog away from me!"

"He's not here for you. I'm letting you go."

"You should have let me go in the first place!"

"You were a promising student; *think* about what happened." Professor Raines took a breath and stood up from her hiding spot, and stepped out into the street, her hands raised. "You manifested while on campus. The guild has never been able to study an elemental's first expulsion. In my position, you would have done the exact same thing."

"It's true. I would have done precisely what you did." A tense moment of silence passed when it seemed like all the world held its breath. Poena looked down at her hands, at the electricity arcing between her fingers. She clenched them into fists and narrowed her eyes at the professor. "But that doesn't make it right!"

She fired another bolt, forcing Professor Raines to dive to the ground as it shot through the air above her head. Constables started appearing from small side streets and alleyways to circumvent Farris' fire. Soon a dozen of them were closing in on Poena from all sides, some wielding batons and others wearing gloves with studded knuckles. They'd made no attempt to arrive unheard, and Poena turned to face them.

Farris struggled against Tamaleon's grip, taking in a deep breath to call out simply to know that he'd done something and not just watched what was about to happen. Tamaleon's withered finger was touched against his temple.

Farris' head swam, his vision went cloudy, and the deep breath he'd taken in wheezed out of his lungs pitifully. Tamaleon pulled his finger away after only a second, leaving Farris badly dazed but still able to stand. He looked through glassy eyes at the scene unfolding in the square where everything seemed to be happening in slow motion. He mumbled a prayer to whatever might be listening that she would run rather than fight. His prayers went unanswered as Poena let loose a volley of small crackling balls of lightning at the constables. Several hit their marks and knocked them to the ground but, most of the constables were still closing in on her.

From the side street came a vicious cry. "Garion, end this!"

Poena turned back to the roof where she'd last seen the marshal, but he'd already descended to street level. She let loose an intensely focused bolt of blindingly white energy, but without the time to properly aim, the bolt grazed past his shoulder and exploded the corner of the building behind him.

Garion's flight continued, his scarf down, and his jagged teeth bared. Poena went down hard onto her back, where Garion held her fast by planting his feet on her chest. His teeth went to the side of her neck below her ear, and his hand was at her throat. Blood trickled down Poena's neck and pooled on the ground. Her limbs went limp and the last of her electrical energy pulsed out from her fingertips, skipping harmlessly across a few stones before dying out.

"No," Farris whispered. Tamaleon, gripping his shoulder in sullen silence, turned Farris away from the scene and led him staggering back to the Dragon's Breath.

In the square, Professor Raines emerged from the side street as Garion used Poena's loose rags to cover up the body. Blood was at the corner of his mouth as he pulled up his scarf.

The constables, who'd been frozen in place since the marshal attacked, parted as Sgt. Harmon strode through the scene. "Marshal Cole," she barked. "I would ask you to remove that immediately," pointing to the still rag-covered form on the ground, "and consider your business within this city concluded."

Garion looked to Professor Raines, who nodded. Silently, he picked up the ragged bundle, slung it over his shoulder like a sack of wheat, and headed to the main gate to dispose of it beyond the city limits.

As he passed by Professor Raines, she whispered, "Wait at the edge of Barreth, I'll send for you."

"You will accompany me to the Hall of the Arbiter at once," Sergeant Harmon stated flatly. "And I would advise you do so with as little fuss as possible."

Professor Raines set her jaw and bit her tongue. There was nothing she could say that would help the situation. A pair of burly constables flanked her on either side, leaving her no option but to do as instructed. She motioned for Sgt. Harmon to lead the way.

Chapter 24

As the sun crested over the city walls, Tamaleon and Farris were approaching the Dragon's Breath. Tamaleon kept a hand on Farris' arm while Farris moved in pointed silence with his eyes focused ahead of him. As they approached the front door, not bothering with the side entrance this time, Farris wrenched his arm out of Tamaleon's grasp. The older man shot him a look, but when Farris made no move to run, he simply opened the door. Farris stepped in first, letting his feet hit the floor as loudly as he was able to without putting in the extra effort to stomp. Tamaleon shot him a look but said nothing, and he led the way toward the other end of the hall, winding around tables and chairs. Auria swept in from the bar, where she'd been looking over inventory, and moved to intercept.

Tamaleon leaned toward Farris and whispered, "Just keep up, and don't say a word."

Farris clenched his jaw and made a fist unconsciously but remained silent. There was nothing good that could come of making a scene here.

Auria didn't try to stop them and joined on the other side of Tamaleon, easily matching his stride.

"Can this wait please, Auria?"

She shook her head, and the trio moved three abreast through the hall, prompting the small technical crew working near the stage to clear out of the way. "The staff is on edge after yesterday." She paused and glanced at Farris. "It's not going to happen again, is it?"

"Marshal Cole got what he came for and has left the city. I don't expect he'll be back anytime soon."

They approached the doorway to the maze of backstage area hallways. The passage was too narrow for them to keep walking side by side as they had been, so Tamaleon put his hand behind Farris' shoulder and set the young man back several steps so he could follow behind. Farris kept close to the pair, who weren't bothering to hush their voices in his presence.

"He seemed to know you," said Auria, shooting her employer a quick sideways look. "I've never known you to deal with the Marshal Service."

"As a rule, I don't. And while you manage most of my affairs, some things I still deal with on my own."

After several twists and turns, Farris peered around the pair and recognized the bare hall with the single door to the owner's office.

"How is the day's prep going?"

"We had to scratch the gulnan fish from the menu, and I spent the morning rewiring the lighting rig, but other than that, everything is fine."

"You know we have machinists for that." Tamaleon smirked.

She raised her eyebrows at him and shook her head. "They're not as good or as fast. In any case, I expect no issues, and with permission, I have something that I have to address offsite."

They stopped in front of the office door, and Tamaleon turned, frowning at Auria before nodding. "Do as you will."

Auria turned to leave, paused, and turned around. "I won't question what isn't my business, but please just tell me one thing." She glanced at Farris and back to Tamaleon. "Are we in trouble?"

Farris looked up at the face of the man who seemed to be controlling his fate. He couldn't read Tamaleon's expression, and the pause hung in the air like a lead fog.

Tamaleon gave the faintest of smiles as he shook his head. "No. Everything is fine."

With that, Auria nodded and left while Tamaleon began the job of opening the door. Farris watched him through narrowed eyes. Once the door swung open, Tamaleon nudged Farris roughly into the room and entered behind. Once inside, he walked to the desk, closed the door, and sat back in his chair with his feet up on his desk with infuriating casualness. "Now I just need to figure out what to do with you for the midday hours. Then you can ship off out of my life."

Farris glared. "What is wrong with you?"

Tamaleon didn't answer, and any remaining hint of civility dropped from his face as though it'd fallen through a trap door.

"You could have done something; you could have helped her," Farris said, his voice gaining strength. "You didn't even try. She didn't have to die!"

"She died because she was an idiot!" Tamaleon shouted, shooting up out of his chair. "I couldn't have saved her, and neither could you!"

"You're a coward."

"You're damn right I am! Look at me, boy. I'm losing my color." He pointed to the greying hair spreading from his temples. "Do you have any idea what the average life expectancy of an elemental is?"

Farris gritted his teeth. "No, I don't,"

"Me neither, because most are snatched up and isolated for study or torn apart by panicked mobs before they make twenty-five." Tamaleon fell back into his chair as though the outburst had drained his strength. "What's more, most of them deserve it."

"She didn't—"

"She attacked somebody in the street. She was like all the rest. Too loud and too dangerous. She may not have deserved to die, but she did deserve to be hauled off to the nearest university."

Farris advanced on the desk and slammed his hands as he leaned over it. "You don't know what happens in those places!"

Tamaleon averted his eyes, and there was a hint of apology and shame Farris wouldn't have thought the man was capable of. "What I know," Tamaleon said quietly, "is that the ones being studied aren't hurting anybody anymore. And that's enough for me."

"So why haven't you just turned me in?"

"Don't tempt me." Tamaleon stood up from his chair with a heave and paced around the desk to the bookcase that concealed the hidden bath. He activated the books that slid the panel back and revealed the tiled room. "You might want to take a minute and let some of that go," he said, nodding towards Farris' hands.

Farris lifted his hands off the desk, revealing scorch marks. He fought off the instinct to apologize and walked past him into the bath. Once there, he dropped to his knees and plunged his hands into the water. The flames poured from his hands, writhing around the water like snakes being strangled. The bath began to bubble and steam from the heat. A minute later, all the energies were expended.

Steam billowed out of the passageway as Farris exited. "If you ever need work, I think we could open up a sauna," Tamaleon said with a grin.

Farris didn't laugh; he didn't even smile. "How soon can I leave?"

"Not soon enough." Tamaleon opened the office door and walked out, pausing in the doorway. "You'll stay here, so I know where you are, and this afternoon we can finally be rid of each other. Think you can manage that?"

"To be away from you?" Farris scoffed. "Absolutely."

"That's the spirit."

The door swung closed and left Farris alone in the office that suddenly felt like a tomb. He looked down and saw the empty plate that had been the bearer of Poena's last meal. He picked up a pillow from the couch, clutched it to his chest, and sunk down into one of the chairs, weeping into the soft fabric.

Chapter 25

Sgt. Harmon escorted Professor Raines on a direct route through the city to the Hall of the Arbiter. Moving swiftly through the great domed building, they soon arrived at the double doors of the receiving hall where a mousy official went in ahead to announce them. She couldn't quite make out what was being said though voices were soon raised, and the official scurried back out. They held one of the doors open and waved the pair in frantically.

Professor Raines held her head high and strode in with the air of somebody whose presence had been graciously requested rather than demanded by armed escort. Her long legs took her quickly across the blue carpet with Sgt. Harmon following close behind. The double doors boomed shut behind them, the sound reverberating around the hall.

Arbiter Lorac drummed her fingers on the desk as the pair worked their way toward her. She leaned back in her chair and tilted her head as she was approached. She had the look of a woman who had run out of her daily allotment of patience. She didn't even wait for the professor to get halfway across the room before she started to bellow. "I would say that I've brought you here to listen to your side of what happened out there, except I don't care! I'd be more than happy to hold you personally responsible for the damage."

Professor Raines reached the end of the carpet, several feet from the desk, and stopped dead at the end of it, the tips of her boots perfectly lined up with the square edge. "I didn't cause the damage."

"You may not have fired the shots, but they were aimed at you. And you don't have any business being in my city in the first place!" She took a deep breath and leaned forward in her chair. "I allowed Garion some leeway because he had a certain amount of goodwill with me. *You,* however, have none."

"So, where does that leave us?" Professor Raines folded her arms.

"That's going to depend on your next few answers." Arbiter Lorac raised an eyebrow. "With that lightning bug eliminated, am I correct in assuming you got what you came here for?"

Professor Raines took a deep breath and paused. "No. I had no interest in her, and had I known she was here, I would not have entered your city."

"Well, then the issue is whether I should allow you and the half-breed bloodhound to continue your search for whatever you actually want." She glanced down at the papers in front of her. "So, Professor Draza Raines, you should consider these next few minutes very carefully." She flinched at hearing her full name spoken. This wasn't missed by the arbiter, who smirked confidently. "Professor of Elemental Humanism at Sagaris University. This isn't exactly a day trip for you, is it?"

Professor Raines tightened her lips and lifted her chin defiantly but said nothing.

"I have to say, I've never been the academic type; however, this is a fascinating area of study." Lorac leaned over to look around the professor at the sergeant. "Ever read up on any of this Harmon?"

"I can't say that I have, Good Lady." Sgt. Harmon shook her head.

Arbiter Lorac shrugged and looked back to Professor Raines. "My office received a telescribe that the Guild wished to be notified if you appeared in the city," she said, settling back into her chair. "As I suspect did every other Arbiter within broadcast range of Sagaris. As of yet, I haven't done that, and I'm rather interested to see if you can give me a reason not to."

"I suppose that would depend on what it is you think I can do for you," she replied as coolly as possible.

"How familiar are you with the concept of artificially redistributing the naturally occurring energies generated by a living Feyanic being?" Arbiter Lorac asked, showing off a better grasp of the technical language than she'd let on before.

"Familiar enough to be helpful, I believe."

She tapped a finger on her chin and pursed her lips for a moment before standing. "Sgt. Harmon, if you go out to the lounge, I believe you'll see my niece. Please send her in and consider yourself dismissed."

Sgt. Harmon gave a terse little bow and marched quickly back to the double doors. A heavy silence fell between the two women, the only sound being the muted echoing of the sergeant's boots on the blue carpet. Neither spoke for a moment, after which Auria entered and strode barefoot across the hall. She passed by Professor Raines and the Silent Guard as though they weren't there and joined Arbiter Lorac behind the desk. She leaned down to give her aunt a kiss on the cheek before looking over Professor Raines.

"Can she help?" Auria asked, brushing a bit of her hair out of her face.

"For her sake, I hope so." She moved from behind her desk and turned to the back of the hall, glancing over her shoulder. "Come on then."

Cautiously, Professor Raines walked around the two members of the Silent Guard, who made no move to prevent her and followed Lorac and her niece to a steel door embedded in the back wall. With the pull of a lever, Lorac opened the door, and they entered a lift. Once inside, she shifted several more levers on the wall, and the lift descended. The professor ran her fingers over the lift's frame. While not nearly as streamlined, its basic design had more than a passing resemblance to the ones used to ascend to the upper tier of Sagaris. This particular contraption was less sophisticated and quite a bit older in design and build; however, it had clearly been well maintained over the years.

The professor placed a hand on the frame, feeling it vibrate as they descended. The three stood in silence, and as it dragged on, she took careful note at the pace of the stones passing by in the dim light. At first, she'd thought they were descending slowly, but taking note of the speed, it became clear that they'd instead descended further down than she'd have thought possible: below even the undercity. Eventually, the lift ground to a halt, and the door opened to reveal a solid steel wall. Auria tended to the control levers of the lift. She aligned them in a specific pattern and rotated the handle on one of them in a complete clockwise circle. When she was done, the wall slid to the side, revealing a long metal tube of a hallway that slanted downward.

Auria exited the lift first, followed by Arbiter Lorac, who motioned for Professor Raines to follow. Eventually, the downward slant of the walkway leveled out as the corridor turned sharply to the right. Around the corner, it opened into a spacious, steel-framed glass sphere. Through the glass was an underwater view of Lake Vaettir. The glass was clear, but the murky water limited the visibility. The three women moved into the sphere toward a work bench set in front of an elongated panel. Professor Raines approached it, her eyes narrowed as they passed over the dozens of levers, knobs, dials, switches, and a printed readout coming out of a large outdated inscriptor. There was a subtle hum, though it didn't seem to be coming from the console.

Looking down at her feet, Professor Raines saw that below the grated metal floor was more glass, and just past that, she was able to make out what the monitoring station was connected to. In the dim waters, she saw a large, rounded outline. Kneeling down to look closer revealed it as a concave metallic dish, aimed at the heart of the lake itself. She placed her hand on the grate and felt the vibrations, which seemed to be in time with the low pulsing hum she'd noticed earlier. Like the lift they'd taken to get here, everything in the sphere was outdated in design and constructed with aging material but carefully maintained and preserved.

Auria motioned to the panel, giving the professor silent permission to approach and examine the instruments and readout. Looking over the readout, Professor Raines could easily see that the instruments were monitoring something, presumably whatever the dish was aimed at. The specifics of the data weren't immediately apparent, but a few minutes examining the panel brought a partial picture into focus in her mind.

The Arbiter looked to Auria and then back at the professor skeptically.

Auria cleared her throat. "Do you understand it?"

"It's not difficult to work out the basics." Professor Raines adjusted her glasses. "There was an incoming flow of energy which was being both collected and measured by the dish below, and that collected energy was being redistributed throughout the city." The professor did some quick mental math and frowned. "But not all of the influx was being used as power. A significant portion is being redirected back to the source." She looked up from the readouts and cocked her head at Auria. "Why would so much of it be sent right back where it comes from? Why would any of it, for that matter?"

"That has to do with the source." Auria directed Professor Raines' gaze to an elaborate set of binoculars mounted on a stand near the glass wall of the sphere.

She approached the binoculars, pushing her own glasses up onto her forehead, and looked through them. It took a few moments for her eyes to adjust to the various filters being employed to cut through the murk and darkness of the lake. As her eyes adjusted, she saw the sturdy scaffolding style supports, the arkensteel framework holding up the solid surface level of the dam. This was how Torvec was able to block and regulate travel without stopping the flow of water. She let her eyes drift from the feat of engineering to a small school of fish flitting about the weeds as they waved back and forth in the gentle currents. Past the fish, came a gently pulsating blue glow, like a child's nightlight in a pitch-black banquet hall. The professor adjusted a few knobs on the binoculars to sharpen the image on the glow, and the faint outline of a humanoid body began to take shape before her eyes. It was vaguely humanoid, curled into something like a fetal position. Some more adjustments to the focus, and it became clear that the limbs were too long to be human, and that's when the professor spotted two distinctly short and broad horns on the being's head. She breathed in sharply and stepped back from the binoculars, her glasses dropping back onto her nose. She looked to Auria and then to the arbiter, both of whom nodded to confirm what she'd just seen. In the center of the lake, dormant but radiating constant energy, was the infamous Vaettir water sprite.

"How?"

"Ages ago," Arbiter Lorac said, leaning against the console and looking over the equipment, "before my time and before the Guild became so zealous about scooping up every person with scientific acumen on the continent, there was a brilliant inventor trying to devise a better way to protect this city from that thing's wrath. They knew that Torvec could be so much more than a haphazard dock for merchants, but it would never grow and prosper as it should, so long as the threat of the sprite hung over it. They built this device, which I admit I barely understand—"

"Essentially," Auria cut in, "the inventor discovered that the sprite radiated a near-constant flow of energy. They calculated and broke down the exact nature and frequency of that energy, and with this knowledge, they were able to invert the signal and reflect it back at the creature. This effectively rendered the sprite unconscious, and its continued energy emissions are the source of its own dormancy."

Professor Raines was boggled. The theory of it all was simple enough, but the complexity of the calculations needed to map the exact pattern of the sprite's energy signature would have been staggering and should have been far beyond the means of a single mind. "But not all of its energy is needed to keep it in a suspended state?"

"Correct. Though that wasn't realized until sometime later."

"Auria's father was tasked with maintaining the device. The original inventor passed away without leaving a proper record of their notes or studies. We're not even sure of their name, but her father was brilliant in his own way. He was able to figure out most of it on his own. He's the one who realized that only a fraction of that thing's energy was needed to keep it sleeping, and the rest could be used to power the city."

"Which freed you from the need of the Guild's lightning cages and the hazards of the Alchemist League's combustible engines."

"Torvec has been self-sustaining ever since," Lorac concluded with a smug grin. "The Guild assuming we run on League technology, and the League assuming we run on the Guild's."

Professor Raines cocked her head and placed her hands on her hips. "Why tell me? You must know the Guild would go to great lengths for access to this technology, so why risk bringing me in?"

Lorac sighed. "Because we need your help." Professor Raines furrowed her brow and turned to Auria.

"We have my father's notes, but it's only what he could piece together. We know how the device itself works but almost nothing about the specifics of the sprite's energy output. We can't trust many people with this knowledge, and we haven't been able to reconstruct the original calculations. All we know is that the energy signature is changing."

"Changing?" Professor Raines cocked her head. "How?"

"I don't know." Auria frowned at her feet. "It may be adapting to the signal inversion and trying to break free. Or maybe the changing energy pattern is just part of the creature's lifecycle. Regardless, the nature of the signal has been changing gradually over time. Because we don't know how to recalibrate the dish to compensate, we have to devote a higher and higher percentage of the energy influx to keeping it asleep. It won't be much longer before there won't be enough left over to power the city properly."

"Auria is wonderfully gifted with mechanics and electrics, much like her father was," Arbiter Lorac said with pride. "However, the knowledge we need to keep this city running is beyond any of us."

Professor Raines straightened her posture. "You realize I could easily just tell the Guild what I've seen here."

"But you won't," retorted the arbiter.

"Why not?"

"Because you haven't gotten what you came here for yet, and I can easily see to it that you never do," Lorac said coldly. "What's more, I have a feeling that you wouldn't really want me to tell the Guild you're here. I know there was a burner at the valley outpost a few days ago. So, if the lightning bug wasn't your target, then it's not that hard to guess he's what you're after. The fact that you brought in Garion off the books means that for some reason, you couldn't go through normal channels to catch this boy." Lorac chuckled as a thought struck her. "I'd love to know what you had on Garion to get him to agree to hunt without a warrant."

"Keep wondering."

"Doesn't matter. The point I'm making is that it's clear whatever you plan to do to that boy is beyond even the Guild's questionable standards. I honestly shudder to think what will happen to him in your hands."

Professor Raines uncrossed her arms and looked down at the floor. She felt her stomach knot over the fact that it was better the arbiter think she sought Farris to hid torturous experiments than to know the truth. Knowing Farris was her son and that she sought nothing more than his safe recovery would only give Lorac more leverage.

"However, if you help us reconfigure the energy relay and get this thing running more efficiently again, I'll not only allow Garion back in the city to find the boy, but I'll put a small contingent of the constabulary at your disposal."

Professor Raines perked up at the offer. "And I assume that I won't speak of this device in exchange for you not alerting the guild of my activities here."

"Of course."

"Done." Professor Raines and Arbiter Lorac shook hands. "Garion should be at the outskirts of

Barreth soon if he isn't already. He has full knowledge of the target and can brief whatever constables you're able to spare. They need to understand the boy can be restrained as needed but is *not* to be harmed."

The arbiter nodded. "I'll leave you two to work then. I'll be checking in this afternoon." She turned to leave, and Professor Raines turned her attention back to the monitoring station as Auria joined her.

"Have you tried reversing the polarity of the neutron flow?" Professor Raines asked as she poured over some older readouts.

Auria shook her head. "The flow of neutrons is a byproduct of the inversion process; it doesn't actually affect anything."

Lorac heard their voices fading behind her as she reached the lift and fiddled with the levers until the door closed and it started back up. She hoped Harmon would still be on hand, as the sergeant could be trusted to bring Garion back into the city with minimal fuss.

Chapter 26

Garion had been given a wide berth as he'd carried the limp body down the main artery of Barreth and beyond toward the edge of the Everwood. Once there was some distance between himself and the hamlet, he veered off the road and into the long grass of the fields between the forest and the lake. He shifted the dead weight off his shoulder and down into the grass delicately, placing Poena's body face up. He rolled and cracked his shoulder, sore from carrying the weight this far. He looked around the fields before leaning down and pulling back the hood to reveal her face and the gash on her neck. "You can stop pretending."

Poena's eyes opened hesitantly. She squinted in the light and blinked several times before settling her pale eyes on him. She moved to prop herself up on her elbows, but he placed a hand onto her shoulder to keep her down.

"You're going to want to take it easier than that," Garion advised before sitting on the ground beside her.

"Why…" Poena rasped. She winced and placed a hand to the bloody cuts on her neck left by Garion's teeth. She took a stammering breath. "Why didn't you kill me?"

"I would have if you made me." Garion sliced a strip of fabric from the bottom of his traveling robes with his index finger's talon. He cut off a shorter segment and folded it over several times, then knelt over her, placing the folded cloth against the bite wound on her neck and began wrapping the strip to keep it in place, perfectly balancing the pressure needed to stop the bleeding with her need to breathe.

"That wasn't an answer," Poena murmured once her neck was bandaged. "Why give me a chance at all?"

"Because I'm not here for you. And there was no need for you to die." He looked back to the city and sighed.

Poena propped herself up on her elbows, feeling lightheaded from that movement alone, but she didn't lay back down. She frowned at him. "You made more work for yourself. Killing me would have been easier."

Garion lowered his scarf and pulled back his hood as he turned to look her in the eye. "I'm not the monster you all take me for," he said. "But it helps my work for you to think I am."

Poena met his gaze, ignoring his ashy grey complexion, jagged teeth, and the underdeveloped bridge of his nose. Instead, she locked onto his eyes and puzzled at him. "I'm not the first elemental you've let go, am I?"

"I acquire who I'm contracted for. I don't snipe those who haven't done anything."

"You're not answering me again."

"And I'm not going to." Garion broke eye contact and looked toward Torvec.

Poena glanced in the other direction and saw how close she was to the tree line of the Everwood. "Am I safe here?" she asked, squinting at the shadows moving between the trees.

"Safer than most." Garion stood. "Fey tend to ignore elementals more than humans."

Poena felt a wave of dizziness and lowered her head back onto the ground, leaving her to stare up at the sky as it clouded over. She didn't know how much blood she'd lost, but she was definitely not in peak condition. Before she could say anything else, Garion bent down and placed something beside her. She turned her head to see a small canteen and a cloth bundle. He undid the knot, revealing a bit of condensed bread.

"That, with some hours rest, should get you well enough to move on." He pulled his hood back up and adjusted his scarf back over his face. "And just so we're clear, I don't care where you go, but if you come back to the city while I'm there, I will kill you. No warning, no hesitation."

He turned and waded through the tall grass back to the main road that would return him to Barreth.

Poena took a few deep breaths and propped herself onto her elbows once more, bringing the wave of lightheadedness back in earnest. She could only see the top of his red hood as he moved away from her in the grass. She looked back toward the forest again, wondering if the shadows were really moving south like her eyes were telling her or if her muddled head was playing tricks on her. Unable to decide, she lay in the grass again and felt the tears pool in her eyes as she was left with little more than the sinking reality of what her life had become.

***

The mob of Fey at the edge of the Everwood had only grown more agitated as the morning hours passed and clouds began to blanket the sky. Yet even now, the people of Torvec were oblivious to the force amassed beyond their walls. Skittering among the treshens and pixies were cackling redcaps, kobolds that had traveled from the base of the Celeste Mountains, and a cloaked figure who kept to the shadows.

The Morrighan stood stoic and unmoving with her eyes fixed on the walled city. Though she hadn't moved since the day before, there was a new bristling intensity about her, nearly imperceptible yet distinct. Even this feared creature seemed to be on edge, as though looking over the lip of a cliff at a churning deadly sea. She looked to the city with vicious purpose—a purpose that would be lost on nearly everyone inside those walls. She reached out a hand, palm opened toward the city. A dim blue light, matching the glow of the trapped sprite, gathered between her fingers as if pulled from the air. It pulsed dimly and faded as she let her hand fall to her side once more.

Behind the Morrighan, a slender human-sized figure hidden beneath a vibrantly green hooded cloak emerged from the Everwood. The figure paused at her side, and the Morrighan gave a slow nod. The hooded figure turned and began moving the road that would take it into the city. As it broke off, there was a tense shifting in the trees as they leaned aside and cleared a path for a new approaching entity.

Massive hooves trod the ground, seeming at once to be as silent as death while rumbling like distant thunder. Had any human been unfortunate enough to bear witness, they would not have known what to make of this new arrival. Indeed, their minds would barely be able to conceive of it. It was less a thing to be described than it was a walking absence.

It seemed not to be anything solid or of any definition; instead, it lacked anything at all. It looked no more solid than a shadow yet left distinct impressions on the ground where it walked as it approached from behind the Morrighan's shoulder. Once outside the shade of the forest and in the rays of the sun, the edges of the creature seemed to blur and fade. Yet its overall shape was very clear. Or at the very least, the impression it left on the mind was solid, even if the thing itself was not. And the impression left was that of a great, powerful, terrifying horse.

Chapter 27

Farris paced Tamaleon's office, furiously arguing in his own head. He'd had more than enough of this man, and he'd have been more than happy to leave all this behind. The only thing keeping him from doing that was he didn't know the arrangements that had been made to ferry him out of the city. He doubted he'd be able to arrange for his own passage, and if he left this room now, then he'd still be stuck in the city and no better off. His angered nerves made it impossible for him to sit and wait; he couldn't just be idle, not anymore. He spun on his heels, and his eyes settled on the wooden desk at the other side of the room. He frowned and narrowed his eyes at it. He'd seen Tamaleon put something into a drawer earlier. It could just as easily be a shopping list as a clue to Farris' exit arrangements, but there would be only one way to find out.

He marched to the desk, only to find every drawer and cabinet locked. He couldn't even get any of the component parts to jiggle. Had he not seen the hall owner actually open the drawers before, he might have concluded that they were as fake as half the books on the shelves. But he *had* seen them opened, and at this point, it made little difference to him whether or not he damaged

Tamaleon's property. He looked around the office for something he might use to pry open the drawers. He scoured the shelves, pulled the books to open the bedroom and bathroom, though he had to pause and remember the combination. He considered trying to use one of the lamps but picking one up, he found it surprisingly lightweight and doubted it would hold up to the heavy wood of the desk. And he wasn't quite bitter enough to start wrecking the office for its own sake.

With a heavy sigh, Farris slumped down into the chair behind the desk and drummed his fingers on its leather arms. His thoughts drifted back to the scene in the square, but this time they didn't lock on Poena. Instead, they found their way to the thing Farris had been steadfastly trying to not think about—his mother was in the city looking for him. Part of him desperately wanted to find her, run to her, embrace her, assure her he was alright. But another part of him hastily pointed out she might not let him go, and the need for freedom had gone unsatisfied for too long. He couldn't go back to that regimented life of isolation under her eye in the heart of Sagaris University, fearing discovery of his elementalism not only for his own safety but for his mother's too. Nearly everything he'd gone through since fleeing

Sagaris when the power loss set all the residential doors to open was terrifying; at least, it was new. He'd carried the burden of isolation and protective concealment, and he didn't have it in him to do it again.

He looked at the flat middle drawer of the desk again and frowned, his tapping fingers landing with more force on the chair's leather. He glanced at his left hand, and his fingers stopped drumming. He brought them to his eyes and looked at the burnt crack in the index finger that'd been filed under "deal with this later" back at the public ward. He squinted at the crack, a small fissure of burnt skin that appeared to have started to peel back. At the center of it was the faintest hint of a flickering red and orange glow. His ears pricked up as they caught the pop and crackle of something burning. It was almost distant, as though he heard a lingering echo from the far side of a winding tunnel. Yet it was distinct and to him unmissable. He looked to the drawer again and set his jaw.

With a crack of his knuckles, Farris placed his left hand on the drawer. He didn't have much energy built up, but he could sense the tiniest hints of the familiar hot tickling, similar to the pins and needles sensation of feeling returning to a numb limb. It wasn't much, and he was so used to holding it back, he wasn't sure he could bring it forward, but he was damn well going to try. With a deep breath, he closed his eyes and focused, imagining a scene of a lit fireplace across the room. He imagined coaxing the flame from the fireplace, pulling the fire toward him as though forcing his energies down so deep that it caused its own gravity to pull in any fire around him. His mind was tranquil as he imagined the fire dancing through the air toward him. He felt a twinge of hesitation but forced a slow, steadying breath as he concentrated on how it felt to pull it in closer. A small bead of sweat descended from his temple as he imagined the fire touching his fingers. Farris frowned in concentration as he imagined forcefully expelling the fire back into the fireplace.

When he caught a sour whiff of smoke, Farris looked down at his hand. Grey smoke rose from between his fingers while the varnished wood beneath them began to blacken, crackling as the blackness spread. He scrunched up his face in concentration, trying to force the energies out. He kept his eyes locked for any signs of the wood actually catching fire. Farris began to shake from the concentration, and after a few moments, he fell back in the chair and caught his breath. His hand left behind a charred black patch, with the wood starting to split at the center of it. He grabbed the lip of the drawer with both hands where he'd singed the wood and pulled with all his might. The wood, which had been as solid as stone before, creaked, groaned, and finally snapped off so hard it nearly tumbled Farris backward out of the chair.

Farris looked down at the charred section of the drawer in his hand and couldn't help but grin at his own handiwork. He set the broken piece down on top of the desk and found the drawer now slid out easily. Inside, he found pens and a smattering of documents. Some were folded, some were loose, and there appeared to be no real rhyme or reason, as they were spread unevenly about the drawer. He pulled them out and began to sift through them quickly. Most appeared to relate to the running of the Dragon's Breath and were in a kind of business shorthand Farris had little luck deciphering.

With a deep sigh, Farris began to go through each document methodically. If speed had failed him, that only left thoroughness. He didn't think he could truly figure out what most of the abbreviated terms meant, but he scanned for anything he recognized. He found a few pieces of paper from an apothecary, one noting caution against prolonged use of "sleepless drought." He set these aside and soon had narrowed it down to three documents. Going through these carefully, he arrived at what looked like a pre-printed form with handwritten fill-ins for certain portions. The handwriting was atrocious, but it didn't take him too long to work it out: rubbish removal via Hellion, 4pm, slip 13.

A scowl crept across Farris' face as he landed on the conclusion that he was the "rubbish" in question. He couldn't even feign surprise at this point, and it only strengthened his resolve in leaving now rather than waiting for Tamaleon to come back.

"Probably will be grateful not having to babysit," Farris huffed as he pocketed the form. He pulled the lever that opened the door and left the office for the last time, not even pausing to give it one final look.

Now, he was confronted with the labyrinthine corridors of the Dragon's breath. He couldn't remember exactly the way through the winding halls, but as he moved, he kept careful track of how many times he turned to the right or left to help ensure he was steadily moving further away from where he started and didn't make any complete circles.

Just as he was starting to second guess whether or not he'd miscounted somewhere along the way, he heard echoing voices. Cautiously following the sound, he soon arrived at the end of the hall that led into the main dining area. Tamaleon and Auria stood in the middle of the otherwise empty space.

"Oh, and you'll probably be needing this," Auria said, opening a cloth sack that was slung over her shoulder and removing a heavy bottle filled to the brim with vibrant orange liquid. "I picked this up for you when I swung by the apothecary's for my adjustments."

"How did you know?" Tamaleon took the bottle and placed it into his own shoulder bag, hidden under his coat.

Auria didn't answer; instead, she slightly cocked her head and shrugged.

The two stood there for a time, just looking at each other and saying nothing. Farris felt a sick guilt in the pit of his stomach, feeling deeply that wasn't a moment to be witnessed. He'd only wanted to get out, not to spy on what was feeling like an increasingly personal moment.

Auria's gaze dropped to the floor, and she sighed. "I have to run out again. I'll be back in time to let the preppers in."

"You look like you're wearing yourself a bit thin. Sure you couldn't use a hit for yourself?" He patted the bag under his coat.

Auria shook her head, causing a curly strand of hair to come loose, which she quickly tucked behind her ear.

"That aunt of yours demands too much of your time."

"I do what I must." Auria sighed again as she moved past Tamaleon, their hands and shoulders touching as she brushed by. "As do you." She lowered her head and moved toward the exit.

Farris pressed himself against the wall of the hallway and swore under his breath, feeling a sudden certainty that Tamaleon was heading toward him. His anxiety bore a hole in his stomach. He took in a slow breath and closed his eyes, and to his immense relief, he heard the sound of footsteps growing quieter rather than louder. Tamaleon must be using another exit point from the main hall. Farris waited for the sound of echoing steps to die out completely.

He moved across the open space of the hall as quickly as he could while keeping his footfalls light, which was not nearly as quickly as he wanted to exit the building. He reached the door to the street, paused for a steadying breath, and stepped out into the city. He'd squinted in preparation for the sunlight only to be greeted by the dull grey of encroaching clouds. There were some pockets of blue sky off in the distance, but the sun was veiled. A chilled wind cut across him, and Farris instinctively thought he should go back in for a coat before remembering he didn't have one. He shook his head and scolded himself for even absent-mindedly thinking homey thoughts about the Dragon's Breath. He wrapped his arms around himself and headed down the broad boulevard to the fountain square.

As he put distance between himself and the entertainment hall, a crow perched on the top of the building followed his movements. It started taking short flights from building to building, its bright green eyes never blinking or looking away from Farris.

Entering the fountain square flooded Farris with unpleasant memories of his collapsing there just a few days before. It felt like ages ago now and yet tangibly real in his mind as he recalled the heat rising in him. He stood in front of the fountain with its high spray raining gently down into its basin and looked around at the pedestrians. He'd been in such a haze of fire and panic the last time he'd been here; he hadn't registered anything besides the fountain itself. Now, he was able to appreciate just how full it was.

Merchant carts dotted the perimeter of the square, most selling foods, but mixed among them were craft jewelers and even a merchant in a dapper hat selling "exotic liquors." For as many people as there were in the square, it still felt open and spread out, with some bustling their way hurriedly to other destinations while others lingered at the carts or on the benches spread about. Near the fountain, a fiddler played to accompany a dancer tapping their feet on the cobblestones. Two women around the age of his mother, one in a flowing eggshell dress and the other in a red waistcoat and grey slacks, held hands and smiled as they walked. Children played in the fountain under the protective eyes of their parents a few feet away. The draining grates that lined the fountain made Farris wonder if the scene in the undercity below was as lively as the one up here. A wave of shame overcame Farris as he realized if it's this crowded on a day so gloomy, it must have been full to bursting when he'd been here before. His eyes settled on a cluster of hunched-over boys only a little younger than him, rolling dice and playfully shoving each other. He couldn't stop his mind from flashing the image of this game being consumed by flames. He shook the thought out of his head as the scope of how many people might have been burned or even killed if he'd lost control crushed down on his chest. His breath came in stutters and starts at the thought of what he might have done. This was a mistake, a terrible mistake.

Part of him wondered if he should just find his mother and let her take him back. He held his hands to the side of his head and pushed the thought out. The need to leave would only rise again; he had no doubt about that. Even if this had all been a mistake, he was here now. He couldn't undo the choice; all he could do was secure his exit and get away.

He frowned as he looked at the fountain one last time, then turned west where the docks lay some distance away. He caught the very tip of the golden dome marking the Hall of the Arbiter marking the exact middle of the city but had no time to admire it. He was blasted in the face by another gust of wind coming off the water as he stepped off the cobblestone streets onto the elevated wooden walkways of Torvec's lakeside district.

In many ways, the lakeside was nothing so much as a scaled-down model of the shoreside, with all stone and metal building materials replaced with wood. The bridges were sturdy hardwood, though the shade would sometimes vary even from plank to plank. The buildings in the lakeside were never higher than two stories, but there was still the same energy as bridges connected on wide platforms that served as small squares, with small buildings on the edges and merchant carts darted amongst the congregating residents.

Farris weaved between pedestrians as he kept moving steadily due west. He quickly found while some of the streets of the shoreside would wind or tilt at odd angles, the lakeside was laid out as a grid, and he had a straight shot to the wall and the docks beyond. In less than a half-hour, he was closing in on the section of the city wall that extended out into the lake.

As Farris approached the wall, he took in the numerous gates spread across the curved structure. They were far smaller than the massive main gate on the shoreside, and people were traversing through them freely in both directions. There were constables about, but they weren't paying particularly close attention to the citizens and pedestrians around them. They appeared to be a bit laxer on the lakeside, more a presence in case of trouble than an active guard force. Farris wondered about this and suspected it meant it was the vessels docking and departing were the things being scrutinized rather than the individual people.

Farris looked at the gates, suddenly unsure about which one might take him to his destination and which might delay him enough to miss his ride. Uncertainty gripped his throat, but he swallowed it down.

"Not going to just guess," Farris told himself. "Not again."

He approached a constable leaning against a railing while she surveyed the walkways halfheartedly. "Excuse me?"

The constable glanced down at him and arched an eyebrow. "Need help?"

"I just wasn't sure the best gate to get to slip 13," said Farris sheepishly.

The constable's face softened into a kind smile, and she jerked a thumb to the appropriate gate. "North side docks, right through there."

"Thanks," said Farris before heading off.

He breezed by a pair of constables as one was telling another about a show he'd gone to the night before. He easily passed through the gate to the north side docks without incident.

Once on the other side of the wall, the diverse array of ships almost stopped Farris in his tracks. To his left, the massive dam stretched out across the length of the lake, while spread out before him were more vessels than he'd ever imagined seeing in one place. The refreshing scent of the lake was mixed with the smells of sweat and the odd puff of smoke. Heavy boots clomped across the docks as some of the more utilitarian ships were prepped and loaded. The closest ship to Farris was a sleek metal skimmer shaped like a javelin with a pot belly, highlighted with gold trim, with someone sunning themselves on the deck. Farris started to walk along the dock, taking it all in. He passed by an old-fashioned wooden paddleboat in desperate need of a fresh coat of paint. Next to it was a tarnished grey metal ship composed of sharp lines and held together with rusted rivets. Farris drew a deep breath and couldn't help but feel a thrill of excitement. Adventure stories of sailors, smugglers, and unexplored lands pop into his memory from years ago, before his elementalism manifested.

Glancing around, he couldn't spot anything denoting the slip numbers; however, every ship had its name emblazoned on its hull, even though some were harder to make out. He went systematically along the dock, looking over the names on the vessels. He kept getting his hopes up every time he approached one of the newer sleeker models, even as he remembered Tamaleon's words that it wouldn't be a pleasure cruise. After ten minutes and only a handful of ships checked, it occurred to him he was running the possibility of missing his ride altogether at this rate. He stopped and took stock of the people around him, trying to narrow down who might be able to offer him any kind of direction.

A stout bronzed figure in horn-rimmed glasses stood beside a docked ship and noting something down on a clipboard. They were dressed in the dark blue of the constabulary, but the coat design was shorter and with far fewer silver accents, giving off the impression of being some kind of official but not part of the law enforcement arm of the city.

Farris approached them with as much confidence as he could fake, which meant he barely managed to not look at his feet when he spoke. "Excuse me?"

They turned to him and looked him over from head to toe with a quick nod of the head, but they didn't say anything in response.

Farris gulped. "Sorry, I'm just not sure the best way to figure out where I'm going. I'm trying to find slip 13?"

"Oh, is that all? It's just down that way. Take a left onto the fourth dock, and you can't miss it. Oh, hang on a second…" They consulted their clipboard, and the smile broadened. "Ah, that lot. If you're new, just ask any crewman for the captain, and they'll get you sorted."

"Thanks." Farris sped off, noticing the official was shaking their head and chuckling to themself. He didn't have time to ponder why that might be the case.

He walked briskly along, his boots clomping on the wood. He spotted the ship almost immediately, and his heart sank. It was little more than a huge floating crate with a single pointed side that marked the bow. Stained wood with metal fixings along the sides, all of which were rusted and discolored. It was clearly built for cargo with little to no consideration made for whatever passengers might be on board. At the dead center of the ship, rising into the air, was a massive smokestack that belched a black ball of smog at the sky. The badly worn and barely legible plaque on the ship's side marked it as "Hellion."

Farris sighed and tried looking on the bright side. Decrepit or not, it was still enough to get him out of the city and far away from his pursuers. He was going to have to disembark the earliest chance he had. The smokestack meant it was powered on combustibles rather than lightning cages, which made his fire an even greater hazard than usual, but he'd made it this far, and he wasn't going to turn back now. There would probably be some kind of stop the next morning; he could make it the night.

He spotted a gangplank leading up to the deck of the boat. It was hardly pristine but appeared solid enough. With uneasy steps, he worked his way up it until he was on board. It took him a few moments to adjust to the new rolling sensation caused by being on the water. On the deck, crewmembers in breeches and shirts that were probably white at some point in the past moved about with purpose. Some of the burlier ones were hauling crates and barrels, others fastened lines, while others seemed to be going through some kind of checklist of departure preparations under the supervision of a towering olive-skinned man in a faded green coat with big silver buttons and a shaved head. No one stood idle; it was all movement and bustle. Perched on the green-coated man's shoulder was a wyrette, a diminutive dragon species that resembled a winged serpent. This one was faded orange in color with its tail coiled down the man's right arm and had a bit of a pot belly.

"Oy!" A middle-aged man with a skin-like leather approached Farris. "Whatcha doin' there?"

Farris sputtered for a moment before blurting out, "I think I have passage on this ship." His voice cracked, and he turned a soft shade of pink as the crewman looked him over suspiciously.

"Cap'n!" he hollered over his shoulder without taking his eyes off Farris.

The man in the green coat turned his head and approached unsettlingly fast with his long stride. The rest of the ship had gone quiet, and the man's heavy boots landed roughly with each step. He stopped a foot from Farris and glared down at him. The wyrette on his shoulder matched the man's glare with its oddly squashed face and under bite, showing off some of its lower jaw fangs.

"We takin' on pass'ngers this trip, Cap'n?"

Farris desperately wanted to melt into the deck under the scrutinizing gaze of the two men and the small dragon. He swallowed hard and tried to puff up his chest, though he wasn't sure the huge man would even notice.

"If you're who I think, I was expecting you to have an escort," the captain grumbled.

"He was… indisposed." It was a pathetic non-explanation, but it was all he could think of to say.

"Well, that explains why you're actually here on time," the captain barked with a sudden grin before throwing his head back in a throaty laugh. The crewman joined in, and the laugh reverberated through the rest of the deckhands. The captain thrust a meaty hand out at Farris and proceeded to shake Farris' hand with a bit more vigor than was strictly necessary. "You look small enough to keep out of the way. Think you can manage to not get tripped over, boy?"

"Yes, sir," Farris said with a nod. The wyrette snorted, causing a small whiff of white smoke to blow from its upturned nose and making him jolt back a step.

The captain chuckled. "Don't let Brigand scare you. She's not really mean. That's just her face."

The small dragon huffed again before unwinding from the captain's arm, sliding down to his chest, and flicking out a thick tongue that ran across Farris' chin. He couldn't help but smile as he wiped the slobber from his chin. He felt some of his excitement return to him, with such a colorful character commanding the ship. Any sense of intimidation melted away as the captain radiated a warmth that put him at ease.

"That's the spirit!" the captain bellowed as he clapped Farris on the shoulder, nearly knocking him over. "And I get to thank you for putting me square with that favor-hoarding slickster. Welcome aboard the Hellion!" He gestured proudly at the deck and the crew, who were starting to resume their duties. "This fine vessel is under the command of the one and only Captain Notram Dreyard! I see you travel light, so feel free to head on down to the bunks whenever it suits you." He waved his hand in the direction of a hatchway that led below deck.

With one more clap on the shoulder, which Farris was better prepared to absorb this time, Captain Dreyard strode off and began barking orders to ensure the boat could depart within the next hour. Brigand curled around the back of his neck and laid her head down on his left shoulder with a protracted sigh before closing her yellow eyes.

Farris was too anxious and invigorated to go below deck, so instead, he went to the port side of the ship. He kept to the edge to stay out of the way and alternated between watching the crew prepare and looking at the open expanse of the lake and the rivers beyond.

From the lookout tower of the streamlined transport ship docked next to the Hellion, the green-eyed crow watched the young man. Its piercing eyes flashed black, and it silently took to the sky in the direction of the Everwood tree line.

Chapter 28

Professor Raines stood once more before the arbiter in the receiving hall, having toiled away the mid-day hours with Auria coming and going for reasons that went unshared. The light coming in through the skylight was dull from the overcast sky, making the hall appear monochrome but for the blue rug. Though even that seemed dull and washed out. The professor glanced at the electrical lights which lined the hall, all turned off to conserve energy. She rubbed the palm of her right hand to relieve the aching. Fresh nicks and scrapes dotted her hand, mixed in with the nearly healed cuts from Poena's explosive escape. She was making a bit of a show of the wear and tear to make clear the work she had put in.

Arbiter Lorac double-checked some of the printed readouts her niece had left. "Auria was quite impressed by what you were able to accomplish in just a few hours. I have to say, I share that sentiment. I would have been happy with a slowing of the energy degradation, but there's actually been a slight increase in available power."

"It's a temporary fix. I was able to streamline things and increase the efficiency, but that will eventually be offset as the energy frequency continues to shift. I need to study the inversion further before I can devise a more permanent adjustment."

Lorac nodded. "How long would you expect that to take?"

"It's impossible to say, but with Auria's assistance and existing knowledge of the mechanics, I would think this can be resolved in relatively short order." She paused. "Your niece is quite remarkably talented. I must say I'm stunned she never received university training."

Lorac smiled and nodded on her niece's behalf. "She has a gift, but I'd be damned if I ever let the Guild get their hands on her. Her father would tear me open when I see him on the Otherside, if that ever happened. He was always protective of his son"—she shook her head— "his daughter, I mean, even if he didn't know that when he passed." Her gaze drifted upwards to the skylight. Professor Raines cleared her throat to bring the arbiter back to the present. Lorac refocused and met the professor's gaze again. "I wouldn't want you to think I haven't been doing my part. Both the main gate and the waterways are on lockdown." She interlaced her fingers on the desk. "This means that your burner could not have left the city since your arrival, assuming he was ever here to begin with."

"He's here."

"Then the issue becomes ensuring he doesn't leave. The main gate is the most easily monitored, but I doubt that's his exit point. Most who are looking to run away have their eyes on the docks and passage on a ship."

The booming sound of the receiving hall doors being thrown open echoed throughout the large open area. Garion strode in with Sgt. Harmon close behind him. He lowered his hood and scarf before Arbiter Lorac reminded him and stood to the right of Professor Raines. She peered down at him in silent acknowledgment that the hunt was still on. Arbiter Lorac leaned forward at her desk and glanced to Sgt. Harmon as she stood at Professor Raines' left. "I've issued orders that any ship docked on either side of the dam must submit to a search of its decks before a permit of passage will be stamped. Garion, I'm putting Sgt. Harmon and her squad at your disposal. This should facilitate the search of any vessel you think a likely hiding spot for your burner." Lorac raised a finger in warning. "I expect a much cleaner capture than what happened at the main gate square yesterday."

Garion nodded solemnly.

"Anything you care to add, Professor?"

She turned to Sgt. Harmon. "The capture of this subject is of the utmost importance, but he is to be delivered to me alive and healthy. I'll accept him being forcibly subdued, but I expect to receive him with nothing worse than a light bruise." She narrowed her eyes at the sergeant.

"Understood," Sgt. Harmon said through tight lips.

Arbiter Lorac nodded to Garion and waved him on his way. "Lead the hunt." He pulled his scarf and hood back up to cover his face and strode out of the hall with Sgt. Harmon close at his heels. "As for you, Professor, Auria should be by shortly to take you back to the collection disc. In the meantime, you can wait in the outer hall."

"Thank you, Good Lady," Professor Raines replied with a nod before spinning on her heels and moving to the double doors.

"There is one last thing, Professor." Professor Raines halted and faced Lorac. "I realize even as I ask that I may not wish to know the answer. However, I've never heard of an academic as…" She paused to find the right word. "Keen… on retrieving a lost specimen as you appear to be. I know the Guild values its assets, but this would seem to be beyond the norm."

Professor Raines stood rigid, neither confirming nor denying the arbiter's comment.

"For the sake of my own conscience, what fate awaits him?" After a moment of silence, she added, "I can't help but feel you either plan to do or already have done something that your superiors at Sagaris would not approve of and having a general sense of what is considered sanctioned science... well, I can only imagine the worst."

"You're right. You don't want to know." She turned her back once more, her jaw quivering once she was no longer looking the arbiter in the face, and left the hall.

Lorac sighed heavily before turning to the Silent Guard. "Want to trade jobs for a day?'"

***

The green-eyed crow soared away from the docks on the strengthening winds. The stiff breeze carried effortlessly to the edge of the Everwood. There, the great shadowy mare paced, appearing to be some wicked mockery of a natural life and movement. Since the creature had arrived, all the gathered Fey had put distance between it and themselves. Dense clusters of fluttering pixies, chattering treshen mingling with redcaps, and sapling dryads stretching across the tree line in either direction. All gave the creature a wide berth, all that is except for the Morrighan standing stoic and unmoving even as the wind whipped her wild hair around her.

As the mare paced, its heavy hooves left markings on the grass, the nature of the markings changing with every step but in no repeated pattern. Sometimes the mark would appear burnt and charred; other times, it left behind frost or even stripped away the grass completely, leaving bare stone. In its wake, some of the grass grew longer and more vibrant while some of it withered into dried husks.

As the approaching crow drew closer, the mare halted its pacing and assumed a position next to the Morrighan, its hot breath causing the air to waver and bend with each heavy exhale. The green-eyed crow began a downward dive, streaking through the air toward the Morrighan. In response, she lifted her black feathered cloak with one arm without any other inch of her body so much as quivering. The crow dove into the curtain of black feathers and vanished within the shiny darkness. The Morrighan's eyes flashed green as everything the crow had witnessed in the city and on the docks poured into her.

She turned to the mare. The beast was restless, shaking its head and pawing a hoof at the ground. The Morrighan reached out a hand to touch the side of its long semi-tangible face. Her hand seemed to fade out of existence in the hollow blackness of the creature. The tiniest glimmer of light in the very center of its impenetrably black eye twinkled for a moment before disappearing just as quickly.

Behind them, the assembled masses of Fey were more active than ever. Treshens swung from the trees and gnashed their jagged teeth. Redcaps wrung their hands and tapped their needle-like fingers together. Pixies darted back and forth in the air as brightly colored blurs. A few kobolds crouched low to the ground, gripping their hands the dirt. The dryad saplings began to shake, causing the leaves at the ends of their twig-like fingers to turn brown and drop off. All were making ready for what was to come.

The Morrighan turned to the walled city of Torvec. She opened her black feathered cloak, holding it high behind her. Her porcelain flesh glimmered in what little light was penetrating the grey clouds. The wind blew the cloak about for a few moments, then faded and was soon gone completely. The garment hung limply in the air, and the Morrighan let it drop. The instant it hit the ground, it exploded into a frenzy of bright-eyed crows, flapping and screeching. The birds scattered outward in all directions and then regrouped as they flew toward the city.

As soon as the cloak had landed, a call rang through the Everwood. It was a deep and rumbling call that shook the air—a call to battle. The Fey, which had been waiting along the tree line, launched themselves forward. The treshens dove from the trees and into the high grass of the fields between the trees and the city. They dashed forward, visible as advancing lines in the tall grass. The pixies followed behind, low to the ground as they trailed in the paths the treshens were cutting through the grass. The redcaps hopped into the air and spun around, becoming thinner and thinner until they vanished completely in small puffs of mist. The kobolds laid themselves flat on the dirt and merged with the very earth before slithering forward as shifting piles of dirt and rocks. The dryad saplings drove their wooden fingers into the ground and burrowed into the dirt, traveling as roots through the ground.

Even after the Morrighan had dropped the cloak, her arms had remained raised. Her pale skin was flawless and unblemished. There was not a scratch or a scar on her body, save for two black marks on the palms of each hand. Each was a thick black line that crossed the width of her palms. The blackness was not unlike that of the mare beside her, more of a bottomless gash than a simple discoloration. She turned to that frightful creature again, and once more, she laid a hand upon its cheek. She closed her eyes and let out a slow breath. From the center of the beast's head, a wicked twisted horn emerged, piercing the grey light with utter blackness.

The mare reared back and let out a cry, only vaguely resembling a whinny. The sound was deeper, hollow, and somehow twisted. It was as though the noise had passed through a labyrinth of echoing stone before emerging as a haunting memory of what it started out as. The mare's mane went wild, strands of hair moving like tendrils with wills all their own. At first, the hairs were as black as the rest of the mare, but soon they erupted in flame, as did its tail and the longer strands of hair that surrounded its heavy hooves.

The mare broke into a run towards Torvec. With each step, it appeared less solid and more dreamlike. Soon, the edges of the beast faded and lost definition. The pounding of its hooves continued to echo across the field even as the mare itself faded until there was nothing to see but a tiny wisp of black smoke. That, too, soon vanished.

The Morrighan stood silent, with her hands resting on her bare hips. As if responding to a silent command, the wind returned to whip her stark red and black hair once again into a wild frenzy. The sky grew darker, and a rumble of thunder cut through the sound of the rushing wind. Flashes of lightning began to play amongst the clouds on the far side of Lake Vaettir. The first drop of rain landed on her cheek and ran down her face.

The Morrighan leaned forward, almost bending her body in half. As she did, her milky skin shifted to a shiny blackness. It was not like the impenetrable black of the mare, but the slick, reflective black of obsidian. As she continued to bend forward, bringing her head to her knees, feathers emerged on her skin. They broke through the flesh bloodlessly and soon covered her entire body. Her form curled forward and contracted sharply. Her wild hair drew itself in and lay flat against her back. A wing unfurled, uncovering the head and beak of a large crow with a shock of red feathers running down the length of its spine.

The Morrighan took flight, rising high above the field that separated the forest from the city. She soared higher than the wall, higher than the buildings, and higher even than the flock of crows ahead of her. She glanced down at the encroaching Fey and at the human settlement that would soon know their wrath. Her crow body dove in a straight line toward the city's "impenetrable" wall.

Chapter 29

On the deck of the Hellion, Farris felt the first drops of rain and was comfortably sure that a full-on storm would commence soon, but he didn't want to retreat below deck just yet. It was only a few random splatters of rain so far, and he was enjoying the sights and sounds of the crew making ready. The energy, the sense of purpose, the anticipation, all did wonders for his spirits, even as the back of his mind reminded him of what he'd gone through so far. From what he could tell, the last of the cargo, most of it large wooden crates, had been stored down in the hold. They'd been lowered down a large square opening in the deck near the smokestack. He'd looked down the hole and watched the cargo get strapped in and secured.

Farris took a deep breath and looked out over the lake. His spirits had been steadily lifting since setting foot on the boat, but there was a lingering sense of unease. It didn't even feel like his own doubts or anxiety; it was something that felt strange and unfamiliar, as though he was slowly becoming aware of some dark omen. He took a moment to stand against a railing of the ship and close his eyes. He tried to filter out the clomping of heavy boots on the wooden deck, the feeling of the sporadic drops of rain on his head, and his own anxiety over how he'd been spending the last few days and his excitement at his imminent departure. He calmed his mind and let all those things drift away. Still, something remained, something ominous and heavy. It weighed him down on a level that was beyond physical or emotional, weighing on his very essence.

He concentrated, and it was as though he could feel the space around him teeming with energy, but it wasn't the general buzz of activity. It was something more basic, more primal, and perhaps more dangerous. Farris then realized when he'd felt something similar; it was when he was in the presence of another elemental expelling energy. Since he'd only recently been around others like himself, it wasn't a sensation he had immediately recognized, but even making that connection, this still felt different, more potent than anything else.

There was a low rumble, and a groaning metallic cough as black smoke billowed out the top of the massive stack, snapping Farris out of his trance. It was an unpleasant reminder of the ship's combustible fuel. Looking at the other docked ships, he couldn't help but notice how few had similar smokestacks, even the ones that looked to have seen better days. He remembered some of his old adventure books where traders were a notoriously frugal lot, and most would run a ship until it fell apart before retiring it and buying a new one. Though, until today he'd had no way of knowing if that was a fictional flourish or true to life.

Captain Dreyard appeared to fit the mold formed in Farris' head by those books almost too well, like he might be intentionally trying to live a fantasy version of his own job. Farris turned back and saw the captain standing over the shoulder of his bookkeeper as the last of the cargo was loaded. He nodded, satisfied that everything was aboard, and strode to the bow of the ship where he stomped his foot on a red panel in the floor. A high-pitched horn sounded across the deck, making Farris jump. Brigand was awakened from her slumber on the captain's shoulder, and she slithered up into a coil on top of his head as the crew began to scurry about and line up along the port side.

Farris wasn't sure what, if anything, he should do. He was nudged to one side by a broad-shouldered deckhand, only to be bounced off the hip of another, for which he offered an apologetic smile. He approached the rapidly forming line, but nobody made any room where he might squeeze in.

He wandered back and forth aimlessly for a few moments before he heard a sharp whisper from one of the more wizened-looking crewmembers with what looked like flakes of paint in his beard. "'Cher name mate?"

"Farris."

"Rov. Passengers t' the stern side," he said, nodding to the end of the line.

"Thanks," Farris muttered with a smile before dashing down to the end of the line and taking up a position. Given the rapt stance of attention everyone else in the line was standing in, it wasn't hard for him to deduce that he was the only person on board who wasn't part of the actual crew. Trying to fit in, he adopted his own attempt at the same stance, imitating a young crewman next to him.

Captain Dreyard poked at the wyrette on his head, and she moved to her previous station on his shoulder as he strutted down the line. When he reached Farris at the far end, he grinned. "Good boy," he said before turning again and taking a position at middeck. By then, even Brigand appeared to be standing at attention, pinning her wings back and puffing out her chest while her long tail coiled down the length of the captain's arm for support. "Morning, deck-scum!" the captain hollered.

"Morning, tyrant!" the crew responded in unison.

"Hope you enjoyed shore leave because we're not lingering. Goods secured?"

"Yes, sir!" said the dozen deckhands who'd been loading the hold.

"Engine primed?"

"Yes, sir!" the team of five mechanics responded.

"All persons accounted for?" There was a painfully conspicuous pause as the bookkeeper stepped out of line and skittered over to the captain, showing him a list and pointing to a name. "Where's Turrin?"

"Securing permit of passage, sir!" called out the older crewman who'd directed Farris earlier.

"That shouldn't be taking this long." As if on cue, a spindly man came clamoring up the gangplank, his shoulders heaving as he caught his breath. "Well timed!" The crewman pulled Dreyard to the side to speak to him. Farris couldn't make out what was being said, but the captain's face tensed. "What do you mean holding for inspection? We were cleared at docking!" he bellowed.

The crewman gestured and whispered more details. The captain turned sharply; his steely eyes fixed on Farris. Dreyard stormed forward with thundering steps, and Farris instinctively backed up until he bumped against the railing behind him. With nowhere to go, the captain grabbed him by the collar of his shirt and raised Farris onto his tiptoes. Any and all pleasantry was gone from Dreyard; he looked ready to bite Farris' face off at any moment. Brigand appeared to be mirroring her master's mood and let out a deep rumbling growl from her perch on his shoulder. Farris went white and gripped at the captain's wrist for support. "Are they looking for you, boy?"

"I... I don't..." The swing from hopeful optimism to being reminded of how quickly all that could be taken from him left him dazed.

"They're searching every ship that's setting out today for a fugitive, and word off the books is that it's an elemental. Now I hope that damned snake wouldn't be so brash as to stick a time bomb on my boat, but I'm going to ask again. Are they here for you?"

Farris shook his head frantically, but his eyes told a different story.

The captain could see the truth on the young man's face as plainly as if it were scrawled in ink. He lifted Farris completely up off his feet with his tree trunk-like arm. Farris kicked and squirmed, but it did nothing to loosen the man's iron grip. Brigand narrowed her eyes at the young man, and the whiff of smoke from her nostrils darkened. "I don't know if there's a reward for you, boy, but I've got half a mind to toss you in the furnace right now and be done with it!"

Farris dangled and looked around feverishly. Too much was happening too fast, and he barely had time to think, much less react or take stock. But underneath the adrenaline, panic, and fear, the heat within him rose.

Chapter 30

The Morrighan crow landed silently on the shoreside wall directly above the main gate, gripping its claws onto the metal railing along the wall's edge. Beneath her, the incoming traffic moved steadily into the city, but the flow going out was barely a drip-feed. She peered down into the crowded square where constables were stopping and inspecting all persons and vehicles attempting to exit. The bird's glinting eyes darted about, surveying the scene, but otherwise, its body took on the rigid properties of a statue or some odd bit of decoration placed up on the wall to break up the view.

The red shock of feathers on her back bristled as she peered down at the latest to pass into the city. A slender figure in a green hooded cloak moved smoothly, practically floating over the cobblestones toward the center of the square. Once there, she stopped and stood nearly as rigidly as the crow staring down at her. None of the people bustling about the square took heed as the figure glanced up at the Morrighan crow perched on the city wall. Her face was that of a young woman, practically glowing with youthful beauty, not at all dampened by her solemn expression. The two locked eyes as the sounds of hooves became just loud enough for humans outside the gate or atop the wall to hear it.

A few yards from the Morrighan crow, a watchman squinted out at the fields and forest road. The bird slowly turned her head to observe the human, who frowned as he looked for a source of the sound he was hearing. His mortal eyes saw nothing unusual, but the sound kept building. It was reverberating through him as if the hooves were thumping on his chest through layers of thick padding, and it kept getting louder. He shook his head, trying to clear the sound, and when he looked out again, he saw the lines of depressed grass in the fields. Multiple lines stretching back to the Everwood cut their way through the fields toward the city. The sound of hooves grew ever louder. The Morrighan crow seemed to smirk as it tilted its head at the watchman, taking in his anxiety giving birth to panic as just outside Barreth, there appeared the vaguest shadow of a mighty horse. The shadow would form only to fade again, but the sound of its hooves was unbroken and by now thundering.

The watchman's eyes went wide, and he turned to alert his fellows. The turn brought him face to face with the Morrighan crow, perched only a few yards from him. His breath caught in his throat as the bird tilted its head at him and stared into his eyes. There was infinite rage and infinite sadness dancing together in those eyes, and it threatened to swallow the watchman's being entirely.

The sound of hooves leaving the dirt road and clapping onto the cobblestone street before the gate snapped him back to his senses. He lunged to the railing, nearly toppling over the side, leaned down, and hollered into the square. "Close the gate!"

The crow sprang into flight with unnatural speed, spiraling straight up into the air where it began to circle the square, leaving gusts of wind in its wake.

"Clear the square!" hollered a wiry corporal. The constables clustered near the gate divided, some ushering the civilians to the perimeter of the square while two went to the control for the gate, leaving the remaining constables to take positions facing the main gate to try and spot the threat.

As two constables reached the control shed, a piercing shriek cut through the square, stopping them in their tracks. Constables and civilians alike clapped their hands to their ears, some crumpling to their knees on the cobblestone. Their faces tensed up, trying to stop the noise that seemed to be shaking their skulls from the inside.

The Morrighan crow crossed over the center of the square where the woman in the green cloak stood. People turned to look at her: the source of the debilitating screech. She lowered her, letting her golden blonde hair whip about her, and her mouth was open wider than any human could manage.

From behind the woman, a merchant lumbered unsteadily, fighting against the effects of her cry, putting a rough hand on her shoulder. Her fist whipped around and clocked the man in the head, without any other part of her body moving and with no break in her horrific cry. The punch landed with a wooden *clunk,* and the man was knocked to the ground. But his hand still gripped the cloak, and as he fell, the garment came apart as interwoven strands of grass broke apart and fluttered to the ground.

Screams erupted in the square, barely audible over the debilitating sound the uncovered huldra was making, as those standing behind her could now see that her exposed back was not flat or uniform or even flesh. Instead, it was a hollow wooden pit, like a rotted log from the deepest corners of a forest; just beneath it, a cow-like tail flicked back and forth. Even as the sound of panic built all around the square, the pounding of hooves kept drawing nearer.

Fighting desperately against the cacophony of noise that the huldra was emitting, a constable stumbled to the heavy lever that would close the main gate at the guard station, but they didn't get more than a few faltering steps before collapsing to the ground with their hands clamped over their ears. Around them, other constables had tried to draw their shock rods only to let them clatter to the cobblestones as they too tried to shield themselves from the noise.

One figure in tattered rags with platinum blonde hair did not double over; instead, they bent down to pick up a dropped rod.

The huldra arched its back, pointing its gaping maw to the sky, and grew even louder. There was a sudden crack and a flash of white as a bolt of electricity slammed into the creature's hollowed out back, silencing the shrieking. The huldra rounded on the attacker.

Poena, panting heavily through gritted teeth and with a trickle of blood running from her ears, gripped the shock rod in her right hand, drained the electricity from it, and let that energy flow through her left hand at the huldra, which dropped down onto all fours and skittered sideways into an alley. Behind her, two of the constables managed to pick themselves up and pull the gate lever, which gave way with a deep grinding of gears. The massive metal gates began to swing closed.

The Morrighan crow dove low across the square, inches above Poena, causing her to fall to the side and roll as the strength went from her legs. The sound of hooves was now drowning out everything else. Still, the constables at the lever kept pulling it into its lock position.

Just as the thick metal barrier was about to close completely, the deafening fall of hooves was shattered by a dreadful noise. It would be inadequately described as a horse's whinny only because no words existed to classify it better. It was far deeper and echoing than anything any of the humans in the square had heard. It was as though the sound had originated from the very bowels of the earth itself, echoing for countless eons before finally arriving at their ears. The gates were blasted apart and left hanging precariously on their massive hinges, and for the briefest instance, the figure of a large black mare with a single twisted horn was clearly visible as it ripped through the gate.

Once in the square, sight became incorporeal, nearly vanishing completely. Yet the impression and feel of the beast was unmistakable as its nearly invisible hooves crushed the cobblestones beneath it. As it ran across the square. Every human that it passed found their minds flooded with terrors and pain. The experience was unique to every individual present. Some saw visions of their loved ones twisted in death. Some felt the renewed burn of some long-forgotten pain. Others felt a deep sense of utter nothingness, the empty hollowness of being truly alone. The experience faded as soon as the creature had passed, leaving only a sense of some deep horror scratching at the back of their minds. The specifics of what they had experienced became less concrete, but the feeling of fear and emptiness that it left behind would not be so easily shaken.

Tears streaked down Poena's cheeks as she tried to crawl out of the square before anyone thought to detain her, but she had almost nothing left and collapsed on the cold stones. She didn't lay still long as she was picked up by a small group of rag-wrapped figures and spirited away down a side street and out of sight.

The Morrighan crow circled the square once more and let out its piercing war cry. The few people still in the square looked up along the edge of the wall that was meant to protect them. Perched along the edge of the mighty barrier was a line of treshen. The furred beasts had scaled the wall with the thorny talons on their fingers and toes to look down upon the humans they loathed so deeply. There was an unbearable moment of near silence which ended when the child-sized Fey launched themselves off the wall and attacked everything in sight.

One of the constables made a mad dash to the security booth and pulled a red lever, setting off a siren that sounded from all parts of the wall and could be heard throughout the city. The Morrighan crow ignored the sound and fury, soaring high and moving in the direction the hooves now stampeded—to the docks.

Chapter 31

Garion glowered at the ships, trying to cut through the energy in the air and zero in on Farris, but there was too much going on. Forces invisible to humans were gathering around the city, and his senses were left confused and unfocused. He snarled and turned toward Sgt. Harmon just in time to catch the tail end of what a dock official was telling her.

"Have been informed of the situation, but I think we only have an hour before captains start getting unruly."

Garion advanced on the man before Harmon had a chance to do anything. "Do they know why they're being held?"

The official looked to Sgt. Harmon nervously.

"Answer him." Harmon frowned.

"Not officially, no," the official said, directing the statement to Sgt. Harmon to avoid looking the marshal in the eye.

"What does that mean?" Garion pressed, moving a step closer.

"Well… People talk. With that business at the gates this morning, there're whispers of an elemental. That can't be helped."

Garion shot his attention to Harmon. "Then, he may already know we're searching ships! We can't let anybody disembark from any of these vessels until we've had a chance to get on board."

Sgt. Harmon leaned down and spoke in a harsh whisper. "I don't have the manpower for that. *You* need to narrow it down." Garion's eyes narrowed at her, but she didn't give him the chance to interrupt. "If you can single out half a dozen likely ships or less, I think we can manage that."

The marshal let a low growl before he turned his attention back to the docked ships. He closed his eyes and took a slow deep breath, trying again to ferret out any trace of the fiery elemental energy that Farris exuded. Through the energy of the gathering rain and the unknown forces he was trying to block out, he thought he caught a hint of what he was after. He looked in the direction his instincts were guiding him to. He shot out a pointed finger and began to direct it at a number of ships. "That one, there, there, and the one behind," he said tersely, pointing at a cluster of vessels that included two cargo ships, a ferry, and a private schooner. With his directions given, Garion sprang up onto the side of a two-story shack where officials stored their belongings and scrambled to a higher vantage point, trying to survey the decks of the ships he'd selected.

Noting each ship, Sgt. Harmon turned to issue orders to her squad when a piercing siren rang out. All of them looked about in confusion and shock, knowing what it meant but having never heard it sounded. Sgt. Harmon looked up to the walls, seeing the lights along the top flashing in sequence toward the main gate.

"The city is under siege!" she shouted, her voice bringing focus back to the confused squad. "You lot, to the main gate! Defend the people!" None of them hesitated, and the squad moved out, drawing weapons as they went.

The sergeant called up to Garion, who was holding a position on the roof of the shack. The marshal either didn't hear her or chose to ignore her. His eyes were focused on a ruckus erupting on the deck of a clumsily built cargo ship in the grouping he'd singled out. A burly man was holding a young man in the air by the scruff of his shirt. The marshal's eyes narrowed in concentration, and he dropped down the roof onto the docks.

"Stop!" Sgt. Harmon bellowed, stepping in front of Garion. For the moment, he held his ground, though his posture remained prepared to run. "We're under attack; this hunt is over!"

"Not for me!" snapped Garion. He leapt over the sergeant, already in a run toward the ships as he landed behind her.

The members of Sgt. Harmon's squad looked to her in confusion. "To the main gate, all of you! Defend the city!"

The squad of constables turned and passed through the archways into the city and made for the shoreside as quickly as they could. Sgt. Harmon didn't join them, turning back to follow Garion. She ran after the marshal directly toward a cargo ship bearing the designation of "Hellion."

***

Chaos exploded on the Hellion's deck as the sirens blared from the wall. The captain held fast onto Farris when a piercing shriek cut through from the sky. Both Dreyard and Farris shot their eyes upward, just as a crow dove directly at them. The bird shifted its body as it closed the last few feet, leading with its clawed talons. The captain didn't have enough time to react before the crow scratched at his face, tearing a gash across the right side. Captain Dreyard howled, dropping Farris onto the hard wood of the deck as he tried to swat the bird away. Brigand uncoiled her tail from the captain's arm and snapped her jaws at the crow, missing it by inches. A half dozen more crows swooped in, assaulting the captain's bald head. Brigand was able to wrap her tail around one of the bird's legs, and the two began wrestling in midair.

Farris hit the deck roughly and quickly got up into a crouched position. The captain was still trying to fend off the remaining crows, which were flapping their wings wildly and pecking at him. Even as she struggled to hold onto the leg of the one crow, Brigand snapped her crooked jaw at the others as best as she could manage. The crew didn't seem to know what to do. Some were still standing at attention while a handful of others leapt forward with no sense of organization or direction. One of the crewmen grabbed an oar from one of the lifeboats and tried to smack the crows out of the air, but the birds deftly dodged the attacks.

Farris scrambled across the deck, ducking under the arms of one crewman who made a grab for him. He tried to sharpen his madly racing mind by focusing on one thing at a time, ideally a small, immediate goal that kept his mind from flying into absolute panic. He knew getting off the Hellion was the first thing he had to do. He sidestepped another crewman who made a grab for him and dashed to the gangplank that would take him off the boat. He was nimble enough to evade several more awkward attempts to stop him from sailors who hadn't fully committed to whether they should be stopping Farris or helping their captain fend off the crows.

The black birds continued to dive and scratch not only at Captain Dreyard but any assisting him. The wily birds easily dodged the feeble attempts of the crew to smack them out of the air with whatever they had to hand. Only Brigand was having any luck deflecting the flying pests. She managed to take the crow wrapped up in her tail and whip it at another bird that was making for the captain. The crows seemed to be intent on occupying as many of the sailors as they could, but most of the actual damage they were causing was little more than superficial scratches. Farris filed the attack from the crows under "think about this later" and kept his head down as he reached the gangplank. When he looked down to the docks, he stopped dead in his tracks. Lunging toward the plank on all fours was Garion.

The marshal's eyes burned with a predator's focus as he hit the bottom of the gangplank and scrambled up. Farris tried to move in several directions at once, stumbled, tripped over his own feet, and fell onto the deck. The timing was in his favor as Garion leapt up the last stretch of the plank and ended up sailing over his head. Farris got back onto his feet just as Garion skidded to a halt and turned to face him. The young man's eyes darted about, trying to find any means of escape.

Garion held rigid in his crouch, ready to spring. He seemed to be waiting for Farris to make the first move, but even though he wasn't advancing, the hunter twitched and growled with animalistic rage. Most of the crew continued to try and fend off the crows, but the few who'd noticed Garion moved back and gave him a wide berth.

Farris took a few steps back toward the gangplank, thinking if he were lucky, he could still get off the confines of the boat and have better luck on the docks. That thought was dashed by the sound of heavy boots stomping up the plank. Farris locked eyes with Garion as the marshal reared back for a forward leap. Farris dove to the side and immediately regretted his choice of direction as he tumbled down into the opening to the cargo hold. The marshal's talons missed him by inches, but Garion rebounded almost immediately off the starboard side railing and redirected himself down into the loading hole after his prey.

Sgt. Harmon reached the top of the gangplank just as Garion shot down below deck. She turned her attention to the chaos of the crows. In one smooth motion, she unslung her bolt rifle from her shoulder and took aim. There was a flash as she discharged a bolt of electricity at the cluster of black birds. The cloud of feathers burst outward as the white-hot bolt cut through the air. The crows gained altitude and began to fly an ever-widening circle over the docks.

With the crows gone, a few crewmen saw to the captain while the rest turned their attention to Harmon. All were on edge, and the tension between the rough and tumble crew and the sergeant was palpable. When one of the crewmen tried to inch toward the cargo hold, Harmon cleared her throat loudly to get his attention. The crewman looked down the barrel of her bolt rifle and shuffled back to join the rest of the crew now crowding just behind Captain Dreyard as the burly man was picking himself up.

A few crewmen tried to help the captain to his feet, but he shook them off. Brigand fluttered down onto the deck and curled around the captain's ankle. Despite the rapidly swelling cut across his right eye, which was forcing it closed, he stood tall before Sgt. Harmon. The sergeant let the barrel of her rifle dip down to the deck, ready to be raised and fired at a moment's notice. Nobody moved as the sirens continued to wail, and lights flashed along the mighty wall.

Below deck, Farris had first landed atop stacked wooden crates. His momentum caused him to roll off the crates awkwardly, ultimately landing on the floor with a rough thud. He groaned as he picked himself up, then swiftly fell silent when he heard the muted sound of Garion landing lightly on his bare feet elsewhere in the hold. He scurried away from his initial landing spot and pressed his back hard against a wooden crate.

The sound of the crew stomping about the deck above had stopped, and all Farris was left with only the gentle creaking of the Hellion's planks as it bobbed on the water. Keeping his back pressed tightly against a crate, Farris took in his surroundings. There were no lights in the hold, or at least they weren't turned on, so he had to try and get his bearings by the faded grey light that came in through the loading hole, which did very little to illuminate the damp gloom.

Farris tried to keep his breath slow by matching the rhythm of the light splashes against the hull. As his eyes adjusted to the dim light, he was able to better make out the crates of varying dimensions stacked and strapped down to the floor in rows. They formed narrow paths running from the bow and stern. The stacked rows were not uniform in their height; some nearly reached the ceiling, while others were shorter than Farris.

Turning his head to the stern, he could make out a doorway some distance down. The actual door was ill-fitting, and through the cracks at the top and bottom, he saw orange light. Bending his ear towards the door, he could just make out the chugging sound of the boat's engine idling away, waiting to be opened to full power. The engine room, with its flammable fuel cylinders, was the one place he had planned to avoid at all costs.

Farris kept looking back and up along the top of the crates for any sign of Garion. It was taking all his focus to keep his pace both steady and quiet. The stress and panic of the last few minutes had sped up his elemental energies, and he could feel the heat tingling in his fingertips. The wooden surfaces of the crates were being singed by his fingers brushing over them, but he forced that fact out of his head. One thing at a time was more than enough right now. When he was only a few yards away from the engine room door and contemplating sprinting to close the distance, a hand clamped down onto his chest from above him. He looked at Garion, clinging to the side of a crate a foot or so above his head.

"Don't run," hissed the marshal in an icy tone.

Farris tried to pull away, but before he'd moved more than an inch, he felt cutting pain in his chest as the inwardly curving barbs on Garion's grey fingers emerged and embedded themselves through his shirt into his flesh. He howled in pain, instinctively grabbing at Garion's gripping hand, now held tight to his chest by the barbs. With his concentration diverted by pain, the heat began to flow unchecked through his hands. He gripped the hunter's wrist, and smoke wafted from between his fingers as the skin charred under his touch. The marshal's grip held fast, and Farris thrust his other hand upward over his head, where he touched the hunter's scarf.

With a flash, the scarf caught fire like it had been made of dried straw. The barbs retracted back into Garion's fingers, and his hand shot up to his face, tearing off the burning scarf and hood and throwing them aside. They landed on the floor and continued to burn a few feet in front of the door to the engine room.

Farris made a dash for the burning garments, determined to stamp them out before anything else caught fire. Garion snarled as he leapt from his perch and landed between Farris and the small fire; his jagged teeth were barred at his quarry. Just behind the wild marshal, Farris saw the fire from the scarf spread to one of the wooden crates. Desperate to prevent the flames from reaching the engine room, an image flashed across Farris' mind—the memory of Poena draining the electricity from the constables' shock rods. With barely more than a desperate hope, he thrust his hand outward, aiming his palm just above the head of the low bent hunter at the growing flames.

Time itself felt as though it was slowing to a crawl. Farris could feel the growing intensity of the fire; he could feel the wood begin to crack and burn at its touch. He watched the flame bending itself towards his palm. The tip of the flames formed a spike that shot through the air towards Farris' open hand. He went rigid with both the effort of what he was doing and outright fear. He'd seen this spike of fire before in his dreams, and it terrified him now just as it had then. But he felt himself drawn to the flame, just as it was being drawn to him. He knew he would not be able to break away. And for all his fear, there was a part of him that needed to connect with the fire.

Garion looked back to see the fiery spike piercing the air toward him. He leapt from the floor, flipping over in mid-air and clinging to the ceiling of the hold, not far from the opening they had both dropped down through. Craning his neck from his new perch, he saw the spike of flame touch the hand of the young elemental, who was now locked in place. The instant the tip of the spike touched Farris' palm, there was a roaring sound as the entirety of the growing blaze was sucked violently into his hand. It was over in one violent instant, and once the last of the flame was absorbed, Farris doubled over. He clenched his hand at the wrist with all his might. The fire was coursing through his body, demanding release, but this fire he'd absorbed was different from the fires that originated from his own energies—less primal, less intense. It was almost as though Farris could tame it, yet there was still no doubt in his mind he would not be able to hold it back for long. This was all too new for him to be able to control.

Farris' eyes shot upwards toward the cloudy sky through the hole in the ceiling. An idea came to him through the burning fog in his mind, and he shifted his gaze, catching Garion's eye. He gritted his teeth and growled. "Run."

Chapter 32

The deck of the Hellion was locked in a tense tableau, with neither the crew nor Sgt. Harmon willing to make the first move. Eventually, it was Capt. Dreyard who stepped forward, separating himself from his subordinates and raising his hands peaceably. Brigand stayed behind on the deck, letting her tail unwrap from his leg with a huff. "I'm sure we're to be detained and all that," said Dreyard casually as though this was just a minor inconvenience. "But it'd be lovely if you'd let us off the boat."

"And why would I?"

"Because of that." He pointed a finger to the cargo hold's opening.

Sgt. Harmon shot a quick look at the opening and was greeted with the sight of black smoke emerging from the cargo hold. Her eyes shot back to the captain, who shrugged at her. Harmon frowned and stepped to the side, clearing the way to the gangplank. "Everybody off this heap," she barked. "Now!"

The crew looked to their captain for guidance. "You heard it, lads," he ordered. "Abandon ship!"

The bulk of the crew dashed past the sergeant and down the gangplank, several being knocked into the water by the rush. A few of the elder members held their ground. Rov approached the captain. "What about the Hellion? We might be able to put the fire out!"

Captain Dreyard threw his hands in the air. "If you want to go down there with a wild half-breed and a walking bomb, be my guest." With that, the captain looked to his pet still on the deck. "Brigand! To me!"

The wyrette fluttered her wings frantically and took flight, landing on Captain Dreyard's arm and curling her tail loosely around his neck. He marched to the gangplank, and most of the remaining crew followed him, with only Rov and one other crewman staying behind and moving to the edge of the cargo hold opening.

Rov leaned over the edge of the opening, trying to get a better sense of the fire and whether it could be contained. He was knocked to the deck almost immediately as Garion came scrambling up out of the hold and shoved him aside. The marshal was off the boat and onto the docks in two quick bounds. The standing crewman looked to Rov weakly and fled the ship.

While Rov was picking himself up from the deck, a column of fire erupted from the cargo hold. The shaft of flame rocketed into the sky, forming a fiery pillar that cut a neat hole in the grey clouds. As it rose, it also widened, weakening and dispersing into the air as it climbed higher into the sky. The murder of crows, which had been circling the city for the past few minutes, pulled into a tighter formation around the column of fire.

The shock and force of the flaming spire jolted Rov, causing him to lose his footing and tumble down into the cargo hold. He landed roughly on his back, and it took him a moment before he could pick himself up with a pained groan. He looked over one of the shorter stacks of crates to see the source of the fire. Through the heat haze, he was able to make out a single point from which the column of flame was erupting—from the palm of Farris, whose legs were locked in place, sweating, and gritting his teeth. What he saw was Farris with his left hand pointed at the sky and the column of flame spewing from his palm.

Farris' arm shook from the force of the energies he was unleashing. The fire he'd absorbed, as well his own elemental flame, was all being shot upward. He stood rooted to the spot as much from astonishment as the effort of what he was doing. It was exhilarating, empowering, and terrifying. He wanted this to not be happening yet didn't want it to stop.

Out of the corner of his eye, Farris spotted Rov. The young man gritted his teeth, and the fire spewing from his hand tapered off. There was still some of his own energy left stirring inside of him, and it did not want to be held back. But right now, escape was more important. Farris started to crawl on top of some crates to reach the opening to the deck.

Rov clamored over the crate in his way and lunged at Farris, grabbing him by the leg and yanking him back down. He crashed face down onto the hard floor, the impact knocking the wind out of him. Unable to breathe or even think clearly, Farris lost control of the small amount of fiery energy still in his body. As soon as he hit the floor, the last of his elemental energies radiated out in a wave from his hand toward the engine room. Farris clutched his stomach and gasped for air, forced to watch helplessly as the coursing flames blasted apart the doorframe and entered the room filled with explosive mixtures.

"No!" bellowed Rov, making a desperate dash to the engine room.

Time once again slowed to crawl, and Farris could hear the distinct crack of a fuel capsule as the heat broke it open. He covered his head and curled up into a ball as a thundering explosion shuddered through the vessel. Rov was hurled through the air over Farris' head and slammed into a stack of crates before crumbling to the floor in a limp heap. Farris clenched his eyes tightly as he heard the hull of the Hellion crack and the water rush in.

An eruption of flame and burning fuel burst from the ship's massive smokestack. The initial shock of the explosion funneled upward through the massive metal funnel before blowing it to pieces and showered the surrounding area with red hot shards of metal. Those on the dock, including the disembarked crew of the Hellion, dove for cover as burning shrapnel rained down around them. Only Captain Dreyard stood and watched. Brigand looked from the fiery destruction of the ship back to him and slathered his cheek with her broad tongue.

Once the smokestack blew, the explosion reverberated through the hull and split the ship into two halves, the bow where Farris was still huddled on the floor, and the stern. Water flooded in around him as the floor broke apart. Uncurling his body and finally opening his eyes, Farris saw Rov's still body on the floor. He waded through the rising water to the fallen crewman before he could second guess the wisdom of what he was doing. With considerable effort, Farris heaved Rov clumsily onto a crate that had broken from its straps and was positioned under the opening in the ceiling. Farris couldn't climb the crate without it tipping Rov off into the water again, so he steadied it as best he could while the rising water carried the crate, Rov, and himself through the opening.

As the ship broke apart, its heavier components and metal fittings sank into the lake while the splintered wooden debris floated on the surface. Doubting he could do anything to better secure Rov, Farris paddled a few feet and flung his arms onto one of the larger sections of the destroyed deck. He strained to pull himself up, but he had nothing left and resigned himself to simply clinging to a hunk of wood. Around him, some of the wreckage was smoldering, but any fires were being dowsed by the rain.

Farris rested his head on a bit of deck when there was a thud, and it rocked underneath him. Glancing up, he found himself face to face with Garion, who'd just leapt from the docks. The marshal crouched down until his snarling flat face was level with that of his prey. Farris could only look back at him; he had no more fire and no more strength. Hope drained from him as the water lapped at his neck.

Garion grinned in triumph and reached out to Farris, the thorny talons emerging from the tips of his fingers. Then, the descending hand froze, inches from making contact, and the hand began to quake. Farris looked up at Garion's face, but the vicious hunter wasn't looking at him anymore; instead, his eyes were fixed on something behind Farris, out in the water. Garion's look of triumph dissolved into a deeply rooted sadness that bordered on fear, making the marshal appear almost childlike.

Farris twisted around to look across the water behind him. The lake was blanketed in a veil of smoke and steam from the burning pieces of the Hellion still smoldering on the water's surface. Through the haze, Farris was able to make out the figure of a woman. Though the details of her body remained blurred, her skin was radiantly pale, and a wild tangle of red hair crowned her head. She appeared to be walking across the surface of the water. The crows that had been circling above began to swoop down out of the, diving down at the woman. As each bird reached her, it lost its form, and black feathers began to drape the woman's body. By the time Farris was able to bring her into full focus, the Morrighan was adorned in a long cloak of black feathers.

Farris' breath caught in his throat. He snapped his head to Garion. The marshal erected himself to a standing position as the Morrighan approached. Part of Garion demanded that he flee, run as far and as fast as he could without ever looking back, but another part of him needed to stay. More than that, this side of Garion needed to devote itself to the frightful goddess striding across the strangely still surface of Lake Vaettir.

The rain was falling silently, and the air went still. Even the sirens at the wall had stopped blaring, but there was a sound still to be heard, a faint rumbling that soon coalesced into the rhythmic beat of hooves on the ground. The noise snapped Garion out of his trance, and his eyes narrowed. He lunged for Farris. The Morrighan's cloak exploded in a flurry of beating wings, sharp beaks, and clawing talons. A cloud of crows swarmed Garion, raking and pecking at him. He cried out and tried to leap away, but the crows kept on him. The mass of raging birds held him in the air as their claws tore at his robes and their beaks cut at his skin. Drops of blood fell from the cloud of black feathers.

Then as suddenly as they'd attacked, the crows flew out in all different directions leaving Garion's battered body to fall through air and *thud* onto a floating piece of the destroyed Hellion. Farris was breathing in short, shallow bursts, looking at the fallen form of the man who'd hunted him, now barely moving among the debris. Farris turned back to the Morrighan as the crows reassembled into her cloak. She was inches from him now, and the thundering of the hooves was louder than ever, but Farris couldn't bring himself to turn and see the source. He was terrified; he already knew what it was.

The Morrighan knelt on the water's surface and placed a hand upon his cheek. The hand was cool and gentle, like the feel of damp moss or morning dew. There was something calming about her touch even in all the chaos, destruction, and terror. She looked into his eyes with a sense of sadness about her, as though she was trying to apologize. The young man lost all sense of time looking into her eyes, and it took him a minute to realize that the sound of the hooves had stopped. In its place now came the heavy, labored breathing of a great animal from directly behind his head.

The Morrighan glanced up at the creature behind Farris. His eyes welled up as he twisted his body back around and found himself confronted with a massive black mare. The creature was standing on the floating piece of the deck, even though it should not have been able to support the weight of something so large. It was completely and hollowly black, appearing more as a horse-shaped hole in the world than a living thing in its own right.

Farris felt dread return to him in force as the creature lowered its head. It huffed its hot breath, causing the air to waver and bend as it touched the tip of its single twisted horn to Farris' chest. "Please," Farris begged. "Don't."

The mare's mane burst into fire as the beast drove its horn forward into his chest. Farris felt pain unlike anything he had ever experienced before, but it wasn't the pain of the horn piercing his flesh; it was the pain of his own fire. It exploded through every cell of his body. He felt as though his very soul was burning.

He let go of the floating debris and curled into a tight ball, trying to fight the surging flames, hoping against hope that submerging himself might quell them, but it was more powerful and more ferocious than he had ever felt before, more than he could ever hope to control, or even direct. His curled-up body sank beneath the surface of the water down until he could no longer contain the fire the mare had ignited inside of him.

Farris stopped fighting, and his entire body went stiff. His arms and legs spread wide as fire spewed forth from his fingers, his toes, his mouth, his eyes, and even the hole in his chest left by the beast's horn. The fire shot outward into the dark waters of the lake but did not writhe and die out as his flames always had before when submerged. Instead, the tendrils of fire swam through the water with purpose and headed downwards toward the very center of the lake.

It was over a minute before all the energy had drained itself from Farris and his body went limp in the water. He started to sink deeper, and all sensation faded. Above him, a hand plunged into the lake, grabbed him by the collar of his shirt, and pulled him roughly out of the water.

Chapter 33

Far below the surface of the lake, oblivious to the turmoil that was engulfing the city above them, Auria and Professor Raines continued their work on the reflector. Auria poked at a cluster of wiring with a prong, but the professor had drifted from the work. She sat before the thick glass, looking out into the murky lake, glancing between the leather-bound notebook she'd pulled from her pocket and the stillness of the water. She looked over her notes and observations on her son from his first manifestation and frowned. She snapped the book shut, loud enough to startle Auria and cause her to knock over a tool kit.

The sound of the tools clattering was lost on Professor Raines as she gazed out into the lake as if she were willing time to pass more quickly. Auria picked up the wrench and watched the other woman for a few minutes before she tossed it at the professor's feet. The wrench clanged on impact and bounced off Professor Raines' shin. This finally got her attention. She glanced down at the tool and then back at the woman who'd tossed it.

"Pick it up."

"I beg your pardon?"

"If you get your hands dirty, it'll take your mind off… whatever it is that's weighing you down."

She tucked the book away into her coat pocket and picked up the wrench, and walked back to the heart of the device, taking a moment to once more appreciate the craft which had gone into it.

"It really is amazing, isn't it?" Auria asked as she swapped out the prong for a clamp.

"I still have a hard time believing this machine is so old." Her voice gave away her sense of awe.

"For me, it might as well be ancient. It's like it's always been here. First, my father tinkered with it, now I do, and I'm sure that…" She paused and frowned for a split second. "That somebody will be messing with it after me."

Professor Raines moved in closer.

"Whoever it is, it'll be your legacy to pass onto them."

Auria smiled weakly. "And, what's your legacy?"

"I…," Professor Raines paused and blinked, nearly mentioning Farris but thinking better of it. "I expect it'll be my work with elementals."

Auria furrowed her brow. "Do you mind if I ask you something about that?"

"On the understanding that I might not answer."

"Does the Guild ever try to cure them?"

"No."

"Why not?"

The professor opened her mouth and closed it again, her eyes fixed on the machinery in front of her as she drew a slow breath. "The Guild believes there is much it can learn from observation and experimentation. Curing them removes their value as specimens."

They lapsed into a fresh silence that hung heavy in the room for several minutes, neither woman knowing what to say. The silence was broken by a sudden pop and a flash from the monitoring station. Paper spooled out from the readout. The professor and Auria looked at each other quizzically. Auria moved over to the station and where a small waft of smoke was rising from a spot where an indicator light had burst.

"What's that mean?"

Auria glanced at her with concern. "I don't know. That light's never lit up before. That's why it blew; the bulb degraded." She grabbed the readout and scanned the data.

Professor Raines was about to join her when something out in the gloom of the lake caught her eye. Some distance away, an orange glow up near the surface was moving deeper into the lake.

"You should look at–" started Auria, still holding the new readouts, but she stopped short when she looked up and saw the glow in the water.

The professor swiveled the mounted binoculars toward the glow and peered through them. The filters cut through the murk and gloom to zero in on the spiked tendril of fire surging through the water.

"What is it?"

"I don't know." Professor Raines tracked along the length of fire with the binoculars to find the source. "It looks like—" She shot up from the binoculars and ran out of the capsule to the tunnel that led to the lift.

Auria rushed to the binoculars and set them back to their original position just as the tip of the flames touch the coiled creature that had been powering Torvec for years. The sprite began to, a warm yellow light pulsing around it. A limb twitched, and the curled-up form began to unfurl itself slowly. Auria abandoned the binoculars and hurried back to the readout. Glancing at the data once more, the picture of what was happening became terrifyingly clear in her mind. She fled after the professor.

Professor Raines slammed against the wall next to the lift and tried to pull it open, only to realize Auria had the key. She pounded the palm of her hand against the wall in anger and turned back to see Auria running full tilt up the corridor, fumbling the keys out of a pouch on her belt as her bare feet slapped on the metal floor.

"We need to go now!" Auria shouted. She opened the lift, and both women rushed in, with the professor closing the lift gate behind them. Auria adjusted the levers, and the lift started to move at the pace of molasses. From down the corridor came the echoing sound of cracking glass and then the rushing of water. The lift shuddered to a halt, and water began to pour in from the gaps in the floor grate. Auria flipped several levers, but the lift didn't budge. The light above them began to flicker as power started to drain.

Professor Raines turned to her. "Give me your shock rod."

"What—"

"The one your aunt gave you to subdue me, give it to me now!"

Auria fumbled under her long skirt as the water inched past her ankles. She unstrapped a short shock rod from the holster on her thigh and handed it to the professor.

Professor Raines twisted the rod and sparks began flying between the two forked prongs. "Restart the sequence as soon as I jolt the system."

Auria nodded and reset the levers to their starting positions. By now, the water was up to their knees and still rising. The professor opened a panel in the wall, took a quick survey of the circuitry, and jammed the rod onto a contact point. The light above them lit up brightly once more, and Auria hurriedly flipped the levers in the appropriate sequence. The lift began to rise again, the water draining out of the bottom.

"It's the sprite!" Auria panted as the lift carried them to safety. "The fire touched it. It's like opposing energies jolted it awake and stalled the entire system."

If Professor Raines was listening, there were no indicators. Her eyes were locked on the lift door, and as soon as they reached the ground floor, she yanked it open and dashed out with Auria close behind. The two women exited the lift into the receiving hall, and their hurried steps echoing solemnly. The artificial lights along the outer perimeter of the room were dimming and stuttering, soon dying out completely and leaving them with the grey illumination coming in from the skylight.

Auria looked around the hall for any sign of the arbiter or her staff, but Professor Raines went straight for the double doors. She stopped in her tracks as a high-pitched screech echoed across the hall. Both women stopped women looked up to the source of the sound. Atop the skylight were a half dozen treshen, their thorny talons scraping across the glass. The creatures weren't lingering on the skylight, instead scrambling across it and leaping off in other directions. Auria's hand shot up to her mouth as one of the Fey glanced down at the pair of them. It bared its jagged teeth and started to rake its claw at the glass, leaving white streaking scratches on its once pristine surface.

Professor Raines set her jaw and resumed her dash for the door with Auria close behind. She burst through the heavy wooden doors out into the hallway and nearly collided with a man in a grey suit who'd been coming from the other way.

His face twisted, and he grabbed the professor by the collar of her jacket before slamming her against the nearest wall. "Always wondered what it'd feel like to get one of you lot alone," he growled between labored breaths.

"Tamaleon, no!" Auria shouted as she ran to him, grabbing his forearm, forcing his attention away from the professor and onto her. "I don't know what's going on, but *this* is not important right now."

Tamaleon frowned and released Professor Raines. She moved toward the main entrance of the building, but Tamaleon caught her arm. "Much as it would amuse me, you really don't want to go that way." He let go of the professor's arm and clutched Auria's hand, leading her down a narrower side passage.

Professor Raines took one more glance down the main hallway. From the far end came the sounds of bolt rifles firing, shouting, and chaos. She turned to follow the others down the side hallway, which twisted around in a lazy fashion as it went, nearly barreling into Auria and Tamaleon, who had stopped short.

A red cap perched atop the slumped-over body of a Silent Guard. The upper half of its bald head had a distinctive blood-red hue from which the devious Fey got its name. There were several shards of metal from a destroyed bolt rifle dancing in the air around, and its pointed ears twitched and when it saw the trio. It let out a high-pitched cackle, and one of the shards shot at them, carving a gash in Tamaleon's cheek, causing him to duck his head down into his hand. The creature laughed its screeching stutter of a laugh, but it stopped when Tamaleon took his bloodied hand away from his injured cheek and zeroed in on the creature. Suddenly, the chaotic joy drained from its sharply angled face, and the metal slivers dropped to the ground with small, impotent clangs. The redcap leapt backward and faded away into the marble wall.

Tamaleon led the way down the corridor once more. After several junctions, he shoved open a door that exited into an alleyway. One end of the alley was blocked by a cart, so the trio made for the other end, which deposited them into the small square in front of the Hall of the Arbiter.

As they reached the square, the full scale of the chaos became clear. Pixies zipped about in the air, exploding balls of searing light as they went. Treshen were perched on nearly every building, constantly in motion; some leapt from structure to structure while others descended to ground level and mauled whoever was within their clawed grasp. One was clawing at the back of a man who was bent forward to shield a small child when it was suddenly jolted by a constable with a shock rod. The creature screeched and leapt away while the constable helped the man up and led both him and the child to a hastily built barricade across the square. Boxes, barrels, and a pair of merchant carts turned on their sides served as a barrier between constables firing their bolt rifles and the rampant Fey tearing through the city.

It took Professor Raines a moment to get her bearings before setting off to the docks and finding herself in tailing behind Auria and Tamaleon yet again. As they reached the edge of the square, the cobblestones behind them erupted upward and tore the wooden carts that formed the barricade to splinters. The constables who'd been resting their rifles on the carts were thrown onto their backs, and a pair of kobolds, two feet tall and lanky, stood where the carts had been. They chuckled with a sound like rocks being split with a pickaxe as the cobblestones began to rain back down to earth. As they fell, the stones gathered around one of the kobolds and formed stone armor. The other dropped to its belly and merged with the exposed dirt. One of the constables got up quickly and fired at the remaining kobold, only for the bolt to ricochet off the makeshift armor.

Tamaleon cut across a slight mound of grass, maintained for aesthetic purposes, with Auria at his side and Professor Raines close behind. As he reached the peak of the bump in the earth, a twisted root shot up from the ground and wrapped itself around Auria's ankle. She fell to the ground while the professor stumbled to a halt as a sapling birch dryad, the owner of the gnarled root, sprang forth from the ground between the two women.

It took Tamaleon several steps to stop his momentum and turn back. The creature raised a thick branch-like arm above its head, prepared to bring it down onto Auria. In one smooth motion, Tamaleon removed the glove from his right hand, uncovering the withered fingers, and thrust the hand toward the dryad. A whip of festering black shot from the index and middle fingers, wrapping itself around the dryad's raised arm.

The creature let out a hollow echoing bellow as its white, bark-like skin turned sickly grey and fell away, leaving a pulsating green inner core exposed. The dryad uncoiled its root from Auria's leg, and Tamaleon retracted the vicious black whip into his fingers as the creature dove into the dirt and vanished.

Professor Raines lost herself in the moment of what she was seeing. Tamaleon gripped his wrist and rushed to Auria, who was still on the ground with her eyes locked on him. Tamaleon shoved his right hand into his trouser pocket and offered his left to help her up, but Auria scooted backward on the ground away from him and got to her feet as quickly as she could.

"Please," muttered Tamaleon, barely able to speak.

Auria shook her head, turned back toward the heart of the city, and fled. Tamaleon fell to his knees and slumped forward. Whatever had been driving him before had simply left him.

Professor Raines snapped herself out of the moment as the skies above them opened, and the rain began to pour down in earnest. She ran past Tamaleon and made for the first bridge that would lead her toward the docks. She pushed and elbowed her way past panicked civilians who couldn't seem to decide if they were safer on the water or heading for the shoreside. She ducked as a pixie shot toward her head and knocked a constable over the railing of a bridge with a burst of green light in his face. She did not slow, and her rust-colored coat billowed behind her as she broke through a cluster of huddled dock workers.

The crowds on the wooden walkways of the lakeside thinned, and Professor Raines barely registered that the pixies around her had started to all fly toward the walls and out of the city. Treshens were climbing the walls' inner edge, and all signs of the Fey were evacuating the city. Still, she pushed onward; this was not the time to wonder. In the back of her mind, the analytic part of her realized the retreat was too sudden and coordinated to have been the invaders being beaten back. The Fey were leaving because they chose to.

A deep rumble emanated from the lake, and the water across the entire surface of the lake began to churn and bubble. Waves splashed onto the bridges and lapped at the professor's feet as she ran. The rumble built in strength, the surface of the water vibrated until a shockwave radiated out from the center of the lake with a *boom* that shuddered the lake and everything on it. Professor Raines was knocked off her feet, within sight of the archway to the docks. A deep resounding *crack* could be heard across the entire length of the dam as a vicious fissure tore through it, wrenching apart stone. A figure shot out of the lake in a flash of blue and white light, trailing a stream of water behind it. It stopped dead in the air, high enough to be seen over the walls of the city.

A tower of water held like a waterfall with no point of origin, and at the top of it hovered the Vaettir sprite. Its skin was a pale, sea green, and its limbs were unnaturally long and slender. Its hair was a slow-moving descending wave of water cascading down its back and forming the pillar of water underneath it. Protruding from its upper forehead emerging through the waterfall hair were the two distinctively short broad horns that marked all subspecies of sprite. Though little more than tipped mounds on its head, the horns white pulsed with energy.

Professor Raines scrambled to her feet and sprinted towards the docks. The sprite looked out over the docks, the dam, and the lakeside of the city and slowly, delicately, raised a thin hand. Columns of water thrust themselves skyward. The sprite swung its spindly arm down sharply, and the columns swung in turn, crashing with devastating force onto the southern docks. The professor gritted her teeth as she was nearly knocked off her feet by the shuttering walkways under her, but she pushed onward toward the archway that would bring her to the northern docks.

Chapter 34

When Farris had been pulled from the water, he'd barely even registered his body being heaved up onto the wooden docks. When the world began to fade back into focus, he felt himself being renewed and rejuvenated. He opened his eyes and saw Matron Branford kneeling over him. She held her hands inches above his chest as a yellow and white light passed from her into his body. Warmth radiated into him, gentle and comforting. He was tempted to linger in the feeling and stay there, but the Matron's face was one of borderline panic—a panic shared by the few still remaining on the docks, who were rapidly fleeing in a disorganized stampede.

"Can you move?"

"If I have to," groaned Farris.

"You definitely have to." She helped him to his feet.

The sprite towered above the lake, and the murder of crows were circling again, this time in tight formation over the freed sprite, swirling the clouds into a vortex over it as thunder cracked. The columns of water were brought crashing down onto the southern docks, making the wood beneath Farris' feet shutter and groan. There was a rumbling from out on the water as part of the dam broke off and slid into the lake.

Matron Branford grabbed Farris by the hand and pulled him after her, guiding him away from the archways to the city proper and along the outer curve of the great wall. They passed an abandoned guard station set before a narrow stretch of walkway, only wide enough for two or three people to walk abreast. The walkway stretched around the outside of the wall all the way to the shoreline.

As they fled for their lives, the sprite began its assault on the walled city itself. The hovering Fey glowed and clapped its delicate hands together. The sound was thunderous, and a visible wave of force rushed forward from the sprite's clasped hands. The ripple of energy slammed into the walls of the city, which stood strong against it, but on the other side of those walls, the waters under the feet of the lakeside residents churned violently. Waves climbed up from the surface of the lake, crashing into the bridges and walkways. As the waves intensified, supports and structures began to snap and shatter, the sounds of wood breaking and metal splashing became lost in the rush of wind and water.

On the other side of the wall, Farris ran with all his might, with the matron only a few steps behind him. The planks under their feet strained and groaned as they began to snap as the assault of the waves grew ever fiercer. Above the lake, the wrathful sprite unclasped its hands, and the circling crows rocketed outward in all directions. One final blast of energy flew out in the wake of the crows, sweeping across the lake, undeterred by the impotent structure that had kept the city safe for so long. The whole of the lakeside crumbled under the force, leaving a thick layer of floating debris and only a handful of the strongest reinforced structures standing, and even some of those were stripped down to their foundations.

Farris and Matron Branford were only a few strides away from the shore as the final shock of energy struck them from behind and threw them clear of the walkway as the wood disintegrated underneath them. They hit the solid earth roughly and tumbled along a worn dirt path. Water splashed over them as the lake's surface shifted restlessly, but soon the water was little more than a gentle lap on the shore, leaving Farris and Matron Branford dripping on the damp earth.

Farris rolled onto his back, coughing up water and sputtering as the sprite descended silently into the water from whence it came, its dominance over the lake once more fully asserted. As Farris sat up, he looked about for any sign of treshen or pixies or any other Fey, but there was nothing. Even the crows were nowhere to be seen. And the mighty horse of Farris' nightmares was little more than a shadowy terror in his mind, the memory of it fading rapidly even as the pain it ignited remained indescribably vivid.

Matron Branford stood over him and offered her hand to help him to his feet. Farris made several failed attempts to say something, but there were no words that felt right in the wake of everything that had just happened. The matron offered a sad smile as she was ringing out her robes and then knelt on the grass and began to pray. Farris felt horribly intrusive watching this, so he moved silently along the worn path around the outside of the city wall.

As he rounded the gentle curve, he was greeted by the sight of a steady flow of soaked and dispirited people passing through the main gate and out of the city. Barreth appeared fairly unscathed by the forces that had devastated Torvec. There was a growing cluster in the space between the small hamlet and the wrecked doors of the gate; people with no sense of direction beyond not wanting to be in the middle of the battered city.

Farris stopped on the muddy path and sighed. He didn't know why he'd headed back this way; there was nothing for him there. Not safety, not shelter, and definitely not escape. He had no business being among people who'd already suffered so much. He was a hazard, and he was unwelcome. The need to keep moving hadn't gone away. He still had strength in his legs, and as long as that remained, he would keep moving. He nodded his affirmation to himself and returned up the muddy path that brought him back to the kneeling matron as she finished her prayer and stood up.

"You alright?" Farris asked as he approached, not knowing what else to say but fed up with the silence.

Matron Branford nodded and smiled somewhat weakly. "You?"

"Yeah, thanks to you."

She reached out and touched her hand to Farris' chest. The still dripping tatters were failing to cover the hole in his chest pierced by the equine phantasm. It was only an inch or so in diameter, and there was no blood, but it had a reddish-orange glow coming from deep within.

"You'll want to cover up," Matron Branford said somberly. "I can't heal that."

Farris nodded, and she pulled her hand away.

"Selane. You saved my life, but how were you even there?"

"Tamaleon had told me when your boat was supposed to depart, and I'd just been planning to wave you off," she said with a slight shrug and smirk. "But then the constables arrived. There wasn't much I could do, but I couldn't just run away."

"I don't know how to repay you."

"You can repay me by not treating this like a transaction to be balanced. I did what my conscience told me to do."

"So, what happens now?"

Matron Branford looked back at the floating remnants of the broken docks and the pieces of splintered ships and cargo crates that were now washing up on the shore. Exhausted and slumped forms were emerging from the water, as well as some bodies that did not move except for how the small waves off the lake pushed them. She turned back to Farris. "You need to leave." She pointed north along the edge of the lake. "Follow the shoreline, and you'll get to the Ilyria River. It'll be slow going, but it will take you north like you wanted."

"Is that a good idea? Going on foot?"

"More so than staying." She sighed. "It's not safe for you here."

Farris' eyes dropped down toward the ground. "You know you… you could…"

Matron Branford looked at the young man quizzically.

"You could come with me," Farris finally managed to blurt out.

Matron Branford reached out and put a hand on his cheek, bringing his eyes back up to meet hers. She was smiling even as she shook her head. "You're a sweet boy," she said. She leaned forward and kissed him on the forehead, a gentle kiss that lingered for a moment. She kept her hand on his cheek as she pulled away. "But you have so much still to learn, so much living to do. And I'm needed here."

"But if they find you…"

Matron Branford waved away the concern. "I'm in no more danger than I ever was. You, on the other hand, need to get going before somebody washes ashore who saw your outburst on the docks."

Farris frowned and nodded. He couldn't find any more words, only managing a half-smile and a "thank you" before starting to head north along the shoreline. After a few yards, he looked back one last time. Matron Branford gave him one final wave before turning her attention to the people crawling out from the lake amongst the debris. He turned away from the city that was supposed to grant him his freedom and set out to seek it on foot.

The matron began tending to those emerging from the water. Most were fine physically; exhausted, angry, and crying. As the matron bent down to a battered heap of red robes, a tall woman in a rust-colored coat and cracked spectacles practically knocked her over. She stormed away north after Farris.

Chapter 35

Farris trudged through fields of tall grass that ran along the eastern shore of Lake Vaettir. He had made the conscious choice to keep off the road that laid a little further west of him, opting instead to keep a comfortable distance from both the water and the main route of travel. He held his hands out and let the tips of the grass brush along his palms. As he made his way, he heard a faint voice behind him.

"Farris!"

He frowned, but he didn't turn around, nor did he quicken his pace; he simply continued moving forward.

"Farris Connor Raines, turn around!"

He stopped in his tracks and drew a deep, slow, difficult breath before turning around. As she neared him, his gaze dropped to his own feet. "I'm not going back," he said softly.

"Yes, you are." She closed the distance between them. "Do you have any idea what I've gone through to try and find you? What I've risked?"

"You could have just let me go."

The professor stopped mid-step a few feet from her son, tears glistening in her eyes. "You're not safe out here," she implored. "I'm trying to protect you."

Farris straightened and looked her in the eyes. "The way you protected Poena?"

"She…" The color washed from her face. "What happened to her is exactly what I'm trying to shield you from. If another university ever got hold of you—"

"Then I would be put through exactly what you did to her and countless others."

"I won't apologize for my research," she said, frowning, taking another step toward him. "It's my job as a scientist to seek out new knowledge for the betterment of all. And it's my job as a mother to protect *you*, even if it's from my own work and those like me." She reached out a hand and placed it on Farris' shoulder, tears rolling down her cheeks. "Why did you run?"

Farris reached his hand across his chest and placed it atop his mother's. "I couldn't stay locked away like that anymore," he said. "It may not have been a containment capsule, but I wasn't any freer locked in our dormitory suite."

"I was just—"

"I know why you did it," Farris said, squeezing her hand. "And I know it's dangerous out here. I've seen it." He gently lifted his mother's hand off his shoulder, like it was an injured bird he might crush if he handled it too roughly. "You're the only family I have, and I'm sorry for hurting you. But when the power went down, and the doors opened... I couldn't just stay. I need a life that's my own, even if it's an uncertain one. And I need you to let me have that."

She didn't fight when her son took her hand off his shoulder. Tears were flowing freely as she looked to the ground, suddenly lacking the strength to hold up her head. After all she'd done and risked reaching her son, she couldn't bring herself to talk him out of his choice. Farris leaned forward, going up on his toes to kiss his mother on her cheek. She looked down at his kind young eyes, and he smiled at her.

"I love you," he said. "And I'm going to be alright."

She reached out a hand and brushed her son's hair from his face. "I know you are."

The two embraced, each clutching to the other with the desperation that comes with not knowing if it's for the last time. They stood as one in the gentle breeze, both waiting for the other to loosen their grip. Ultimately, it was Farris who eased off first, and his mother followed suit, stepping back to look at her son's face once more.

"I love you," she sobbed.

"I love you, too."

Farris, his own eyes damp, turned to make his way through the field north to the river. He sniffled as he went, but he couldn't look back this time. Behind him, Draza Raines stood frozen in place until he was out of view over a slight crest. She turned, almost mechanically, toward the lake and walked to the water.

She soon came to a stretch of rocky beach leading down to the lake. From her coat pocket, she pulled the notebook she'd removed from her office, the one containing all her notes on Farris' elementalism. It documented every action she ever took, trying to slow or reverse her son's condition, and detailed notes as to any other research that might allow her to cure him. It was a record also of her sins against the Guild—her unauthorized experiments on Poena undertaken in her desperate search for a cure.

If they had known she sought to reverse the condition, the first question would have been "why?" and that question would have inevitably led to Farris. But for everything she did, she never found anything that indicated a cure was even remotely possible. Even as she felt her failure crushing her, she clutched the tome tightly, as though the book itself was standing in for her son, but she couldn't keep it. The information's very existence put Farris at risk. And if she could not keep him safe, she could at least cover his tracks.

From an inner pocket, Professor Raines removed a petite flask with a stopper and a button on the side. She pressed the button, and a small but vibrantly bright flame emerged from the flask and danced about. It was a tiny essence of Farris' own elemental flame, captured and held in stasis within the containment flask. She watched the point of fire curve back and forth, feeling about for something to latch onto, and held the edge of the notebook. The Guild's scientific notebooks had been designed to resist intense heat, but elemental fire was different—more powerful, more primal, and more than the pages could withstand.

The flame curled around the corner of the book almost lovingly before igniting the pages. The professor dropped the burning tome onto the rocks and sand and clicked the button on the flask, replacing the stopper and containing the flame. She watched as the pages turned brown, curled up, and burned away in the dirt.

She would have much to answer for back at the university, especially for leaving campus in the middle of an inquisition, but so long as the administration never learned of her true reasons for leaving, it would amount to no more than a loss of lab privileges, another semester or two in the lecture hall, and a slap on the wrist. Even if it came to much more than that, she could take it. The dark clouds broke, and the late afternoon sun sparkled across the surface of the lake. Professor Raines did not notice. Instead, she sat down in front of the burning book with her knees drawn, clutching the flask to her chest, and softly wept.

Chapter 36

Arbiter Lorac stood on the roof of a four-story building after having been holed up on the top floor as a defensible position when the Fey had attacked, and evacuation was ruled unsafe. A member of the Silent Guard, his robes torn and stained with dirt and grit, stood behind her with his bolt rifle slung on his back. Lorac surveyed the city streets, littered with the remains of broken merchant carts, shards of glass from smashed windows, and a heavy air of loss. The sky was starting to turn a darker shade of blue as the sun hung ever lower, but none of the streetlights were lit. She sighed, knowing the city would spend a night in near-total blackness now that its source of energy had broken free.

"I think it'd help if you were seen."

The arbiter whipped around in surprise at hearing a member of the Silent Guard speak for the first time since taking up her position.

"Since when do you talk?"

The guard shrugged. "We're not in the hall. Figured that would give me some leeway."

"Think your commanding officer would agree?" Lorac asked with a raised eyebrow.

"I won't tell if you don't."

Arbiter Lorac smirked and looked back down at the streets. "Only a few bodies," she said, the smirk vanishing as quickly as it had come.

The guard stepped up next to her and peered down. "The Fey seemed to be going for breadth of damage over depth."

Lorac scrunched up her face. "What does that even mean?"

"They opted to damage more things over completely destroying a few things."

The two lapsed into a customary silence that suddenly seemed inappropriate and awkward.

"I've always wanted to ask one of you lot this," Lorac said, turning to face the guard. "Have you got a name?"

"Billi."

"Reina." She extended her hand. Billi accepted it and shook her hand with a surprisingly gentle touch. "Nice to meet you properly."

"You as well, Good Lady."

"Now that's a phrase I don't want to hear out of your mouth again," she said, wagging a disapproving finger even as she smiled.

"It would really help for you to be down there. For them to see you, know you're safe, that you have a plan."

Lorac laughed bitterly. "Do you honestly think I have a plan after this?"

"No, but you always were good at faking that you had one."

The arbiter shook her head. "Have all the Silent Guard been this observant, and I just never noticed?"

"Kind of the point, isn't it?"

"You know, I'm half tempted to get you dismissed so we can talk again." Lorac looked down one last time and turned to the stairs that would take her off the roof. "Alright," she said after a slow breath. "Button it up, and let's pretend like this job still means something."

She made for the stairs, with Billi close behind.

***

The public ward was overwhelmed, with the intake lounge so packed with injured and terrified the staff barely had the space to move among them. Under the supervision of the somehow still composed Matron Branford, they did the best they could, separating those with minor injuries from those in more dire need. Each prospective patient had been given a numbered tag on a rope to wear, to help the staff keep everything straight and clear.

Selane stepped away from the soaked pile of wet red rags on the cot she'd been tending and surveyed the room when her eyes landed on a sullen form strapped to a carrying plank and propped against a corner. She shook her head and weaved through the throng to the adept healer in white robes tending to Tamaleon.

"Tobie," she said, tapping the healer on the shoulder. "Situation?"

"He hasn't exactly been cooperative," huffed Tobie. "But it looks like he might have been caught up in one of the waves that crossed the shoreline and slammed into something. I had him strapped down to keep his posture and not damage his spine further."

"Did he fight that?" Matron Branford was pained by the hollow look on Tamaleon's face.

Tobie sighed and shook his head. "No, he just didn't do anything to help with the process either."

"I'll see to him from here. If you could tend to the family with number 76, we need to figure out if the youngest child is truly injured or just scared. And please send me two orderlies."

"Yes, Matron." Tobie bowed before shuffling off.

Matron Branford looked around her quickly to be sure no one was paying particular attention to her, then placed a hand to Tamaleon's back. His posture relaxed slightly, but his eyes continued to look out blankly without focusing on anything.

"He got out, you know," she whispered. "He's safe."

"I don't care."

"You've been saying that for as long as I've known you." Matron Branford looked in his eyes and frowned. "This is the first time I actually believe you."

Two orderlies approached and stood at attention next to her.

"He'll need a single room. We know we're doubled up, but that's *not* an option here. Something with a plant in it." The orderlies looked at each other and back to Matron Branford. "It's important," she stressed. "Please just trust me." The orderlies nodded and went to take positions on either side of Tamaleon to move him when she held up her hand to stop them. "I think someone is here to see you. Let's give them a minute."

Auria watched as Matron Branford and the orderlies stepped away then went to Tamaleon. "How're you?" she asked, nervously running a hand through her curls.

"I was thinking of going dancing later tonight," mumbled Tamaleon with a weak smile.

"You told me a long time ago that you didn't really trust anybody." She wrapped her arms around her own waist for want of anything else to do with her hands. "So, I suppose that makes me the fool for ever thinking I might be the exception."

"I—"

She held up a hand and stopped him. "You saved my life. But the way you did it…" She shook her head and frowned. "I can't deal with this right now."

"If not now," Tamaleon breathed, "when?"

"I don't know. Maybe tomorrow, maybe in a year, maybe never." Her glistening eyes met his. "Just not today."

With visible strain, Tamaleon tried to reach out a hand to her, but Auria turned away and hastily retreated out of the ward.

The matron and orderlies returned, but he turned his head away, refusing to look at any of them. Matron Branford sighed and motioned for the orderlies to execute her earlier instructions. They carefully shifted the board Tamaleon was strapped to until it was parallel with the ground, and they set about moving him to a second-floor room.

Selane put her purple hood back up and turned her attention once more to the sea of people she might actually be able to help.

***

Poena opened her eyes in the dark and cold, feeling unyielding stone beneath her. The wall that came into focus was also stone, stretching up to the high ceiling that somehow seemed protective rather than encroaching. In the distance, she heard the idle dripping of water splashing rhythmically into a pool, setting a soothing tempo to the area. The effect didn't last, as her memories of the square and the huldra rushed into her mind. She bolted up in a panic, only to go light-headed and slump back down onto her elbows. Around her, a cluster of people in ragged clothes took a step back, many with their hands raised to show them as empty. From there walls came the dull glow of green flames emanating from clean burning lanterns, seeming to pulse in time with the drips of water.

"It's ok," said a soft voice as a woman with greying hair stepped forward. "You're alright."

"Where…?"

"Don't worry, it's not a prison," the woman said calmly as she knelt beside Poena. "This is the undercity."

Poena tried to process this thought, and her head drooped to see that the dancing electricity across her chest wasn't properly covered by her robes. She hastily shifted the beaten fabric to conceal it.

"You don't have to do that. We're not going to turn you in."

"How did I…?" Poena started, her voice trailing off.

Two men took a step forward, one of them clutching a hat sheepishly. "We saw you up in the square," he said with red cheeks. "Saw what you did. You fought that huldra. Didn't want to leave you to be captured like a criminal. Not after that."

"But… I'm dangerous," Poena protested.

The other man scoffed. "No more than half 'o us here. Least according to them up top."

Poena looked back to the woman, who was smiling reassuringly. "I'm Cecily Branford," she said. "You don't have to tell us your name if you're not ready."

As the weakness in her arms became too much, Poena let herself drift down onto her back, looking up at the high ceiling. For the first time in what felt like ages, the tension she'd been holding onto, the feeling that she needed to be ready to flee at any moment, started to fade. "My name is Poena."

"Welcome, Poena," said Cecily, with an echoing chorus of "welcomes" chimed in from the gathered residents of the undercity.

***

The Morrighan crow landed on the stump at the edge of the Everwood and uncurled from her bent position, head emerging from under a wing and the feathers reforming as her cloak. All was silent around her but for the whistle of the wind through the long grass. Fading into being at her side came the shadowy hollow of the mare.

She reached out a hand to the beast's cheek, touching for a moment but then passing through as though through mist. The creature's fierce horn was no longer adorning its head, and as the sun set, it became less and less corporeal. The Morrighan looked out to the lake and the city, dark and dim with no electric lights springing to life to fight the darkness like there had been for so long.

The mare turned, and its form flitted away like dandelion seeds blown on the wind. The Morrighan let her cloak fall from her shoulders. Hitting the ground, it broke into the murder of crows, all flying in different directions. She turned her back on the Locket of the Lake, on man's "great progress," and vanished into the wood.

***

The walk to the north side of the lake had taken longer than Farris had anticipated, but as the last of the clouds cleared and the sun neared the horizon, he spotted where the lake connected to the Ilyria River, which flowed the length of the continent to the ocean. Choosing to go through the fields of grass hadn't made it any easier, though the brush of the grass against him had been comforting in a way that he couldn't explain. The few lonely clouds that remained were lit up in vibrant reds and oranges as though they were burning away in the sky.

For the first time since encountering his mother, Farris turned to look back in the direction of Torvec. He could just make out the glint of the wall and could see a slight plume of smoke rising from within the city. He couldn't be sure if something had caught fire, but the optimist in him chose to believe it was city workers burning away some of the debris. A gust of wind tossed the young elemental's hair into his face, and he brushed it back with his left hand. Once his hair was out of his vision, his eye lingered on the burnt tips of his fingers. He rubbed his thumb against them, feeling the rough and cracked skin and detecting a distinct twinge of warmth that his other digits were sorely lacking. He sighed and turned northward once more.

Farris didn't have a clear idea of where he was headed, but he'd decided it was best to just keep moving forward. The worst thing he could do at this point was stay in one place. Based on what Tamaleon had told him before, he knew that there would be the occasional trading post along the river and that eventually, it would empty out into the sea. He had absolutely no conception of how far such a distance would be by foot, but since he couldn't possibly know that he knew worrying about it wouldn't help. Glancing off to the east, Farris thought he could see the edge of the Arid Wastes, but in the fading light, he couldn't be sure if it were truly sandy dunes he was seeing, or just grassy hills lit up red by the setting sun. The amount of things he didn't know or couldn't be sure about was something that would have held him back, not all that long ago. But for all the uncertainties in the back of his mind, there was one thing he knew, and that knowledge was a soothing balm over any other facts. He knew for the first time since his elementalism had manifested, he felt in control of his own life.

His legs were aching by the time he reached the edge of the forest that ran along the river. Glancing up, he saw a crow perched in upon a tree branch. He met the bird's black eyes and looked at it directly, not blinking. The crow seemed to nod, almost as if giving the young man permission to enter the forest, or at least that was what he chose to believe. The bird flew off into the sky and away to the north, soon disappearing from sight. Farris took a deep breath and stepped in amongst the trees. His sense of freedom did not diminish as he entered. If anything, it grew stronger. Any lingering fear served to only temper his resolve. He did not know what awaited him, but he knew finally, his fate was in his own hands.

The End

About the Author

Nathaniel Wayne hails originally from Northern California, but is happy to call Vermont their home. They're the oddball brains behind the YouTube channels Council of Geeks, its subsidiary channel Break Room of Geeks, and Vera Wylde. *Dreams of Fire* is Nathaniel's first published novel.

Printed in Great Britain
by Amazon

75805207R00232